Praise for the w[...]

"One thing is almost as certain as dea[...]   [...]icano
angst. You'll find plenty of all three in h[...] [...]u and delirious whodunits,
which stand as an unparalleled achievement in American crime literature."
—Ilan Stavans

"Manuel Ramos is one of my all-time favorite authors and in *My Bad* he delivers
everything I look for in a noir tale. Gus Corral is the guy I want on my side if I'm in
trouble and Ramos proves once again he is the master of creating great characters.
Clear your schedule and be prepared to read this blitz attack of noir in one sitting."
—Jon Jordan, *Crimespree Magazine* on *My Bad*

"Ramos explores issues of the border, identity, violence and slights from outside the
community, as well as within. They are thought-provoking and unpredictable. Many
linger long after they end; and often they contain depth charges that explode in the
reader's mind after the story has ended. His novels belong on your book shelves."
—*Los Angeles Review of Books* on *The Skull of Pancho Villa and Other Stories*

"Manuel Ramos has a well-earned reputation for writing gritty stories about Latinos,
stories that grab you by the throat. The richness of Ramos' work is evident in *The
Skull of Pancho Villa and Other Stories*, a collection of previously published short
stories. The stories are clever and sometimes funny, but their real strength is the way
they capture today's Latinos—the talk and humor, the swagger and irony. Ramos has
a rich voice. He nails it."
—*The Denver Post* on *The Skull of Pancho Villa and Other Stories*

"Ramos puts Latinos back in the picture. He is known as a crime writer, but that does-
n't quite capture what he does. His books are love stories, political dramas, mordant
cautionary tales. Characters who are Latino, black and white, artists, professionals and
laborers, are described in staccato chapters, like a catchy corrido."
—*Los Angeles Times* on *The Skull of Pancho Villa and Other Stories*

"The Godfather of Chicano noir hits us hard with this collection. Great range, dark
visions, and lots of mojo—much of it bad to the bone. A fine book!"
—Luis Alberto Urrea, author of *Into the Beautiful North*,
on *The Skull of Pancho Villa and Other Stories*

"As invigorating as a dip in a Rocky Mountain stream."
—*Mystery Scene* on *Desperado: A Mile High Noir*

"A dark mix of North Denver gangsters and Catholicism, but it's [the] setting that
really grips readers. Nostalgia is combined with reality . . . Ramos gets it right."
—*Denver Post* on *Desperado: A Mile High Noir*

MY BAD

A Mile High Noir

Manuel Ramos

Arte Público Press
Houston, Texas

My Bad: A Mile High Noir is made possible through a grant from the City of Houston through the Houston Arts Alliance.

Recovering the past, creating the future

Arte Público Press
University of Houston
4902 Gulf Fwy, Bldg 19, Rm 100
Houston, Texas 77204-2004

Cover design by Mora Des!gn

Names: Ramos, Manuel, author.
Title: My bad : a mile high noir / Manuel Ramos.
Description: Houston, TX : Arte Publico Press, [2016]
Identifiers: LCCN 2016025123| ISBN 9781558858336 (softcover :
    acid-free paper) | ISBN 9781518500978 (ePub) |
    ISBN 9781518500985 (kindle) | ISBN 9781518500961 (pdf)
Subjects: LCSH: Private investigators—Fiction. | Murder—
    Investigation—Fiction. | GSAFD: Mystery fiction. | Noir fiction.
Classification: LCC PS3568.A4468 M9 2016 | DDC 813/.54—dc23
    LC record available at https://lccn.loc.gov/2016025123

16 17 18 19 20   7 6 5 4 3 2 1

This story is told by two people—Luis Móntez, the lawyer, and Gus Corral, the investigator.

For my son and daughter Diego and Verlyn.
Shout-out to #1 fans Veronica & Darold and María & Neil.

Mil gracias to Guillermo Garibay, attorney-at-law, for his
legal insights about an early version of this book.

Prologue

The big man waited at the back door of the low ugly building. He stood next to a pickup. The snow was light but it would be heavy in another hour. Grab the money and run.

The double-sized door opened and a bearded man dressed in jeans and a greasy flannel shirt walked out. A cloud of vapor floated from his mouth. "Hey, it's cold out here," Eugene Eccles said.

"Yeah, tell me about it. You took your sweet time about opening the damn door."

"You are Toby King, right?"

"You expecting someone else?"

Eccles thought that Toby King did not look like a Toby King. More like a José or a Juan or a Carlos. Gonzales or Martínez, maybe. Something Mexican. But the customer was always right.

"No. It's just that usually we load through the front, Mr. King. We don't often use this back door. Since you said you had a bigger load . . . guess it's okay. Hope it fits in the unit. How big is your box of stuff?"

He peered into the truck's empty bed.

"Uh, where's your stuff?"

King pulled a gun from the deep pocket of his coat.

"Get back in. Number one forty-three. Now."

Eccles led the way down the narrow hallway until they stopped at door 143.

"Open it."

Eccles used the ring of keys hanging from his belt. The door opened with a loud grating noise.

King pushed Eccles into the small room, then smashed him on the side of the head with the gun. Eccles collapsed on the concrete floor. A red line of blood creased the side of his face. King rushed to the box in the middle of the floor. He grabbed the top flaps and tore them open. Something was wrong. The box was too light.

"Where's the goddamn money?" he shouted at the unconscious Eccles.

King grabbed Eccles under the shoulders and dragged him to the hallway. He closed 143, found the right key on the bleeding man's key ring and opened 144 across the hall. He pushed Eccles into 144, shut the door and locked Eccles and himself in the dark.

He didn't want to, but he had to wait for the lawyer. Goddamn Luis Móntez. He knew something about the money. Why else was he coming to this place? Toby King spit on the wall.

"I'll have to kill him, too," he whispered to the man on the floor. He hoped he'd be finished by the time the storm hit.

Part One

What's The Worst That Can Happen?

1 [Gus]

stone free to do what I please
stone free to ride the breeze

I stepped away from prison trying to convince myself that I was on the way to a new and better life. My mind had turned to mush but my body was hard. The pen will do that. I told anyone who asked that I was okay, considering. And I had every intention of doing the right thing.

That first night out was weird. Not sure what I expected. I wasn't ready, that was obvious. Corrine, my sister, picked me up at the halfway house right before lunch, nervous about what to say to me. She'd organized a welcome home party and several of her friends began dropping by in the early afternoon, more for Corrine than for me. Eventually Max, another sister, and my long-time pals, Ice and Shoe, walked in. Max's girlfriend, Sandy, aka La Sandra, showed up a few minutes after Max. Jerome, one more old friend, popped in for a hot minute, then he split. Said he had a business meeting. We didn't know whether to believe him.

Shoe, real name Tony Vega, was the jock of the group. Taller than the rest of us, he still looked like he could play a mean pickup game at the rec center. Ice, real name David Zamarripa—a name I'd almost forgotten since I never used it—was the would-be musician, which made him the lover boy in the group. He worked for the City and County of Denver as a maintenance man. I wasn't sure how Shoe made his living.

I'd missed these guys. They had my back since high school, and I had theirs. At least, that's the way I thought about them.

The partiers were in a good mood and they all took pains to make me believe they really cared that I was back. The stories about my arrest and the whole mess with the Mexican gangsters and the kidnapping and Corrine's awesome escape were told again, but this time we could laugh about some of what had happened. None of us talked about the blood or bodies or the fear. The party went late but I didn't drink too much. One half-hearted beer, if you can believe that. You'd think I would get all crazy and loose. You'd be wrong.

I worried about showing too high of an alcohol level when I met my parole officer and he gave me the mandatory tests, but that wasn't the reason I held back.

Of course, booze wasn't the only available drug. Shoe asked me if I wanted to get high.

"I have some bud, bud. All legal, too."

"I guess that's how it is now, right?"

"It's like the world changed overnight," Ice said. His red eyes and goofy grin gave away that he'd already sampled Shoe's product. "Marijuana stores popped up everywhere. Over on my block, there's three different ones. Opening day was a circus. Lines of pot heads around the block. I got really stoned." He giggled, tried to cover his mouth with his hand. He couldn't keep it in and he gave up and walked away.

"I better pass," I said to Shoe. "I have to meet with my P.O. tomorrow. You know what that means."

"But it's legal," Shoe insisted.

"Except for me," I answered.

The highlight of the night turned out to be Max excitedly announcing that she and Sandy were finally getting married. We toasted the couple and cheered the progressive voters of Colorado because Max's marriage would be legit and official. The party turned into a celebration of Max's longest-lasting relationship until the happy pair had to leave for their band's show at a club in Capitol Hill.

A vibe floated through the remaining group, something gray and heavy that laid on my shoulders like a sack of dead fish. Maybe it was only my imagination. I fought the feeling, but the tricks I used in prison when the dark took over were missing. No weights for lifting, no yard for running, no sympathetic counselor who would listen to anything I said until her shift was over.

I was thankful when the party finally ended and I made my way to Corrine's basement, my new home until I found something I could manage on my own.

"You can stay as long as you want, you know that," Corrine said. She carried blankets and a pillow.

"Yeah, I know. But I don't want to mooch. That's got to stop, know what I mean?"

"You're not mooching. I want to help. You got a bad deal with the cops, you took the hit for everything but I know you didn't do all that stuff that the cops, especially Reese, said you did. You're my brother, Gus. In this house, that means something."

I smiled at her, gave her a hug and said, "Without a doubt. Thank you."

She hugged back. We finished making the bed.

"Goodnight, Gus. I'm glad you're home."

Home. What a concept. But all that time I'd had to think prison, you know, made my hard head open up to the idea that I needed, and wanted, some of the comforts I'd never given much thought to in the past. Like a home. Family. Decent job. Peace.

I shared the basement with a cat or two and Corrine's CDs and record albums. Stacks of Chicago blues, sixties and seventies rock, Tejano and Mexican, and a handful of Waylon Jennings, Willie Nelson, Bob Dylan and other outlaws were scattered against walls, on makeshift shelves, and in a scratched and peeling cabinet. She'd inherited my father's vinyl collection and added a few of her own CDs to the mix. I dusted off and plugged in an old turntable. When I turned it on, the knobs lit up and the needle arm moved so I figured it worked. I found a pair of gigantic headphones that plugged into the turntable. Then I spent an hour listening to scratchy blues legends. I read about many of the musicians and their songs in prison. I read a lot in lockup. Thanks to Corrine's basement, I finally heard the music. The blues seemed to fit my lifestyle, attitude, outlook on life in general.

I had only one nightmare that night. In my opinion, I slept like a baby—first time in months.

The next day, I finalized the details of my parole at an office across from the courthouse. First, I met the man who ran the program, Ed Dillings. Thin wispy curls circled his ears. He didn't have enough hair to cover the shine beaming off his huge forehead.

"Mr. Agustín Corral? You go by Gus?"

"That's me."

"I'm Ed Dillings." He extended his hand and I shook it. He held on to my fingers rather than shake them. "I'm the director of this office. Any problems, issues, controversy—you bring them to your assigned P.O. If he can't handle them to your satisfaction, come to me." I jerked my hand loose. "But don't try any ex-con bullshit. Be real, that's all I ask."

"Yeah, sure, okay. But you're not the person I report to?"

"No. Your regular contact will be Harold Mills. You'll meet him in a few minutes. He's been with the office about five years now, so he knows the deal. I'm sure you do, too. I won't waste too much of your time today. I just want to be clear that our job is to ensure your transition back into the world is as problem-free as possible. But we can't do that by ourselves. You have to be invested in your future, your own life, if you hope to avoid recidivism. We got programs for everything from drug rehab to computer tech. Our counselors are trained in psychology, sociology, and some can even run a yoga class. We'll give you leads on jobs, apartments and used cars. Hell, we'll teach you how to swim if it's something you need to survive. But it's all for nothing if you don't care, Gus. You have to give a damn. You do that and you might make it out here."

I nodded with as much energy as I thought would impress him. "No one wants it more than me," I said.

Someone knocked on his office door. He shouted from his chair, "Come in."

A woman walked in. She was about thirty with a slight stoop in her back and long dull brown hair that hung across her face. Bony angles jutted from her chin and elbows. Her clothes didn't fit right.

"Barbara. You still here?"

"I wasn't sure we were finished. I'm gonna go now. I guess I'll see you later, at the house?"

He stood up, wrapped his arms around her shoulders and walked her out of the office. I waited for a minute or two until he returned and shut the door.

"Sorry about that. My daughter, Barbara. She's not feeling well."

I nodded.

Dillings finished his pep talk and moved me on to the man who would be my official parole officer, another white guy I immediately nicknamed Dirty Harry. He was young, younger than I, but his squint was old and cold, without sympathy, not even a "let's work together" cliché. All business.

"You check in every week. You got my card. Call if there are any issues."

"What's that mean?" I asked.

"You'll know when it happens. Don't waste my time. That's all I ask. I got too many files to worry about the screw-ups. If you make this work, we'll have no problems."

"It's gonna work. No doubt about that."

"Every guy who's ever sat in that chair said the same thing. Know how many of them really made it?" He tapped his stack of papers on his desk like they were a deck of cards.

I took a wild guess. "Not many?"

"Right. Very few, in fact. To be honest, Corral, the odds are against you."

"I been fighting the odds all my life."

"Yeah? Where'd that get you?"

I had no answer.

"Just remember," he said, "I got eyes on you and if you miss a beat, it's over. I'll turn up when you least expect it, so you don't get second chances with me. You pay attention to the rules, you get a job, keep your nose clean, everything will be okay. First sign of you out of step, you're violated, and back you go. Simple and easy, right?"

Whatever, boss.

"I got a job." I sounded boastful but that was all right.

He looked up from his inch-thick pile of forms. "You do? Already?"

"Yeah. My attorney, Luis Móntez. He hired me."

"To do what? It has to be a legit job, Corral."

I ignored his rude assumption about the arrangement Luis and I might have worked out.

"It's real. I'm going to be his investigator, process server, janitor, all-around go-to guy. He said he'd send over the papers you need for your records. And he also said you can come by and check us out whenever. We got nothing to hide."

He rocked back and forth in his office chair. "That's good, Corral. I like that. I'm actually happy to hear the news. I know this guy Móntez. I've worked with some of his other clients. That could be a good fit for you." He picked up his pen and chewed on it for a few seconds, like a man carrying a nicotine monkey. "On the other hand . . . "

"What?"

"On the other hand, I heard about some of Móntez's capers in the past. That guy was almost disbarred. He's been arrested. Nothing ever came out of his legal troubles, but you have to stay away from anything that's off-center. You understand?"

"What you have to understand is that I'm going to do all I can to get back on the right path. That's what you want, right? I ain't gonna do anything to screw that up. You don't have to worry about me."

"Good. I hope so. But they pay me to worry about you guys." Now I was one of the guys. "One other thing. You can't participate in his criminal cases. Might put you in contact with felons, ex-cons. That would not be good."

"Luis said we could work around that. He's done this before. He knows how it has to be."

"No problem then."

We set a schedule for visits and reviews and a few other things that were required by the State of Colorado in return for me being back on the streets. Harry went through all the rules and regulations, again, and itemized each and every act of life I was prohibited from doing. He finally asked for my urine.

When I left Harry's office I felt like I'd been back in prison for a few sweaty hours. I didn't like that feeling.

But I didn't feel like a criminal. I didn't feel much else, to tell the truth. One day I was locked up, the next I wasn't. Whatever happened to me the last few years was over. My prison adventure ended and that meant that all the alliances and conflicts and enemies and games that I'd created and played to survive were finished. Out of sight, out of mind. Now what?

2 [Luis]

well baby I can never be satisfied
and I just can't keep from cryin'

I didn't think Gus was much of a gamble. Yeah, he had all that excitement when the cartel hoodlum set up camp in Denver and he did end up in a shootout in a hotel parking garage, but Gus came from a good family and for me, that's important. The guy did his time and paid for his crimes, or at least for some of them. There was more to his story than he let on, but I was too old to get all up into somebody's business if that person didn't want to share. As long as he did what I asked around the office, we'd be good.

I'd been burned by ex-cons before. In my line of work that shouldn't surprise anyone. Most of the time the problem blew up because I went against my better judgment and I trusted someone who didn't deserve it. Gus struck me as reliable. If he was half as steady as his sister, he'd have it made—as much as a guy fresh out of prison can have it.

It wasn't my idea to hire him. That came from Corrine Corral. I begged off at first. I told her I was winding down my practice so I could retire from the lawyer racket, and that I wasn't sure I had enough work to keep Gus occupied. Did no good. Corrine was persistent, for months. She didn't want Gus to have to go back to work at his ex-wife's secondhand store where he'd sold junk to customers and slept in the backroom at night. She talked to me every other day about what I could do for her brother when he was released. If I saw her somewhere, Gus would be the topic of our conversation. She even wrote a note about Gus on a Christmas card she sent me. That woman . . .

What's there to say about Corrine Corral? A Chicana legend and somebody who's easy to trust. She swore and promised that I wouldn't regret hiring Gus, that, in fact, I would one day kiss her for bringing him to me. So taking on her brother wasn't much of a gamble, like I said. I asked for one thing. I made her promise that he would dress appropriately for the office. When I first met Gus he looked like an out-of-work gangbanger, which he might have been a few years ago.

"I know what you mean," Corrine said during one of her visits to my office. "I used to talk to him all the time about his image, which he absolutely did not care about. Prison changed that, I think."

I nodded. "Prison changes the strangest things in people."

"I'll bet. I'm worried about him, after he gets out. Gus hasn't exactly fulfilled his potential, if you know what I'm sayin'?"

I had a pretty good idea. "Some men grow up in prison, others regress. Depends on what's there in the first place."

"Guess we'll have to hope for the best," she said. "Anyway, he has two suits. An old one that I'll make him throw away and the one I bought him for his trial. That good enough?"

"It's good. But he doesn't have to wear a suit every day. Not sure he's the same size as when he went in, anyway. We'll play it by ear. As long as he doesn't show up in T-shirts and flip-flops."

"No problem."

I worked with my accountant to arrange a way to pay Gus the minimum wage that he was willing to work for. We could do it because we cut back on weekly orders of office supplies and a few other expenses that I didn't think we'd notice. Well, maybe Rosa, my secretary, would complain, but she saw that as part of her job anyway.

"We'll buy stuff as we need it," I announced. "If I want to retire in less than a year, we have to eliminate some overhead."

Rosa let me know from the beginning that she was against hiring Gus. "I remember that guy from when you represented him. There's something about him that's not right." She crossed her arms and leaned against a wall, ignoring the fact that she pressed against my framed *Zoot Suit* movie poster.

Rosa could be a pain but I didn't deny that she brought a certain . . . uh . . . charm to the office. Nothing like a homegirl chola to make clients feel at ease, to be reassured that they were getting the finest professional legal services. We'd worked together through the lean years when I couldn't pay her unless she agreed to not cash the check until after the weekend, and she rode the high with me when times were at their all-time best. She warned me about my failed romances before they failed, and guaranteed success for my biggest legal victories. She talked me through the former and drank me under the table for the latter.

"He's okay," I insisted. "Like so many of my clients. Not a saint, but not the devil either."

"You sure about that? I wouldn't be surprised by anything he might do. There's an edge to the guy." Rosa prided herself on her ability to read people.

She and I had a good understanding. I was the guy who signed the checks, but Rosa ran the place. The arrangement had worked for several years. I felt like we'd grown up together. It was just her and me, no partners or associates. I started out on my own and that was the way I would finish.

Forty years out of law school and I ended up with a reliable secretary and a comfortable office in the heart of Denver. There were times, especially in the first ten, fifteen, maybe twenty years of my practice that those two things were elusive fantasies of Móntez, the Chicano lawyer barely keeping his head above water. Somehow, I'd made the proper corrections.

My office was on the first floor of a fairly new building in Denver's Golden Triangle, about three blocks from the courthouse where I occasionally appeared. I'd cut back on courtroom work—too expensive for most of my clients, and too much potential brain damage for me. I was at the stage where I could be pickier about my clients.

The location didn't have the prestige of an address in the middle of downtown Denver, but in my mind the office was the outward representation of what I tried to carry inside: professionalism, competence, quality. Leaving it would be hard. But why not quit while I was ahead?

"We don't know everything about Gus," I said. "I can handle that. How many of our clients ever tell us the complete truth?"

She nodded.

"The reality is that I need some help. I'm slowing down, Rosa. Can't do all the legwork I should for my clients. Gus can go places for me, plus he knows the playground. He's lived in Denver all his life, his sister is well-connected and his family has a solid reputation."

"And he comes cheap."

"There's that. He needs a job. I think it'll be all right."

She walked away shaking her head.

Then I tried to think of things to keep Gus busy.

That first day on the job he was a wreck. He walked and talked and evaded like an ex-con. His shoulders slumped under the weight of past sins and continuing penance. He reacted to everything I said with an over-eagerness that annoyed then frustrated me. One of my long-term clients asked if "the guy out front" was "okay?" I nodded, half-heartedly.

"Relax, Gus."

We sat in the conference room where he would interview clients.

"It'll take a few days to get used to how we work around here. Ease into it. There's no rush." I wanted Gus to make it.

He folded his hands together, almost closed his eyes. "Yeah, I get it. You're right. I'm letting all the free air and sunshine and moving around get to me. I'll be okay. No need to worry."

"I'm not worried. It's cool."

He drank from a plastic bottle of water. He finally smiled. I thought we would be all right after that.

His first big job walked in the office as a new client, someone I didn't know but who presented a classic legal problem. Gus had been on the job about a week. Mainly, he threw out trash, shredded documents, served a few subpoenas.

The client introduced herself as María Contreras. She wore a simple black blouse and dark blue pants. An oversized purse hung from her shoulder.

She started the conversation. "Maybe you knew my husband, he was about your age. His name was Anselmo but everyone called him Sam. Sam Contreras."

A couple of things happened. First, I twitched when she brought up my age. How old did she think I was? Second, I twitched again because yeah, I knew Anselmo "Sam" Contreras. And he was about my age, north of fifty-five but south of sixty-nine.

Sam Contreras was the kind of guy you either hated or loved, and sometimes in the same day. He owned and managed the old Roundhouse Bar that used to be a busy, busy place near Union Station, back in the days before that part of Denver got all prettied up and civilized. I knew many stories about Sam and his bar. Hell, I'd played a major role in a few of them. I vaguely remembered that there was a widow in the picture. She had to be at least fifteen years younger than Sam. Sam's bar was not the kind of place where you showed off your wife, so there was no reason for me to recognize her.

"Yes," I said. "I knew Sam. I went to his memorial service. That must have been what, three, four years ago?"

"That's right. I guess we didn't meet then."

I shook my head. "I don't think we did."

I almost said, "I would have remembered" or some other lame automatic male reflex, but I didn't. Luis Móntez, Renaissance man.

"You know, they never caught the guys?"

This time I nodded. "Yeah, that whole thing was a mess."

She pinched her lips together. "You know the story?"

"What everyone else knows. Sam was on vacation, fishing from a boat off the southern Baja coast. Him and a guide, someone he'd used over the years. They were attacked by pirates or smugglers, somebody. The boat sunk along with the two men. The Mexican police figured that the pirates made a mistake, thought Sam had drugs or bags of money onboard and then killed him when they didn't find anything. As I recall, the cops dredged up pieces of the boat, but that was it. There was a storm that same day and most of the boat was swept away, along with Sam and his guide."

She nodded. "Yes, that's what happened. They found Sam's body, eventually. I had him buried in Mexico. He loved it down there."

"Sam was a tough bar owner. A throwback to wilder Denver times. He acted as his own bouncer and he took that role very seriously. Saw him more than once beat up a belligerent drunk or an underage kid flashing a fake I.D. I always thought that case had strange parts to it."

She stared at her hands while I spoke. She raised her head and wrinkled her face.

"Why strange? Why do you put it that way?"

I recalled Sam's steady stare. He could make you run out of his bar simply by looking at you at closing time, especially if you were drunk. I tried to hang on to her stare but she turned away again. The woman intrigued me. Most of my clients did, in different ways. I watched in hope of picking up a few clues about her that she might not reveal voluntarily.

She appeared to be in good physical shape with healthy skin tone and good biceps so I assumed she worked out, maybe jogged. But I detected tobacco scent. A smoker who tried to stay in shape? Talk about a walking contradiction. Her reluctance to look me straight in the eyes meant that she was embarrassed, or not telling all of what I should know, or lying. There hadn't been any small talk, no real attempt to soften the mood, nothing except business, but I couldn't fault her for that. She spoke about the death of her husband, after all. A brutal, violent death.

"I've been a criminal defense attorney most of my life. It's very rare that someone doesn't eventually talk about a job, one of the perpetrators, I mean. These guys, the professional thieves and robbers, live their criminal lives for a lot of reasons, but most of them want, even crave, credit for what they do. They can't help but brag or tell stories about themselves. That's often how they get caught. I've represented a good number of bad guys whose own words tripped them up. But nothing ever surfaced about Sam's murder. No snitch trying to make a deal, no barroom bragging overheard by a cop, no loose jail talk. Maybe Mexican pirates are different. The Mexican cops didn't have anything, U.S. cops weren't interested and the case shriveled up and died."

I bit my tongue for that last sentence. The woman's husband had been the one who had died.

"No, nobody was ever arrested," she said. "A few years ago I talked to one of the original detectives from La Paz. He said they would question some men they'd arrested who were harassing tourists in the same area, but I never heard any more from him."

"Is that what you want my help with? Following-up on what the cops did in the case? You want someone to solve your husband's murder?" As I said it, I knew I wouldn't take such a job. Butting heads on a cold case with defensive Mexican cops, trying to deal with international legal protocols, and a complete lack of any forensic or physical evidence was not my idea of how to spend the months leading up to my retirement. I was curious about Sam Contreras' murder, but not that curious.

"No, that's not why I'm here." She produced a file of papers from her purse and laid it on my desk. "It's a little more mundane than that. Just a money problem."

Money problems I understood and appreciated. No such thing as "just" a money problem. I had enough of my own to be certified as a money problem expert. Such problems could often be settled with a few phone calls. The debtor thinks he gets away with something if he pays less than owed. The creditor is grateful for anything out of what had been a bad debt.

"Depending on what it is, I can probably help with that kind of problem. What's it about?"

"I'm the only one left from Sam's family. We never had any kids. His only brother died in Iraq. I tried to keep the bar going after Sam was killed, but it was too much for me. I got in way over my head, but by the time I realized I needed to sell, it all went to crap. The bar was closed for taxes and license penalties. Creditors stuck liens all over the title. I didn't know what to do. I tried, but . . ."

"I remember when the bar closed. I heard the family wanted to keep it going."

"That was me." She slumped in the soft leather chair reserved for clients. "I didn't have any experience and I didn't have any money or anyone to help me. I walked away from the bar and let the creditors fight over the bones. I never looked back. Not until recently, I mean."

"What happened?"

"I started getting letters. And then email. They came out of the blue from a man I don't know but who claimed he'd been in business with Sam and that there was some money that should have been split between him and Sam. But he couldn't get to it."

I shook my head. "You didn't fall for that, did you? I hope you didn't."

"No, no, I was extremely skeptical, of course. I didn't do anything with him, not even answer his messages. But then one day this arrived in the mail." She pointed at the envelope and papers on my desk. "That's when I thought I should get some legal help."

"I'll look these over. I gotta say this sounds a long way from mundane. But why don't you tell me what's going on, the way you see it, and what you think you want me to do for you?"

"I'll try." She straightened up and pressed forward. "This guy, he told me his name is Richard Valdez, says that he and Sam had a business together. That Sam provided upfront money and other services, and that Valdez did the actual work."

"What kind of business?"

"The way I understand it, they had an import business. They called it Aztlán Treasures. Folk art. Day of the Dead figurines, pottery, that kind of stuff. From Mexico and Guatemala. Valdez had connections with various dealers, manufacturers and artists around the Southwest. Guess he was an artist himself, when he was younger. He did all the traveling, made the sales to the shops and outlets, built a network with the Mexican artists and exporters."

"Valdez was the face of the business?"

"Yes. The customers only knew him and I guess they thought they were only dealing with him."

She paused.

"You want some water, maybe coffee?"

"No, I'm okay."

"And Sam? What did he do in this import business?"

"According to Valdez, Sam took care of the books, paid the bills, and then he and Valdez split the profits. Sam got fifty percent, same as Valdez. Valdez said they'd been doing this for years but I never came across anything in Sam's things about any import business, or about Valdez. I never heard of Aztlán Treasures or Ricky Valdez. That's what he calls himself. Ricky. But the papers look authentic. There's contracts, receipts, all the stuff such a business would require."

"But now Valdez says he's owed money?"

"Yes. He claims that Sam socked away two hundred and fifty thousand dollars that had accumulated in the business' operating account. He wants half of that."

"This is very fishy, you know that?"

"Yes, yes. But, the papers. It seems to be all there. And that's Sam's signature all over the documents. I know his autograph."

"I've got several questions already."

"That's why I'm here. I need advice. Help me figure this out."

"You don't know anything about this import business?"

"Nothing. I never heard of it. I, uh . . . ah . . . "

"What is it?"

She breathed deeply as though I'd asked her to reveal her darkest secret.

"I only knew Sam for about three months before we got married. And we were married for only three years before he died. Truth is, I didn't really know him."

"But you were married."

She cleared her throat. "Sam and I had been separated for a couple of years. We didn't get divorced but I didn't know what he was up to, in business or anything else. To tell you the truth, we didn't speak the last few years of his life. We had one good year together." She paused again. "Sam and I had a complicated relationship."

"I have experience with many of the complications a marriage on the rocks can create."

"Yes, sure. You're a lawyer."

And I had personal, in-my-face, ugly divorce knowledge, too, but that went unsaid.

"I knew about the bar," she said. "But that was it. I never heard of Aztlán Treasures."

"Why would they split the profits? Valdez was doing most of the work. Sam was only the bookkeeper."

"Because Sam's money was all they had at the beginning, according to Valdez. I asked him the same thing. He says the split was really more like sixty-forty, but to pay back Sam on his investment, Valdez turned over another ten percent. He says all he wants now is fifty percent of what was left of the business."

"Pretty generous." I glanced through the papers again. "Another question. If the story is true, where's he been for the past three years? Why come after the money now? And where is it supposed to be? Why all the mystery?"

"I don't know the answers to some of those questions. But he thinks I know where the money is."

"But why now? Why not when Sam was killed?"

"That's just it. He says he was in prison. He was arrested right around the time Sam was killed. Apparently he imported more than simple folk art. He smuggled rare artifacts across the border, things Mexico didn't want to lose. He basically was a grave robber but he went to jail for failing to declare the items at U.S. Customs. It was a minor charge compared to what Mexico could have done to him. He says he couldn't do anything about the money until he got out. And now he's out."

"And he wants his cut."

"Yes. He thinks I know where the money is, or how to get to it. Sam supposedly told him that." She sighed. "Can you help?"

For a few seconds I thought about the different answers I could give to that question.

"Uh, Ms. Contreras, you sure you want to stay involved in this situation? An ex-con demanding money from an illegal smuggling operation, and the unsolved murder of your husband? Valdez should be satisfied with the fact that he's out of prison, but apparently that's not enough. All in all, it's not a pretty picture."

"I don't think I have a choice. I'm not saying that I have to find the money and pay Valdez. But I have to do something. He won't stop harassing me until I find a way to make him stop. And . . . "

She didn't finish her sentence so I took a stab at completing the thought.

"Valdez says that Sam was also in on the smuggling. That he took the fall for Sam and kept him out of prison. And for that alone he should be paid? Is that close to what he said?"

She nodded. "It really doesn't matter to Sam, I guess."

"Do you know how Sam and Valdez met?"

"Only that they were in the Marines together."

"They see action?"

"Afghanistan. The Korangal Valley."

I again flipped through the papers she'd deposited on my desk. Most of it consisted of communications between Valdez and Sam. Email, letters, notes, some receipts for the import business. Nothing, of course, about smuggling or a vanished pot of a quarter of a million dollars. From my quick review, it looked like the import business was legit and real.

"What's the next step with Valdez?"

She strummed her fingers on the arm of the chair. "He wants to meet. Said he had more information he would show me to prove his claim."

"You can't do that. You shouldn't do that."

"What should I do?"

"Let me look at all this in detail. I'll check with the Secretary of State, make sure this is a real company. Do some other background work. I'll get back to you about whether we can help, about whether our office should get involved. Meanwhile, if he contacts you, try to put him off for a few days. Threaten to go to the cops with his story if he persists. That might reveal whether he's on the level. If he's honest he shouldn't object to a few more days, or to you talking with the police."

"And if he's not?"

She blinked several times. She had a point. How dangerous was a convicted smuggler, a robber of Mexican treasurers? Would bringing up the police put her at risk?

"I just need a couple of days. That's all I can offer for now."

She sighed again. "Okay. I'll wait to hear from you. I would feel better if I knew where he lived. I should at least have his address. Something, anything about him. I feel exposed now. Let me know if you learn anything, as soon as you know? Okay?"

"Sure. No doubt."

I wanted to believe her. She came off as desperate, needy. All my education, experience and so-called smarts had to be enough to help a woman like María Contreras. I wanted to give her a chance, but I had to stop and think it through. I'd been around too long to do otherwise.

Rosa made sure we had all the information we needed to set up a new computer client file including a copy of María's driver's license. Then my newest client slowly walked out of the office. She glanced back at me just before the office door shut. I wasn't sure if it was a look of pain or pleasure. I'd been fooled that way before and learned not to make a judgment until I had enough information to back up my conclusion. I was a long way from that point with Ms. Contreras.

3 [Gus]

when things go wrong, go wrong with you
it hurts me too

At first glance, Luis Móntez's office looked like any other office, or what I thought an office looked like. When someone walked through the door they stepped into a space where Rosa, his assistant, greeted clients, answered the phone and made sure the place presented a serious face. Then the client waited in one of the comfortable chairs, or was ushered by Rosa to Luis or me. Law books and computers, naturally; plenty of leather, dark wood and a conference table and chairs in a separate side room. A general work area and the conference room took up the bulk of the floor plan of the office. My desk crowded into the work area.

But the initial impression was wrong. His office was like no other lawyer's office I'd seen—and there'd been a few—mostly when I was a kid. Móntez squirreled away souvenirs of his cases, clients and history, and oddball stuff spread across tables, book shelves and chairs. Sitting in corners, balanced between books or hung on the walls were things such as a pair of dented hubcaps, native Central American masks, tickets to a music festival in New Mexico. Posters for psychedelic rock groups I'd never heard of shared wall space with flyers demanding peace or justice or both. The place could have looked cluttered, maybe a hoarder's fantasy. Rosa diligently organized everything and worked hard on making the office look busy but professional. It was a difficult and never-ending task.

Móntez looked through several pieces of paper and what appeared to be a bookkeeping ledger. His grandfather clock ticked in the corner and I watched the gold-colored hands move to the precise rhythm. Rosa was at lunch and the office was empty except for him and me. I finally asked a question.

"She denies any knowledge of the money, or where it is, or why Sam would have told Valdez that she knew how to get it?" He put down the pages from the file. "That's her story. Not sure I believe her yet. But I haven't spoken with Valdez either."

Móntez had a reputation for being deliberate, a thinking kind of guy. He didn't jump to conclusions. In other words, the opposite of whatever kind of guy I was. I liked the way he took his time about most things. There were days when he could be frustrating but that said more about me than him.

Corrine told me that when he was younger he was a risk-taker, a guy who would go all out for his clients or friends even if it was dangerous. She had several stories about the Chicano lawyer that made him out to be a real stand-up dude. He had an activist history, a hell-raiser for the old Chicano Movement, the civil rights struggle of Mexican Americans back in the sixties and seventies.

"He was all chingón back then," Corrine explained with a hint of pride in her voice.

He never came off big-headed or high-tone to me. Just another Chicano who saw a lot of life and tried to do his job. Corrine said he'd slowed down, of course. The years added up on everyone. I felt my age myself and I was nowhere near Móntez's.

I picked up the file and thumbed through it. "Getting something out of Valdez? Good luck. That'll be an interesting conversation," I said.

"Tell me about it. Can't guess what Valdez will do. Meanwhile, I'm trying to figure out if the smuggling money was laundered through the import business."

"Logical. But obvious."

"Right. The periodic moving across borders, numerous deliveries, convenient hiding places in the legit folk art pieces."

"Don't forget the stash of money that's at the heart of your client's problem."

"Yeah, too obvious. Maybe not to Sam, though. He was a character and could be an asshole, but I never had the impression that he was a hardcore, experienced criminal mastermind."

"Maybe he wasn't involved. He could have been Valdez's patsy."

"And now Valdez is trying to scam the widow?"

"I've heard of worse."

"The money must be from illegal activity, maybe drugs. That's a huge chunk of change from only gewgaws and curios. There's more to it than statues and vases. The fact that it's been hidden away for years makes it look suspicious, to say the least." He made a note on his legal pad. "Why would Valdez let Sam handle the money, especially such a large sum? Why wouldn't he keep it under his own control, or at least know how to get to it? Doesn't make sense."

Luis' intuition sounded right to me. I thought for a minute.

"Valdez's either lying about the money being part of his deal with Sam," I said. "He found out about it somehow and now he's trying to get his hands on it. Or . . . "

Móntez smiled at me for some reason. "Yeah?" he said.

"Or he thought it was safer to keep away from the cash. He could deny he knew what was going on, easy to blame it on Sam, his partner, especially if no large amounts of cash can be traced back to him. He's been locked up, so if that was his plan it didn't work. Guess we should find out which it is, if Ms. Contreras is our client."

"Haven't totally decided yet. Maybe you can do a check on her, dig up whatever she didn't tell us about her involvement with her husband's businesses, how all that went down. You think you can work on that?"

I didn't think I had a choice.

"No problem. I'll start tomorrow."

"As soon as possible," he said. "She's stalling Valdez but who knows how long that will play."

"Good point."

"It's been bothering me and now that I think about it, I don't like the risk to her. I should tell her to go to the cops even if Valdez holds off on his meeting."

"Doubt they would do anything," I said. "No real crime committed, is there? The money could be from dope dealing but there's no proof of that, from what you've told me. They'd treat it as a civil legal issue between two people, like a debt. Even she described it as a money problem."

He stood up and paced behind his desk. He stared for a minute at his Casa de Manuel calendar, which featured the typical Popocatépetl and Iztaccíhuatl fantasy painting. The half-naked Aztec couple scampered in the moonlight along the shores of Lake Texcoco. I tried to think about what Luis might be thinking, but it was no good. Too many options presented themselves. Did he want to be on a beach somewhere with a scantily clad native woman rather than dealing with somebody else's complicated and potentially dangerous legal crisis? Did he really want to dig into a case that might include a greedy dope dealer on the prowl for a big con? Then I remembered that he was a lawyer, a damn good one, from my own experience. These kinds of problems had taken up most of his adult life. This was what he signed up for when he took the lawyer's oath so many years ago. This was what he lived for, no?

"See what you can find out today," he said. "It's only a little after one. I don't want to be the cause of any trouble for Ms. Contreras."

I left his office to begin work.

I used my desk telephone and called Jerome Rodríguez, the guy who knew everyone and all their dirty business, and the guy who stood next to me when the shit hit the fan and the bullets flew. I figured he should have moved past all that by now, right?

I can't say he was eager to speak with me, but eventually he agreed to meet.

"At your coffee shop in the Northside?"

"Nah. I sold that place. I'm over in RiNo now. You know where that is? I had to escape the Highlands craziness. RiNo's a little more my speed."

"What's the name and address of this latest racket?"

"Strictly honest commerce. Nothing shady. I've learned my lesson. You make a good role model for that kind of education. I'm so clean you can hear me squeak when I walk."

"I'll believe that when I see it."

"Come on over to J's Joint, Washington and Ringsby Court. We serve healthy, organic, mostly breakfast but we have sandwiches, too."

"J's Joint? Sounds like a marijuana cover. That your gig, too?"

"Don't need no cover these days, not in the Mile High City, and I mean high, man. But, no. Not that kind of place. I thought about it, but there's too much . . . uh . . . government oversight in that business for my comfort level. I'm here now. Come on over and we can talk."

RiNo—the River North Art District—was the latest trendy Denver neighborhood. The main landmark of the area had been the almost worn-out National Western Complex where the annual National Western Stock Show and Rodeo happened every January. But, like everything else in Denver, the cow town image was changing. Leave it to Jerome to surface there, on the cusp of the curve, so to speak. Galleries, restaurants, condos, music studios and artist lofts now stood on land where industrial chaos, ragged warehouses, empty garages and dimly-lit, sketchy bars used to dominate.

I drove Corrine's black and red Kia Soul, a car that featured hamsters in TV ads and that made me feel like a lab rat. But Corrine loved the car, told me it was "cute." And to be careful with it. She was dead serious when she said that.

Móntez's office was near the courthouse, almost directly in the middle of the downtown hustle and skyscraper buildings. I followed the heavy traffic on Lincoln south until Lincoln became Twentieth Street, curved around toward the ball park, turned onto Lawrence Avenue and followed it to Broadway. Then a straight shot to Brighton Boulevard. The car did great, but because I wasn't used to driving I uncorked a bit of anxiety about the congestion, noise and rude drivers, all the while silently saying to myself that I wasn't going to let anything happen to Corrine's car. I appreciated that the Kia was easy to maneuver in Denver's rushing streets.

During my time spent in stir I often thought of Jerome. What we'd been through created a bond that neither of us ever put to words, but we both knew that something had passed between us that would remain forever, like a deep scar. I felt guilty for putting him in danger and I knew there was always going to be a barrier between us because he'd warned me about what I was doing; and when I didn't listen it ended up costing him. But still . . . we survived—beaten, bruised, bloodied, for sure, but alive—which was more than I could say about several of the other players.

He waited for me at one of his patio tables. The place looked new, clean and bright. Almost antiseptic. Two customers munched on sandwiches and drank what I assumed was a healthy beverage. The view from the restaurant wasn't much. RiNo was still under development, "on the drawing board" as they say, and large tracts of windswept weedy land littered with trash or rusted machinery competed for attention with the new buildings.

"You look the same," I said as I shook his hand.

"You don't. Older. I hope wiser."

"Don't know about that. I can tell you it's good to be out."

"See, smarter already. Now you just got to stay out."

I didn't intend to bring up that I hadn't seen him since my trial. No visits, phone calls or letters. He told me before I took my ride to the joint that he was allergic to prisons. I didn't really blame him. In fact, I kind of appreciated his absence. While I was locked up there was no one other than Corrine that I wanted to see, or that I wanted to see me.

"No problem, Jerome. Ain't no way that I will ever get into any kind of legal trouble again. Especially anything like what we went through."

He gulped down whatever he was drinking. "You want something? Chai? Espresso? A sandwich?"

"Thanks. Some iced tea, if you got it."

He signaled one of his waiters and ordered for me.

"I'm real happy to hear you've learned your lesson," he said. "I can relax now."

"Relax? What you uptight about?"

"Because it seems that when you got trouble, I end up with the same trouble. I share your pain, Gus, so to speak, if you get my drift."

I laughed. "Yeah, I get what you mean. Not to worry. There's nothing that can happen that's gonna drag you in. I promise."

"You promise? That's it? Hell, I feel better already."

I spread my arms like I wanted to hug him. "Not sure what else I can do. I'm on the straight and narrow, pal. I'm working for Luis Móntez, checking in with my parole officer, staying away from bad influences."

"Except me."

"Yeah, except you."

He took another drink.

"These are interesting times, Gus. You see how Denver is changing." He rotated his arm in a wide arc that included his shop and the mountains to the west.

"Yeah, a lot changed in a few years. Grass is legal. That's big, I hear. But some things never change."

"Like what?"

"The Rockies can't win."

He laughed. "That's true. These days, no one wins, not even the Broncos."

"Except the marijuana dealers."

He slowly nodded. "You can say that again. The pot business is wide open. A guy with the money and ambition can make a lot more money selling weed. And the cops can't do anything about it. It's almost wild west boom times."

"But you didn't want any part of it?"

"No, not for me. I told you, there's a lot of oversight. And some of the people in that business . . . "

"What. They're dopers?"

"Ha, if that was all, no problem. Seriously, it's a tricky business. The state says okay, but the feds still trip on the illegality of kush. Creates logistical problems for the young entrepreneur, and most of them are real young."

"What kind of problems?"

"Like moving the product across state lines. Can't be done, so a guy has to be smart about selling to out-of-state buyers. It can be handled, but it has to be watched."

"What else?"

"What to do with all the goddamn money that's pouring in every hour. Millions, and millions. But many banks won't touch it, because of the feds. So, for now it's mostly a cash business. And where there's that much cash . . . "

"There are people who want to take it."

"Exactly. In the old days, that would've been hard for me to resist. But cold hard cash has created an entirely new business. Security for the pot shops. Temporary storage for money. Bodyguards for boxes and boxes of dollar bills."

"Man. Who does that kind of work?"

"The kind of guys you might expect. Military, ex-police, retired prison guards. And others."

"Hoodlums?"

He stared across the patio and over to the mountains. "Of course. So now we got crooks guarding money against other crooks. Some of these guys are really bad. And I don't mean in a good way."

"Hell, if I'd known, I might have held out for one of those jobs. But I'd probably be too stoned all the time to be much good at guarding the money."

He laughed. "So, what you want?"

The waiter served my tea. I took a long cold drink. Excellent. Not sugary sweet. Spicy but smooth, real strong flavor.

When I finished I said, "Nothing too traumatic. A potential client of the office. I'm doing a background check. I can't talk to you about her. I'm learning that lawyers got their rules about confidentiality and privacy that the good ones follow to a T. But I wanted to ask about Sam Contreras. Remember him? The old Roundhouse? He's part of the picture with the client, so Móntez wants any info I can gather about him. Just in case. Whatever you know about his setup with the bar, and what kind of other stuff he might have been into. Anything, really."

"Damn, Gus. Here you go again." He made a noise like a growl. I thought he might reach across the table and slap me.

"What? Only background info. That's all I'm asking. Contreras is dead. What harm is there in asking about him?"

"You know how he died, right?"

"Went down with his boat in the Sea of Cortez. Supposed to be piracy, something like that."

"That's the accepted version. There are others. The first story was that the boat simply sunk in a storm. Then they thought the two men on board might have had a falling out. The Mexican Coast Guard eventually pieced together that Sam and his guide had been overrun. Those so-called pirates were never caught."

"That's pretty much what I heard."

"So you think it's okay to ask about a murdered guy when the murderers are still running around? You don't think you might draw someone's attention that you don't want?"

Jerome thought like that. "What we're working on doesn't have anything to do with Sam's death in Mexico. This is an entirely different matter. Anyhow, I don't expect any pirates to come sailing up to Denver anytime soon."

"You're testing my patience, Gus. I'm not going through the OK Corral for you again, understand, Corral?"

The play on words was mildly amusing but it told me that Jerome was pulling my chain for the most part.

"There's no risk I know of. That's all I can say."

Jerome grunted. "I should know better." Then he tipped on the back legs of his chair and used his heels to balance himself at an angle. "Contreras had a reputation, you know that. And he deserved it. Guy could be mean, a brute. On the other hand, he sometimes had good intentions. He hauled food and water to the homeless that camped by the Platte."

"I didn't know that," I said.

"Yeah. I saw it. The bar was no five star deal, but it was all right for a dive by the tracks. Longtime customers that returned every week."

"I had heard that. Móntez told me the same."

"The thing is . . . "

"What?"

"His lifestyle away from the bar was not what you'd expect. The Roundhouse was not where the Chamber of Commerce would send tourists. It was just there, a watering hole where the beer was cold and cheap. Mechanics, roofers, construction guys, a few bikers, whores taking a break—that was the crowd."

"Móntez said he used to drink there, when he was a drinker."

"Oh yeah. He could tie one on with the best of the boozers. Didn't matter he was a lawyer. Saw him tangle a couple of times with guys I wouldn't cross."

"He's settled down."

"I don't know about that. He's older, that's probably it. I'd bet that if you put him in the right situation his old reflexes will kick in."

"Can't see el jefe as some kind of bar brawler."

"Anyway, the customers at the Roundhouse didn't flash a lot of cash. But Contreras had a nice house up north by Standley Lake. He didn't live a real big life but I always thought he had to have more going on than he showed."

"How's that?" I finished off the tea.

"Well, he bought or maybe he leased a new car every two years. He spent a few weeks every summer somewhere along the Mexican coast in a place he owned with a few other guys. That's when he went on his fishing trips. They fished, drank, partied. Nothing too extreme, but still it caught my attention when I heard about those things."

"Maybe he had investments that paid off. People do that, I hear."

"Didn't strike me as the type, but could be. He rented out his parents' old house in the Westwood neighborhood after they died. That couldn't have been much but it was something. He married late but he had women around all the time."

"Nothing too fancy, though, right?"

"Right."

"A guy trying to stay under the radar but there's still something," I said. "So he most likely had another source of income?"

"Yeah." He stared at me, smirked. "And you know more than you're telling me about Sam." He paused. "Guy was dirty, right?"

"Can't say much more unless Móntez gives me the okay." I wanted to ask him about María Contreras but Móntez had warned me about tipping off anyone that she might be his client. "Thanks for your thoughts."

He shrugged. "Didn't really tell you anything you didn't know or couldn't guess. You just want back-up for whatever you tell your lawyer."

"Maybe." I stood up to leave. "Tell me, Jerome. How do you know this stuff?"

Jerome squinted at me. "Seriously? You're gonna ask me that?"

"Yeah, never mind. I forgot for a sec who I'm talking to."

"That's right."

4 [Luis]

you can't spend what you ain't got
you can't lose what you ain't never had

Gus filled me in on what his friend Jerome told him, plus he gave me all the information he'd found on Ms. Contreras. The stuff about Sam confirmed my suspicions that there was more to the guy than simply a rough-and-tumble bar owner. I'd known many men like Sam over the years. They presented one front while they worked hard at something else entirely. If they weren't complete outlaws, they often skirted the fringes of lawful behavior, thinking they were untouchable, that their more-or-less honest day jobs insured a type of immunity. It never worked that way, but I didn't complain because those guys kept me in business. Sooner or later they stepped over the line big time, or the police thought they had because of their past history, and the heat would come down on them like the scorching wind from one of Colorado's brush fires on the eastern plains. Then these guys needed the help of Luis Móntez, Esq., Chicano lawyer and cool-down specialist.

Nothing too surprising about the wife. Forty years old, no kids, worked for the Denver Public Library (almost twenty years). She looked like what she offered, nothing more or less.

"The first thing I'll do," I told her on the phone call when we confirmed our attorney-client relationship, "will be to meet with Valdez. Has he contacted you again?"

"Yes. He called last night. I told him I had a lawyer and that he had to deal with you."

"How'd he take that?"

"Not well. He cussed me out, said I was making trouble where there shouldn't be any. Said a lawyer would just take money from him and me. But he stopped almost as soon as he began. Caught himself, I guess. Finally said he had no problem meeting with whoever I wanted. Even the police. He repeated that a couple of times. I told him you would contact him. I asked for his address but he wouldn't tell me where he's staying. I gave him your name."

"Good, that's all good. If he is on the level, and we're only dealing with the split of business assets, then we can work something out, I'm sure."

"But I don't know where the money is. That's the problem. He's insisting that I know and that I'm stalling to keep as much as I can. But I don't know. I don't know where the goddamn money is." Her voice trailed off across the line.

"Then I'll have to convince him that he's wasting his time."

"Exactly. If I knew where that kind of money is, don't you think I would've spent some of it by now? It's been years."

"I won't tell him this, but he has to figure out that he should get a lawyer for a civil action against you or whatever's left of Sam's estate or the business assets, if anything. I'd welcome that, actually. Settling this problem in court is much better than trying to deal with a man who is convinced he's been wronged and will do anything to come out ahead."

"That's what I'm afraid of," she said.

"But he can't force you to give him something you don't have."

I wanted to reassure my client but that was difficult since I was on uncertain ground. I didn't sound all that positive, not even to myself. I hadn't quite persuaded myself that María Contreras had told me everything she knew, and Valdez was still a great unknown. He could be a regular guy looking for his fair cut, or, as I suspected, a slimy con artist trying to wring money out of the vulnerable wife of his dead associate. What I didn't want to think about were the other possibilities, the ones that included the scenario where Valdez had something to do with the killing of Sam Contreras and now was looking to tie up loose ends.

"So you'll take care of it from here?" she asked.

"Yes. I'll call him today, set up a meeting. I'm hopeful I can have some news, good news, for you in the next few days."

"I hope so, too." She didn't sound optimistic. "Thank you, Mr. Móntez."

She said she would send me a thousand dollar retainer that included two hundred for immediate expenses. I explained my hourly rate and all the other details I had to give her to make sure we were on the same page about what I would do, and what I was charging her for. I told her that if I wrapped up the problem with the one meeting, I would most likely return some of the retainer. She said goodbye without seeming to care about what I did with her money.

"You only asked for a thousand up front?" Rosa said when I gave her my notes so she could type the client agreement. "Why so cheap? You in love again?"

"Damn, Rosa, where's that coming from?"

"What? You never got in over your head because of a client, especially a female client?" She folded her arms across her chest and stared me down.

She knew the answer, so I ignored the question. "I don't want to gouge the woman for money. I can take care of this with a phone call and a meeting. I don't need big bucks for that."

"How about your time, my time, even Gus' time? A thousand won't cover the hours we've already spent on this."

She had a point but I didn't acknowledge it. I never was a good businessman, never made the money I should have as a lawyer. But I had no regrets. As they say in the movies, I don't stay awake at night thinking about what might have been or what I should have done. I sleep very well, thank you.

"If we need more, she'll get it for us. She didn't make a big deal out of having to pay me. This guy Valdez is really messing with her head. I'll feel good when I can get him out of her life."

My secretary shook her head. "You'll never learn, Louie. But it's your business, your clients and your headaches. Don't expect me to fix it when we're out of money at the end of the month."

I reminded myself that it was my name on the office door. Rosa worked for me. I kept my thoughts to myself. It was my turn to shake my head. "Whatever. We'll be okay, Rosa. We always are."

I called the number María had given me for Ricky Valdez. He answered on the first ring.

"Hello Móntez," he said before I had a chance to tell him my name.

"Mr. Valdez. You know I'm representing María Contreras. Looks like we should meet to talk about this problem with some money you say is owed to you by the late Sam Contreras."

He laughed. "That's one way of putting it. But let me clear up something. I'm not talking about a debt. I'm talking about my property, my money. The two-fifty grand is money I made and earned for Aztlán Treasures. I was the head of that company. There never was any doubt about that. I gave the money to Sam for him to keep for me, and I would have paid him out of it, as part of our arrangement, if he hadn't been killed. But the money is mine, it's not owed to me, it's mine. Your client has it and won't return it."

He spit out the words like he expected his phone to die in the middle of our conversation and he had to say all he wanted as quickly as possible.

"Are you saying she stole it?" I asked.

"I talked to the cops about that. They said I had to handle it myself."

"So they don't think there was any theft?"

"They didn't say yes or no about that. Just that I had to deal with it with my own lawyer or in court or however I wanted. So, that's what I'm doing. Like the cops said. We'll see how much I get out of doing it this way."

"What makes you think that Ms. Contreras has the money, or knows where it is? She tells me she doesn't know anything about the money, and that she had little or nothing to do with her husband's business."

He laughed again. "She can say whatever she wants. I know different, and so does she. Sam agreed to hold the money for me, like a bank. I was getting ready to do my time. He told me how he gave it to his wife so she could add it to some kind of account or mutual fund so it would earn interest while I was in prison. I believed him, he had no reason to lie to me. Now she won't give it up. She doesn't know who she's messing with."

I wrote notes on my pad as he talked. There's always two sides to every story, I reminded myself. But Valdez's side sounded weak. Or was my other hunch the one I should follow? The one about not trusting Ms. Contreras?

"Before we get too deep into this, let's arrange a meeting. I've got some paperwork, what you sent to Ms. Contreras. I assume you have something else. Let's meet, show me all that you have. Maybe we can resolve this."

"I'll meet, but we ain't resolving this until I get my money, all my money."

We agreed to meet the next day around 11:00 A.M. I suggested that I could meet him wherever he wanted; he said my office was fine.

≫ ≫ ≫

Gus' second case began later the same day we started work for María Contreras.

He introduced me to Jackie O. Later he told me that her original name had been Javier Ortega, but the name, and other parts of Jackie's identity, had been changed years ago—name change petition, sex change operation, new clothes.

"We've been friends since we were kids," Gus explained. "We cruised the Northside in my father's old Lincoln. Two homies looking for action."

Jackie's bright orange lips smiled. She loved color, no doubt. That day in my office Jackie highlighted her orange lipstick with orange capri pants, white stilettos, a subtle violet blouse and an amber scarf wrapped around her head.

"I wore one of my weekend outfits to meet you, Mr. Móntez. You like?" She didn't wait for a response. "I've heard about you for a long time now. It's so my pleasure."

She extended a hand that featured well-manicured orange and black polka-dotted fingernails. I shook it and a few bits of glitter flew loose.

"Gus tells me you're having a problem with your employer?"

Gus and Jackie sat down and I cleared a space on my desk so I could keep notes.

"Former employer," Jackie said. "I finally had to leave."

"What's the problem?"

Jackie took a deep breath. She sat back in the chair and fidgeted with her fingers, like she held a phantom cigarette.

"I've been a bartender at a bunch of different places—from dives like the Holiday Bar & Grill to downtown joints that cater to lawyers and bankers. I even did a minute at the Ship Tavern in the Brown Palace."

I wrote "bartender" on my legal pad.

She continued. "I'm back at it, behind the bar. One of the new places on Tejon, not far from the old Dog House. Remember that place? Anyway, it's not what I ever really wanted to do, you know? Not for the rest of my life. So I went back to school and recently got a degree in Business Management from Metro State."

"Congratulations," I said.

"I'm only saying this because of what happened. I'm not a dummy, or a fool."

I nodded.

"I got a non-bartending gig about six months ago. Working as an administrative assistant for a real asshole. He's my problem."

"Because of your, uh, taste in clothes?"

Jackie squinted like she smelled a rotten piece of meat. "Something like that."

"No, seriously. You get hassled because of who you are, or how you express yourself?"

"Oh, that. That's a given. I dealt with that a long time ago. No, what I'm talking about is related, but different."

"Start from the beginning."

Jackie's long legs stretched across the floor.

"The place is called Dynamic-Tec." She grabbed a pen from my desk and wrote the name of the company on the back of one of my business cards. "They do all kinds of tech support, from cleaning out viruses to hooking up peoples' cable TV and sound systems. All I was hired to do was help the main guy, Joseph Cristelli, with clerical stuff and office management kinds of things."

"Cristelli's the owner?"

"Yeah. The person in charge, and he knows it. He's some kind of genius, at least that's what he tells his employees every day, and I mean every day. He's started up about six different companies like Dynamic-Tec. Sold them all and now he's very rich. He's a young guy, still in his twenties. Dresses like an old beatnik, though. Beard, those skinny jeans, a leather bucket hat. You see guys like him all over the Northside now."

"You worked for him for less than six months?"

"Yeah. I left about a month ago. Gus said I should talk to you, see if there was anything I could do. The jerk owes me a month's salary. He won't pay because he says I quit and forfeited that month. I told him he was full of it, but he just laughed and said to sue him. So that's what I want to do."

"Why'd you quit?" I thought she would have led with that crucial piece of information but clients often surprised me when they told their stories. I could never predict how the first interview would play out.

"The guy's no good." She rushed into the heart of her story. "He can hack anything and he steals private information that could help him or might embarrass people. Then he uses that info to get jobs, or to back off the competition. It's simple for him, but effective. The victims don't even know they've been hacked. Cristelli has it figured out so that it looks like he outsmarted the competition. He thought I was a dummy or a punk or something so he didn't

really hide what he was doing. Thought I would just go along, I
guess. Finally, I called him on it. Surprised the hell out of him, but
I'm not a crook. He wanted me to cover up what he was doing.
Promised me a raise, even a cut of his action. All kinds of stuff.
When I wouldn't play, he went from nice guy to bully. He said I
needed to disappear and shut up, and if I didn't like it he would
have me arrested for sexually harassing his other office workers, if
you can believe that bullshit."

"What did he mean about harassing the other employees?"

"Look, I'm an easy target. Wherever I work, there's gonna be
somebody who doesn't like me. Usually, it's much more than just
dislike. They hate me. The religious nuts are the worst. At
Dynamic-Tec there was a woman who refused to have anything to
do with me; claimed I was an abomination from hell and she
wouldn't sin by working with me. Cristelli told her to ease off, at
first. Then, when I wouldn't go along with him, he told me that the
woman, Clara Villagrana, would be only too happy to talk to the
cops about how I made lewd and lascivious comments to her, and
that I kept tormenting her in a sexual way until finally one day I
exposed myself to her. Like I would be showing off what I had
become. I took a swing at him but two of his pals pulled me off and
threw me out of the building. The next day I got a hand-delivered
letter from him accepting my so-called resignation."

I scribbled notes as fast as I could to keep up with Jackie's nar-
rative. "You never actually quit?"

"Not really. I didn't have a choice."

"You sure you want to stir this up?" Gus said. "He'll probably
follow through on his threat to sic the police on you. And he's
probably also cleaned up his computer history so that there's no
evidence of his hacking schemes. If this woman makes a complaint, it could be difficult for you, to say the least."

"I have to do something. I'm tired of this shit."

"What do you know about Villagrana? Would she go as far as
lying to the police?"

"I don't know. She really hated me. Couldn't be in the same room with me. She might do anything. But I can't say for sure. She acted all religious but maybe lying isn't a sin these days."

I looked at Gus. "Can you check out this Villagrana? If she's Cristelli's leverage, she might be the weak link only because she thinks she's doing God's work."

"Yeah," Gus said. "Either that or she's faking it and in on the whole thing with Cristelli."

"You mean like his partner?" Jackie asked.

"Something like that. Guess we'll find out."

5 [Gus]

go, get out of Denver, baby
go, get out of Denver, baby go, go

After our meeting with Jackie I had to rush to an appointment with Dirty Harry. I wrapped up a handful of details, then drove over to my parole officer's office across from the U.S. Mint.

Frankly, Harry and I had not warmed up to one another. I thought he took his job way too seriously, and I got the impression that he thought I wasn't serious enough about my obligations to the state and him. But I walked the line.

"How's it working out with Móntez?"

"Good. Good. He keeps me busy. I'm learning a lot."

"Anything I need to know about?"

"You mean about what I'm working on with Móntez?"

"Sure. Tell me about what you're actually doing. What's a typical day like?"

"Well, I can't talk about clients, you know that, right?"

"Tell me what you can. You know what I mean." He sounded bothered.

Harry wore a gray tie over a black and gray plaid shirt. The tie hung loosely around his skinny neck and the curled corners of his shirt collar. No jacket. His hair bunched up in several places. I doubted he owned a comb. Stubble dotted his chin, no matter what time I met with him. He looked like a hillbilly dressed up for his annual night out on the town.

"I served a half-dozen subpoenas last week for a hearing Luis has coming up later this month. One guy didn't want the papers. He threw them back at me but Luis says he was served. I signed affidavits that he'll file with the court. The guy has to show up."

"Lawyers, huh? I suppose if Móntez wants me in court, to waste time I can't really spare, and you dropped a subpoena on me, right here, across my desk, I'd have to show up, is that it? Nothing I can do about it?"

He knew perfectly well how it worked. "I just serve the papers, sign the affidavits."

"What else? You more than a process server?"

"I interviewed a few witnesses, wrote up their statements, had them sign. That kind of thing."

He put down the yellow legal pad he used for his notes. "Jerome Rodríguez? He part of a case you're working on?"

I nodded. Harry was good. I'd met with Jerome only earlier that same day.

"Móntez wanted me to talk with him. Possible witness in one of his cases. How'd you know I saw him?"

His smirk irritated me but I didn't show it. "Remember, Gus. I got eyes on you. This Rodríguez is a bit shaky, has a history of interaction with various law enforcement agencies." Jerome would have loved that. "I'll need something from your lawyer that confirms you got together with Rodríguez as part of your work. And the next time you have to see him, because of your job, of course, I need to know ahead of time. We clear on that?"

"No problem, sir. No problem at all." I think my dislike of Dirty Harry turned to hate at that moment.

When Harry was finished with me I headed home, where Corrine waited with a dinner of rice and enchiladas. I didn't care for her arroz but I would never tell her that. It was edible but it wasn't the fluffy, soft rice I remembered our mother cooked. Corrine's enchiladas were a different story. Corrine had never been afraid of eating or cooking with hot chile, and enchiladas were her prime examples of how to work a miracle with corn tortillas, cheese, onions and a velvety red sauce that overwhelmed all six senses.

"You don't know how much I missed your cooking."

"I tried to get some food to you, but the hassle discouraged me. I should have tried harder." I looked up from the food. "I'm sorry," she said.

I wasn't used to this apologetic sister. I hoped that with the passage of time Corrine would return to her old self and we could resort to our much more exciting love-hate relationship.

"I'm here now and the food is here and we're having a great dinner. That's all that matters. Nothing to be sorry about. Prison and everything that went with it is done and it's fading from memory. This is great, Corrine. I can't quit eating."

The rest of the meal went by quickly but Corrine never really perked up. I finished five enchiladas and two beers. I was washing dishes when Móntez called to add something to his earlier message. He told me to find Valdez and watch him.

"What does this guy do? Who does he know? What's his story? Ask around. Anything you learn you give to me before my meeting with him tomorrow."

"I only have tonight to do this?"

"Yeah. What's the problem?"

"Don't expect much. It's not a lot of time."

"Sometimes this work moves fast, Gus. Other times, it's too slow. Justice delayed, you know?"

My very busy day suddenly was a very long day.

"You have an address for him?"

"No. I've asked around but no one knows this guy. At least not the people I know."

"Right. I'll get you what I can."

According to María Contreras, Valdez had been in prison during some of the same time as me. I finished the dishes, then checked the most obvious Internet sources to find his address. Nothing probable turned up under the names of Richard or Ricky or Ricardo or Richie Valdez. Not even Rico Valdez. I avoided the most likely place for information about an ex-con but eventually I had no choice. The night moved at its own quick pace and Móntez needed something now.

I called someone I knew from prison. Eric "Shorty" Macías owed me a favor, something about helping him out when the odds were definitely not in his favor. He sounded happy to hear from me, although I assumed he was high. Drugs were his devil. They were at the core of his trouble in prison but men like Shorty never faced up to that undeniable fact. We had our small talk, our "what's new" chit-chat. When I asked him about Valdez he came across as relieved. I guessed he expected me to ask for something bigger or more expensive. It's a bitch to owe someone you did time with; not a position I ever wanted to be in.

"No sweat, Gus," he said over the phone. "I'll find something. I recognize the name; might have even crossed paths with the dude one time or another. I'll get back to you."

I was about to go downstairs when Corrine emerged from her bedroom, all covered in make-up, sporting shiny new shoes and a relatively new dress that hugged her too tightly in too many strategic places.

"I'm gonna bar hop with Barb and Lucía. I'll be late, so don't wait up. You don't need the car, do you?"

"I'm good." She ran out the front door leaving the scents of perfume and minty mouthwash in her wake. I liked that she wanted to have a good time. Her remorse about me had apparently disappeared.

I went downstairs, found the headphones, wrapped them around my ears and turned on the turntable. I listened to the laments and celebrations of Muddy Waters and Little Walter and Magic Sam. A nervous buzz circled my head but I figured that came from my need to do my job right, and the knowledge that Móntez wanted, needed, information about Valdez that I was expected to find. While I listened to music, I did what I could on the computer, searching for information, finding a little.

Shorty called about an hour later and gave me an address.

"The guy was down in Cañon City, not over with us near as I can tell. But enough people move around the system that I got a line on him. The address is listed under someone else's name, a cousin or something like that. But the guy I talked to swore it's where he spends his days."

"Good. That's what I need."

"Great. Glad I could help." He must have thought we were even now, that his debt had been paid. I didn't agree but I didn't say anything about it.

"You know anything else about Valdez? What's his rep? Friends? Where's his hangout?"

He thought for a few seconds. "His reputation's not square, Gus. He was popped for a small-time smuggling thing and did his time but there's talk he cut a deal early on, and that he snitched on a few guys to cut his sentence."

"Lot of guys get that jacket but it doesn't mean it's true. Could be jailhouse politics."

"Yeah, could be. Unless I was there in Cañon I can't say for sure. I can follow up on that if you want."

Under prison math, then I would owe him.

"It's good for now. If I need something else I'll let you know."

"Okay. You just call. Anyhow, his house is in southwest Denver, off of Morrison and Kentucky."

"Westwood, right?"

He repeated the address and I wrote it down, as well as a note to tell Móntez about the Westwood connection.

I think Macías was hurt when I told him I couldn't meet him later for a drink. I wanted to tell him that I no longer belonged to the club where he and others like him had lifetime memberships. I had let mine lapse even though I'd paid the dues. I said only that I had other plans, and then I hung up. My watch read almost ten.

I texted the address to Móntez, said I would find it and added that, if our guy showed, I would watch him for a few hours. To myself I said, "Waste of time."

I used the office's account with a do-it-yourself car rental outfit. I found one of the mini cars parked two blocks from Corrine's house. The "revitalized" Northside was the perfect area for this kind of enterprise. The hipsters and yuppies and young marrieds must have loved the idea of accessing an environmentally friendly automobile through glitzy technology that included a plastic card that unlocked the car and turned on the timer. Corrine still lived in the middle of the gentrification, although she confessed that it was a struggle, especially with the developers calling every week trying to convince her to sell.

The rental was a blue and white toy, almost too small for me, but Luis told me the rates were cheap and I could park it almost anywhere without worrying about meters, tickets or gas. As I drove south on always-busy I-25 from the Northside to the Westwood neighborhood, I felt exposed, vulnerable, silly. The car was smaller than Corrine's Kia. If any other car or truck hit me, my ride would crumble into a tiny ball of smashed metal and plastic, with me jellied in the middle of the ball.

I knew how I looked to all the drivers who passed me, some honking their horns even though I was in the slow lane. In the tiny car I came off as a brown-skinned, muscle-bound hulk pressed up against the steering wheel of a car that had no business carrying me.

Westwood was one of the few remaining neighborhoods in the Denver city limits where the word "barrio" still fit. Working families who'd been residents for decades, damaged but proud houses and small shops that dealt in everything from motorcycle repairs to marijuana cookies, all mixed together in a crooked rectangle bordered by Alameda, Mississippi, Federal and Sheridan. Tattoo artists collected books for neighborhood kids, Mexican taquerías sprung up and died like mushrooms, while the public art of Chicano artist Carlos Frésquez welcomed visitors to the community at Morrison Road, the diagonal street that cut through the heart of Westwood.

I drove past the address. Valdez lived in a gray aging house that must have had all of four rooms. The dirt yard had no plant life. No life period. I parked the car several blocks from his house, locked it up and electronically closed the account. I walked back to Valdez's house. The lights were on but I didn't see anyone. I wasn't sure what I was supposed to do, or what Móntez expected from me. He'd simply said, "Watch him."

I stood in darkness under a tall pine tree with rough branches and hoped that I would stay awake. I made myself as comfortable as possible. I bent my knees and squeezed into the darkness of the tree. From where I stood I could see the front and a side door, and a large dirty picture window covered with dark blinds or curtains.

The night was filled with throbbing noise. Thumping bass rhythms mixed with barking dogs, ambulance sirens and hollering children. Screen doors slammed, water flowed along the curb and traffic moved on the major streets in a constant hum.

I watched and waited and managed to stay awake until midnight, but I drifted in and out of awareness. Then I must have dozed off because I jerked against the tree when I heard a distant car alarm.

A pickup truck painted primer gray sat on the gravel driveway that ran along the side of the house. It looked like a late 1970s Ford.

The lights were still on in the house but there was no movement, no sign of any life.

I wrote down the New Mexico license plate number hanging on the back of the pickup. I thought I could check that out back at the office and then Móntez could decide how he wanted to use the information, if it mattered at all. I hadn't expected much, so even a license plate number struck me as worthwhile.

I turned to walk to the rental car when headlights lit up my side of the street and I jumped back in the shadows. A dark, late model Camry pulled to a stop in front of the house. For almost five minutes nothing happened. The driver's door opened and a woman stepped out. I couldn't see her face because of the scarf wrapped around her head. She carried a large handbag. She rushed to the side door and tapped on the cracked wood. Light from the house surrounded her when the door opened. A man grabbed her arm and pulled her inside. The door slammed shut.

I walked around the tree and looked for a way that I could approach the house without being seen. Such a route did not exist.

As soon as I entered the street I would be exposed and in clear view from the picture window.

I stood where I was and waited.

Fifteen minutes. The side door opened abruptly. The woman emerged wrapping the scarf across her forehead. I saw her face for a second. María Contreras. She ran out of the house, looked over her shoulder, then jumped in her car. She sped away almost immediately.

Two minutes. A tall man wearing a dark hoody slipped out of the house and climbed in the pickup truck. He backed out of the yard and drove down the street in the opposite direction from the woman. The lights in the house remained on.

I looked up and down the street. I saw no one, not a kid on a bike or an old-timer out for a walk. It was late, I reminded myself. I ran across the street and peered in through the side door window. A man lay on the kitchen floor. He looked unconscious or dead. Then I saw the blood seeping out of a gaping wound on his right temple. I backed away from the door, checked the street again, then ran to my tree and called Móntez.

"Get out of there and meet me at the office," he said.

"Shouldn't I call the cops?"

"I'm calling my client first. I'll see you in about twenty minutes. You sure he's dead?"

"Yeah. That hole in his head is too big."

"Get out of there," he repeated.

For an instant I toyed with the idea that no matter what Móntez said, I should report what I'd seen. But that old feeling crept up my spine and I reacted as I always had. I didn't want to connect with the police right then. I jogged through the Westwood night back to the car, away from the bloody scene. I felt like the kid who was blamed for everything—the sucker, the punk, the kid who never knew what hit him. I couldn't shake the feeling.

≫ ≫ ≫

"You didn't recognize the guy in the pickup, or the dead guy?" Móntez looked worried.

"No. I couldn't make out any face details on the man and I almost didn't recognize Contreras because of the scarf. I wouldn't have known it was her except for her license photo in the file. The dead guy didn't look like much, just dead."

"He could have been Valdez?"

"Sure. He could have been anybody. I don't really know."

The image of the bleeding man stayed in my head. I thought after all I'd been through I was immune to blood, gore and death. I realized I wasn't and I felt better about myself.

"And you didn't hear any gunshots or fighting? Nothing like that?" the lawyer asked for about the tenth time. We were repeating ourselves.

"Nothing. I'm not sure the dead man was shot. Someone could have opened his skull with a hammer or something like that."

"You think Contreras did it?"

"I don't know, Luis. I saw her run in, then run out, followed by the hoody guy. He was there first. He could have been the killer. I'm not sure how long he was in the house."

Móntez arched his eyebrows.

"Or the vic could've already been dead before either of them arrived. I didn't hear anything and I was there for a couple of hours. The action wasn't much, it all happened fast."

"But she was in long enough to clobber someone and make sure he was dead?"

"Yeah, I guess. It doesn't take long to kill someone, does it?"

He looked sideways at me. "Depends, I guess."

"I thought she didn't know where Valdez lived. Wasn't that what she told you? Wasn't she kind of obsessed with knowing where he lived?"

"Yeah. She wanted to know where he was, for her protection, she said. After you left your message about what you found out, I called her. She asked if I had an address and I gave it to her."

"Earlier tonight?" I was wary of where the conversation was headed.

"Yes. She knew what we knew."

"You call your client again? Now that there's a dead person involved? What's her story?"

He shook his head. "I get an 'out of service' message on her cell."

"Christ."

"But that's not all."

"Really?"

"Yeah. On my way over here I drove past the address she gave us on her client information sheet."

I could see it coming.

"It's an empty lot."

I tried to take in all he was telling me. "She planned this whole thing, to get a line on Valdez?" I said. "She used us. And she's already on the run."

"Looks like it. She's moving fast."

We kept at it, going over what I had seen, what it could mean and what it meant for our work for María Contreras. I was tired and sleepy. Móntez looked worn out, but he talked like he could go all night. I decided I had enough.

"I need your legal advice, Luis. So, what do we do, counselor?"

Móntez stood up and stretched his arms over his head like he was greeting the sun. He reminded me of the prison's yoga class. He walked behind his desk with his arms reaching for the ceiling, his fingers vibrating. Gray hair streaked his temples and mustache. His dark jaw tightened and his shining eyes shrunk to black dots. He stared at a poster that hung on his wall: a bunch of deep purple grapes dripped blood. The words "Boycott Grapes!" stretched over the fruit like an ironic halo.

"Time to call the cops."

6 [Luis]

my father said to be strong
and that a good man could never do wrong

Gus and I talked until the sun came up. We mapped out all the possible scenarios that could explain what Gus saw at the Westwood house. None of them sounded totally right to either of us. We were sure that Gus watched María Contreras and Richard Valdez at the house, but unsure whether Valdez was the dead man or the man in the pickup.

I turned on Rosa's computer and ran a quick search of the license plate number. It didn't take long to learn that the plates had been stolen in Las Cruces, New Mexico, along with the late model Honda to which they'd been attached. The guy in the pickup most likely had already tossed them into somebody's dumpster.

We finally agreed that we had to get the police involved but the risk for Gus was too high considering that he'd left the scene of a major crime. Parolees were sent back to prison for far less than that. He wanted to call the police in the first place, but we decided discretion was a better route to go. I tried to reassure him. The worst he was guilty of was following his lawyer's, and employer's misguided directions.

"Let me take you home, Gus. Get some sleep." He rubbed his eyes, looked around the office as though he finally realized where he was.

We drove in silence for the most part. He asked when I would call the police.

"As soon as I let you off. Might as well get them over to the house tonight." I paused. "Uh, this morning." The eastern sky streaked orange and red as the sun made its way up from the distant plains.

When I stopped at Corrine's house, Gus sat in my car without moving. "Something wrong?" I asked.

"Who is this woman, and why did she pick you to run her game? If she wanted to kill Valdez, there had to be an easier way to find him."

"I never met her before. No idea why she would come to my office for help with Valdez. She said she was married to Sam Contreras. I knew him, sort of. I don't remember her from his funeral. But maybe she recalled me or Sam mentioned something."

"People do talk about you," he said.

"That good or bad?"

He shrugged. "Her story about Valdez trying to get his hands on the money? You still buy that?"

"I talked with someone who said he was Valdez. He sounded serious about wanting his money, and that María knows where it is. If he's the dead man, I doubt we'll ever know the whole truth."

"Her story sounds more and more off key."

"I agree. Right now, I don't know what to believe. I'll call the cops, report the killing, and we'll start over tomorrow morning. Get some rest."

He slowly opened the car door, squirmed out of his seat and then he stopped. He turned back to look at me.

"It's just that . . . Oh, screw it."

"What is it? What's bothering you?"

He shook his head. "Can't say this hasn't been interesting. Be careful, Luis. See you tomorrow."

I made an anonymous call to the police department using a public phone, maybe the last one on the Northside. The scarred device hung on a pole near the corner of Thirty-Second and Vallejo. A metal half-shell, covered with graffiti tags and hipster stickers, hovered around the grungy phone. I stood in the dawn shadow of a pre-gentrification building that housed a chiropractor and karate school. The only people I'd ever seen using the phone, early morning or late at night, were hunched-over Latinos trying to find a ride, or drunk young white men, also looking for a ride.

I lived less than ten minutes from Corrine Corral's house. I drove with the window open. The morning air slid over my face and rushed through my remaining hair. I was suddenly fully awake. I couldn't help but notice that the Northside had changed but I'd quit worrying about it. It's a given that change happens to all of us whether we want it or not. I parked in front of my house. As I locked the car, my cell buzzed. Gus. He couldn't wait a few hours to talk at my office.

"What'd they say when you reported the dead man?"

"Nothing really. The 911 operator I talked with pushed for my name, of course. Wanted to know how I knew about the dead guy. I just gave them the address and told them what they would find. Took less than a minute."

"I guess that's all we can do for now?"

"For now. I probably should do more. Never learn, I guess. I'll talk to the police officially, as soon as there's news about the killing and who was killed. If it connects to my client, I should try to find out what the police are doing, even if she has skipped out on me. If it's Valdez, I have a bad mess on my hands."

Gus groaned but I let it slide. I admitted to myself that I was thrown by the turn of events.

"I don't want to screw up, Luis," he said. "I'm on thin ice with my P.O. If he thinks I'm involved in this, in any way, you know he'll send me back."

An idea opened up in front of me, out of nowhere. "I'll talk with Ana Domingo," I said. "Maybe she can help if Harold Mills gets all hot and bothered."

"Who?"

"Ana Domingo. She's the fairly new Community Liaison Officer for the department. Helping parolees is supposed to be one of her projects. That and things like Meet-A-Cop nights and school assembly presentations. Not a fan of mine, guess I've defended too many losers she thinks should be put away for the good of the community. But we have a professional relationship. From what I've read about her job, whatever anyone talks to her about is supposed to be confidential except in the most serious life or death circumstances."

"I think we're there, Luis. Someone got killed. Sounds serious to me. And you're gonna believe that she won't run to her supervisors with what you tell her? You and I know better."

Gus spoke a lot of truth, a nasty habit.

"I'll do what I need to do to protect you, Gus. Beginning with last night when you called me from your stakeout in Westwood, you're my client as well as my employee. I have a duty to you that even the cops can't violate." I don't think he believed me. "But we need to know what's going on."

"María Contreras is your client, too. How does that work?" That was what had bothered him all night. The more I learned about Gus, the more I respected his smarts.

"Good question, Gus. At this point, I have to consider that she's abandoned our relationship. She hasn't responded to my messages or calls, and I can't communicate with her. I don't think I'm crossways with her as long as all I do is help you connect with the police and don't implicate her."

"I don't see how you can pull that off, Luis. This law stuff is crazy. Not sure I understand what you can or can't do. Not sure I want to understand."

"The rules can be tricky. I can only do my best, and what is best for my clients."

"Yeah, tricky." I could hear him move around, switch the phone from one hand to the other. "We start with a simple 'she's got my money and I want it,'" he said. "And end with 'maybe she iced someone and we helped her find the guy she killed, and hope we don't send our client to jail.'"

As I said, Gus had a nasty habit.

7 [Gus]

but don't play with me 'cause you're playing with fire

After I called Móntez I thought I should check the news for any reports on the dead man in the beat-up house. But I didn't turn on the TV because I didn't want to wake my sister. So I waited. I didn't get any sleep. My head ached and my skin felt dirty. The sun was already coming up and I couldn't rest until I knew what was happening. I had the bright idea to have a morning beer from Corrine's refrigerator while I listened to music in the basement.

The music sounded old and gimmicky and I tired of it quickly. All the singers were dead. The beer tasted bad. Flat and sour. I realized that wasn't the beer's fault. I returned upstairs, threw most of the beer down the kitchen sink, and waited some more. I struggled with Corrine's flashy coffee maker but eventually I boiled a pot of coffee.

The dead man had me intrigued as well as worried. Was Valdez the guy bleeding on the kitchen floor or the guy driving the truck? Why had María Contreras needed Luis and me to find Valdez if he wanted to meet with her anyway? Who was the second man? Was María Contreras a killer or a witness to murder? Which client would Móntez protect if he had to make a choice, Contreras or me?

I never expected that my innocent job with the lawyer Móntez would lead to the hole that I felt for certain I had fallen in. I worked myself into a bag of nerves and anxiety. I owed Móntez for saving my ass and for the job. How far would I go for him? How far would he go for me?

My game of a thousand questions I couldn't answer ended when Corrine woke up. She was scheduled to volunteer at Academia Ana Marie Sandoval, the dual language school near

Móntez's house. She worked there one day a week helping a second-grade teacher and her class.

"What's up, little brother?" She was way too cheery. She helped herself to coffee. "Hey, this is good. Thanks." We killed a few minutes drinking coffee.

"You must've had a good time last night with your pals. Anything exciting happen?"

"The usual," she said. "Those women are too much. They do know where to go to meet men, though."

"So you met someone?"

She shook her head. "No one special. Just guys, you know?"

I poured both of us another cup of coffee. "Just guys, huh?"

"Anyway, I gots to go. What you doing today? Need a ride? Or what?" She stopped talking, walked over to the table where I sat and picked up my empty beer bottle. "What're you doing hitting the booze already? What's going on, Gus?"

"Nothing. Really. I worked late with Luis. Didn't sleep. Had a beer to relax while I figure out if I try to get some sleep or I just carry on. It's nothing. No need to worry."

She tossed the bottle in the recycle bin near the back door.

"You screw up and you're out of here, Gus. ¿Me entiendes?"

Corrine sometimes threw in a Spanish word or two to emphasize her concern. She was pissed. One day I was her fave, stay as long as I wanted, she said. The next, I had to consider packing. She was getting back to normal.

"Yes, I understand. I'm cool. I don't drink like I used to. I been dry for a few years now. I'm just working hard, that's all. Your lawyer friend has me out at all hours. I thought lawyers were more ten to four people?"

She didn't buy my soft sell. "What're you working on? What kind of case?"

I hesitated. I could explain everything that was going on, but Móntez had impressed on me to play it cozy with everyone, cops included, until we had a better hold of the facts. I opted for caution with Corrine, mainly because I didn't want her to carry extra

weight on her shoulders about what her black sheep brother might
be up to.

"He wanted me to stake out a potential witness in a case where
one person says the other person has money that needs to be given
back. I watched in the event the second person tipped his hand and
revealed something about the money. But, nada. It was a waste of
time."

"Bullshit. I can always tell when you're lying or not telling me
everything. I been your big sister too long, Gus." She looked at the
clock on the wall. "But I ain't got time now." She fished keys out of
her purse. "Tonight. We'll go over this again. I'll talk with Móntez
myself if I have to. I'm not letting you get in trouble again." She
walked to the door, stopped and looked back at me. "I'm just concerned, Gus. I don't ever want to visit you in prison again."

There went my plan to not have her worry about me. "I'm
good, Corrine. I swear. What's the worst that can happen?"

"Oh hell, you can't say that. What's the worst? Really?"

I hugged her across the shoulders. She stiffened.

"It's all good. I'll be back at work in another hour. Maybe
knock off early since I did double overtime last night. We can get
something for supper. Talk about whatever you want."

She looked satisfied. "You need a ride?"

I didn't know Móntez's agenda, so I faked it. "I'm waiting to
hear from Luis. I think he's picking me up for some kind of meeting on the case."

"All right. I'll grab a Chubby's burrito before I head to the
school. You know you can have whatever's in the fridge."

"Yeah. I'm good. Not all that hungry. Have a nice day."

She left a few minutes later, her attitude switching back to a
smiling and humming version. She definitely had met someone
who'd grabbed her interest.

I retrieved the paper from the front lawn but I didn't expect
any news about the Westwood house. It had happened too late for
the morning delivery. I turned on the TV and waited through four

commercials until one of the morning news programs popped on the screen. And there it was.

The well-dressed and well-groomed blond anchor sorted through papers and then began a report about a fire in the Westwood neighborhood. I wondered how she managed to look so good so early in the morning. I never looked that good at any time of the day.

"According to a statement just issued by the Denver Fire Department, the house has been completely destroyed but so far no injuries have been reported. We're looking at live footage from our News Copter flying over the scene. You can see several fire trucks and other fire department vehicles and numerous firemen working through the debris, much of it still smoking. So far we don't have any information about an owner or owners of the property." She paused while the screen showed billowing smoke from a collapsing house. "Shannon Flanigan has been on the scene for several minutes, let's see what she has to report. Good morning, Shannon. Can you tell us if there have been any developments in the investigation of the fire?"

The screen switched to another smartly dressed reporter holding a microphone and standing near a fire truck. This reporter was black and looked very young. There was a slight pause as Flanigan listened on her earphone to the delayed transmission from the studio.

"Good morning, Kathy. So far there's not much to report, other than this is quite a fire and the house is certain to be a complete loss. I did just finish speaking with the fire investigator on the scene, Brett Montaño. He confirmed that the house is totally demolished. He described the fire as one of the hottest he's seen in a long time. He verified that they are looking for the owner and any possible victims, but so far it doesn't appear that anyone was in the house, which, of course, is good news." She paused and looked at someone behind the camera, then nodded. "And now, here next to me is Mrs. Viola Alcalá, a resident on this street."

The news ticker on the bottom of the shot scrolled an address for the house. It was the same address Macías had given me. The same address where I'd spent a few hours hiding behind a tree like a lost kid, where I saw María Contreras and a man leave in a big hurry, where I saw another man stretched out dead on the grimy linoleum floor.

The camera panned back to reveal an elderly woman wearing a down vest, checkered shirt and jeans. She had wrinkled skin and thin gray hair pulled back under a scarf. The reporter seemed unsure of herself next to the neighbor.

"Can you tell us what you know about this house, Mrs. Alcalá?"

The woman looked at the camera and blinked her eyes. "I been living two houses down for more than forty years. This place used to be owned by Frank Contreras and his wife, Betty. Good people, great neighbors. They been dead for years. One of the sons lived here for a couple years, Anselmo I think his name was. We called him Sammy. Then he rented it to all kinds of people over the years. I heard he died, too."

"Do you know who owns the house now?" The reporter smiled at the camera and held the microphone steady for Mrs. Alcalá, who kept trying to grab the mike and wrench it from the reporter's fingers.

"I seen different people come and go. Not very friendly, if you really want to know. No one takes care of the yard or the house. Real eyesore for a while now."

"Well, thank you, Mrs. . . . "

The woman did not stop talking. "I ain't seen anyone around for a long time, but you know there was someone sneaking around here last night for a while. Didn't see who." She turned her head slightly to look at the burning shell of the house. "Might be better that it burned down." She smiled, then began to laugh, but the laugh quickly turned into a cough that spiraled out of control. She turned her back to the camera, coughing and growling. The camera focused on the reporter.

"Well, thank you, Mrs. Alcalá. Kathy, I think that's it for now. I'll stay here on the scene and as soon as I learn more from the firemen or police, I'll report back to you and our audience." Harsh coughing continued in the background.

I turned off the television set. The report stirred the mess inside my guts from the night before. My headache turned up a notch. The old lady had seen me. What did she tell the cops? I wanted to take action, talk to somebody, but I couldn't fix on exactly what I should do. I waited for something to happen.

8 [Luis]

el tiempo pasa
y no te puedo olvidar

A half-hour after I heard the news about the fire, I pulled up in front of Corrine's house and honked my horn. Gus emerged, locked the door and sprinted to my car. He carried a mug of coffee.

"What the hell is going on?" he asked.

"You tell me. You were there, remember? You get any hint that the place was going to be torched?"

"You know I didn't. I told you everything that happened, everything I saw. Somebody came back to the house after I left, set it on fire and made sure no body would be found. That's the only thing that makes sense."

He was a bit defensive.

I drove to the intersection and headed west on Thirty-Seventh Avenue.

I wanted to believe Gus, but that meant that whatever was going on was not what we'd expected. I told myself that I was too close to retiring to get involved in another bloody caper with a Chicano on the edge.

"Where we going?" Gus asked.

"I need breakfast. Don't know about you, but I can't pull all-nighters anymore without suffering consequences, like not being able to think clearly. I should eat. It'll help balance my system and we can talk about what might be happening."

"Sure. Whatever."

The truth was that I was half-asleep and in a daze. Not really hungry, but I'd pay a steep price if I didn't get something in my stomach. Actually, I thought that a drink would do more for my condition. Not a beer, but a real drink. Whiskey? Maybe a shot of tequila to work wonders for my thought processes. I hadn't thought about serious drinking for a long time. I wasn't sure why the thought came to me when it did. I didn't suggest the idea to Gus.

"In the old days I'd just have a drink and get on with it," he said. "Can't see me doing that now." Great minds . . .

"Yeah," I said quickly. "I know what you mean."

"You don't drink these days?"

"Those days are over. Can't handle the hangover, and there's always a chance that I'll embarrass myself. Too old for that. It didn't seem to matter when I was younger."

"I can't really indulge, you know? The state is watching me like a hawk, with U.A.s and spot checks from my P.O. Anyhow, it's been years, literally, since I hung one on. Not sure I want to do that again. I think I lost the taste for it."

We sunk into our own thoughts for the next several minutes. I turned right on Federal and headed north. At Thirty-Eighth I turned west again.

"Where's this breakfast going to happen?"

"How about Tacos Jalisco?" I suggested. "You like that place?"

"Sure. We used to eat there a lot. Me and my sisters. Big plates, hot chile. You think we can talk there?"

"I'll ask for a booth in the back. We won't say anything earth-shattering."

"We don't know anything earth-shattering."

I nodded and drove the rest of the way in silence.

When we were finally in the restaurant, I asked him something that had been on my mind since earlier that morning when I first learned of the fire.

"What about meeting with that police liaison person?"

"Seeing as no body was found, there's not a reason to speak to her, is there?"

"Only that you don't want any blowback about this down the road. And I still don't feel right about what happened. I should report to the cops. Tell them everything."

"Easy for you to say. You're not on parole."

"But you haven't done anything wrong, and if they somehow find out that you were there and didn't speak up . . . well, it won't go good if Dirty Harry wants to violate you."

He thought about what I'd said.

"Okay," Gus said. "Set up a meet with Ana Domingo. As long as you think it's what should happen."

The restaurant was busy and several minutes passed before a waitress took our order. Old time Mexican music played in the background.

"That's Antonio Aguilar," I said.

Gus grunted but I wasn't sure he knew who or what I was talking about.

"My parents dragged all of us to the Colorado State Fair in Pueblo when we were kids to see him perform. He sang from a shiny silver saddle on his giant horse." Many years had slipped by since then. My parents were gone, Aguilar, too. There were a few of the Móntez clan left in various cities and I added visiting relatives to my retirement bucket list.

We ate eggs, chile, beans, fried potatoes and tortillas washed down with coffee. I asked him to go over what happened at the house, at least what he'd seen. He finally said I asked too many questions. His irritation with me was obvious. It might have been the lack of sleep, or just an ex-con's sensitivity to interrogations and repeated questions.

I'd been through this several times during my checkered career as an attorney. I wouldn't have traded one day of my life as Luis Móntez, Esq., for anything else, but after forty years of rubbing hard against the rough edges of the U.S. legal system, I was tired, and not from just one lost night of sleep. I'd been in tough spots with old friends like Gato Guerrero or new enemies like Tyler Boudin. Different guy staring back at me, different uptight situations, but still the same in many ways. Except that this time I felt the years in my bones and tired legs. The all-nighter with Gus had already cost me. I drank several cups of coffee while I looked at the glowing but puffy face of Gus Corral and thought about my own sagging and wrinkled flesh. Retirement looked too far away and it wasn't getting any closer.

"I'm trying to help, Gus. That's all."

He nodded. "Why not just go to a regular cop and report what I saw? Why use this community service person, or whatever she is?"

"Remember, I know her. And her position is supposed to encourage people to come forward with information about crimes, problems, neighborhood issues, that they might not want to talk about with the official cop driving around in his cruiser. I just think it's an easier and safer way for you to deliver what you know to the police. Minimize the risk as much as we can. But, there is the fact that so far there's no body. We have to think that through."

"They came back and either made sure the body would be completely torched in the fire, or they removed it and had it buried somewhere else. The fire means they're just being extra careful."

"You keep talking about 'they.' More than one. You're sure María Contreras was in on the killing and the fire?"

"Hell, I don't know." He talked as he chewed. "I can only speak about what I saw and guess about the rest. Last night she looked like she was involved. Very involved. This shit all happened in Sam Contreras' house, the house he inherited from his parents and the house your client might have lived in for a year or so, if I remember right. She didn't notify anyone that there was a dead man in her husband's house. And now she's gone, so I don't have much doubt about her role. Do you?" He scooped up a piece of runny egg and chile with the remainder of his tortilla.

"People do strange things," I said. "Unexpected stuff that boils over and explodes without warning. I've seen it. Over the years I've run into twists and turns that I never anticipated, crap that almost got me killed, so I try to never assume too much. I thought my client was on the level, that she needed help and that I could help her. But today, I have to say, she looks guilty."

9 [Gus]

running on empty, running blind
running into the sun but I'm running behind

I didn't respond to the lawyer and I left it at that. There were times when Luis sounded an awful lot like the wise elder who's been through it all and wants everyone else to listen to the lessons he's learned. I wasn't a fan of those times.

I was certain that María Contreras was a killer who used Móntez and me to find the guy she wanted dead. I didn't give her the benefit of the doubt that Móntez thought he had to give to his client. I wanted only to come clean with this community cop, Ana Domingo, wash my hands of the nasty business and try to get on with my life. After all, I was a free man. Free and independent and ready for the next act in my so-called life. I didn't have time for all this latest trouble and confusion.

Móntez had to be in court that morning, and until we talked to Domingo there wasn't anything for me to do. I asked him to drop me off at the Scheitler Recreation Center. I spent the next two hours at the center near faded Lakeside Amusement Park and cloudy Berkeley Lake. I needed to sweat, to feel the strain and pain, to blank out my mind and focus on my body.

I ran around the lake five times, almost five miles, belching and re-tasting green chile and coffee. The running erased the fog from lack of sleep. Occasionally, without any reason, I imagined the bleeding man stretched out on the floor of the house where we thought Richard Valdez lived. Then I saw the fire. I willed myself to concentrate on the run.

I worked up a nice burn in my thighs and lungs. I forced my legs to keep pumping but it was nothing compared to how I felt when I exercised in prison. Back then, everything was a test I gave myself or that I had to pass for others who watched. In the park, no one watched as I jogged past the swampy reeds and the busy and noisy dog run. The sunshine that bounced off the lake and the leaves of the trees created a golden circle of light that followed me as I ran. My muscles relaxed in the heat. My brain let go.

Inside the rec center, I worked with various weights and an elliptical, and I stroked a few laps in the pool. When I finished with all of it, I felt better. I thought that, as long as I played it straight and honest, I should be all right. Maybe that's what I wanted to think.

Móntez buzzed my cell. He was finished with court and had arranged a meeting with the cop liaison person for later that afternoon. I told him I'd be in to work and we could go from there, but first I had something to do for Jackie O.

≫ ≫ ≫

Jackie called to ask if I had anything new on her problem. I had to tell her that, based on her story and the couple of printouts from Joseph Cristelli's computer that she managed to copy before she was fired, I couldn't say that the case against Cristelli was a slam dunk. She said she would see what else she could dig up.

"Be careful," I said. "I'm looking into it. Just might take some time."

She agreed, then hung up.

Jackie O had been one of the boys in our middle school crew. Along with Shoe and Ice, Javier didn't run when we needed to protect ourselves from the bad or stupid—sometimes both—jerks we bumped into on the Northside just about every week. Jackie was a little guy in muscle and height but he was the meanest of the bunch. He had to be. His home life was a nightmare. He learned at a very early age all about survival.

Javier's mother dropped dead when he was about three. He never learned why she died. The semi-official story was that she'd been beaten by Javier's father, a man who didn't live with Javier or his mother, and she died of a broken heart. "Broken jawbone more like it," Javier would say when he talked about growing up without actual parents. He was raised by his aunt. "I slept in her house every so often," was Javier's version.

The aunt shared the house with assorted men. The man who lived there the most while Javier was growing up hated the boy. He especially hated him when Javier paraded around the house in the aunt's high heels and flowery hats. When Javier put on lipstick and earrings, the man's hate grew into a violent obsession to hurt the boy. Javier got hurt a lot.

One day, when we were sophomores at North High, I stopped at Javier's so we could hang out. I walked in on Javier and the aunt's boyfriend brawling in the living room. Lamps were knocked over, ripped cushions from the couch spilled their padding on the stained carpet and the screaming aunt stood in a corner of the room with her fists jammed against her eyes. Javier was covered in blood from a cut across the back of his head. The man bled from his nose. He held a massive kitchen knife that he swung wildly at Javier.

"Drop the knife," I hollered. The man did not even look at me. He lurched toward Javier, then crouched as though he was about to lunge.

"I'll slice your balls off, boy," the man growled. "You don't need them anyway."

I picked up one of the lamps and smashed it against the side of his head. He fell to his knees, then to his back. The aunt quit screaming. Javier ran out the front door. Drops of blood rained from his ponytail and left a trail behind him. I caught up to him as he ran through the intersection at Zuni Street and Thirty-Eighth Avenue.

He stayed at our house for a few days. No one came looking for him. No policeman asked him questions about the fight, no aunt wanted him to come back home. The doctor at the clinic who patched up his head repeatedly asked about the details of the wound, but Javier would say only that he slipped and fell.

About a week after the fight he was gone. Several years passed before I saw him again. By that time he'd reinvented himself as Jackie O.

I never asked her about those missing years and she never opened up about where she went and what she did. We let those days slip away without regret.

So it didn't surprise me that Jackie wanted to fight back against Cristelli. It didn't matter that the odds of winning the fight were slim to none, or that there wasn't any real payoff if she did manage to win. For Jackie, it was about standing up to the bullies.

I calculated that my first action had to be a visit to Cristelli. His office was in one of the retail spaces on the first floor of a massive condo building on Tejon Street, in the midst of developers' wonderland.

The perky receptionist at the front desk politely told me that Mr. Cristelli was out of town but expected back in the office tomorrow. A name plate on the front of her desk said her name was Debra Pagent. I handed Debra a card that had my name and phone number along with the words "Investigator" and "Law Office of Luis Móntez."

"Why does an attorney want to speak with Mr. Cristelli?" She smiled at me while her fingers played with her computer mouse.

I quickly calculated how much I should tell her. "It has to do with a former employee and a complaint that was made against her."

"You mean Jackie?" Her fingers quit tickling her mouse. "I knew there was more to why she left than what Joey said. I knew it."

"Joey?"

"Mr. Cristelli. We all call him that."

I played my next card. "Mrs. Villagrana around?"

"Not since she left. That was another hard day."

She continued to wear her smile but her eyes told me that she wasn't happy about something. "Debra, you been here a while with this company?"

"Going on a year. I liked it, still do I guess. But it's not permanent for me, you know what I mean?"

"I do, for sure. Good experience, though, I bet?"

"Yes, of course."

"Learning how an office works, how all the different people get along, or don't."

"Definitely."

"What do you think happened between Joey and Jackie? That must have taught you something."

"Well, I can't really talk about it, you know. It's a private thing that was handled by human resources. I can't talk about certain people, or give you anything from our files. I hope that's okay?"

"Yeah, I understand that. I wouldn't want you to violate your company's policy. I myself had to get permission from Mrs. Villagrana's attorney to talk with her. But it was worth it. She told me a lot. I was hoping I could confirm some of the details with your boss. I wouldn't want you to tell me anything personal, confidential. Nothing like that."

"Clara talked with you? That's a surprise. She hated Jackie and was so happy when Joey forced Jackie to leave. I thought that was wrong and I told Clara, but she didn't care. But then, not too long ago, out of the blue, she jumped all over Joey. Argued with him about Jackie, about a lot of stuff. I know she wanted Joey to give Jackie back her job. Talk about a big change. Takes all kinds. I've learned that."

"Yes, good lesson. Mrs. Villagrana was very upset."

"I hope it works out for her at the church. She never really fit in around here, even though she was a good bookkeeper."

"She said the change was good, and not much of a drive for her."

"Shouldn't be since it's only a few blocks away. I hope this gets straightened out eventually."

"I'm sure it will be. And I agree with you."

Debra was back to being perky.

Three distinct Catholic churches had existed in the neighborhood for decades, all within a few blocks of each other. I took a leap of faith based on what I thought I knew about Clara Villagrana. "Our Lady of Guadalupe is a better fit for Mrs. Villagrana."

Debra nodded. "I thought it was an obvious place for her, what with all her, uh, religious attitudes."

I asked her to make sure Joey got my card.

She promised she would.

According to Corrine, Our Lady of Guadalupe was a pillar of the Denver Mexican community since the 1930s. It'd been one of the more active churches in the city because the priests were political—progressives who used the church to organize various liberal, even radical, projects. The church hall was used for meetings and propaganda events. Corrine remembered attending meetings in the church hall about third-world struggles, the grape boycott and bilingual education.

But all that changed over the years. Like the rest of the Northside, the church developed a different perspective. A good example of the change involved a work of art. The mural of the Virgin's miraculous appearance to Juan Diego painted on the altar wall by Carlota Espinoza in the politically ripe 1970s had been hidden behind a wall a few years ago. Chicano Catholics protested and demanded the destruction of the wall, but the priest remained firm in his decision. The official reason was that Christ had to be at center altar, certainly not Mary. Many in the Chicano community assumed that the covering up of the mural marked one more line of separation between long-time Chicano residents and more recent immigrants. Others thought the priest wanted a more conservative, less active agenda. Still, others saw the conflict as a gender struggle between Chicanas, who revered the Chicana-looking Virgin in the mural, and the male priest and church authorities.

Corrine told me the struggle was ironic since, bottom line, the Chicano protestors and the immigrant churchgoers were all Mexican. "But that's the way we are," she said. "If nobody picks a fight with us, we'll make one up among ourselves. Always been that way."

I had no problem believing that a woman like Clara Villagrana, who spouted ugly homophobic rants, could find a place for herself in the church. The days were gone when she would have been challenged by one of the church activists. And I'm sure she felt safe from running into another Jackie O at the church.

I walked around the church grounds and checked out a couple of the buildings before I found Clara Villagrana cleaning the toilet in the priest's house. The door to the house was open and I walked in, and then back to the bathroom.

She was a woman of about sixty-five. Plump, dressed in baggy jeans with an elastic waistband. Her faded sweatshirt had the words "Keep Christ in Christmas" printed on the front. Her mostly gray hair was bunched on the top of her head.

"What do you want?" she said as soon as she saw me at the bathroom doorway.

"I was told that Clara Villagrana was working here in the house. Is that you?"

She hesitated, then nodded. "What do you want?" she repeated.

"I work for a lawyer, Luis Móntez. Our client is Jackie Ortega. You worked with her at Dynamic-Tec. You remember her?"

She dropped the toilet brush in a bucket near her feet. She dried her hands on her sweatshirt. She walked past me to the front of the house. I followed her outside and stood next to her on the steps. The cool morning air chilled me, but it had no effect on her that I could see.

"What are you doing?" she asked.

"I'm trying to find witnesses to what happened at Dynamic-Tec when Ms. Ortega was fired. We think she was wrongfully terminated. My understanding is that you know a lot about the situation."

"I don't know anything about any of that."

"Really? According to our client, you made a complaint against Ms. Ortega that got her fired. Are you saying that's not right?"

"Look. I don't want no trouble. I don't know anything. I told Mr. Cristelli that when I left. I'm not involved with that anymore. Leave me alone."

Her lips trembled.

"I'm not trying to cause you any trouble, Mrs. Villagrana. But our client lost her job. Because of what you said she did when she worked with you. Are you saying now that there isn't anything to your complaint?"

"I'm saying I want to be left alone. Now leave or I will call Father Morales. He'll make you leave."

I backed away. On the one hand, it was good news that she was a reluctant witness. But could she make it right for Jackie?

"You understand the damage you caused with your complaint?"

"Look, mister. I don't care if he goes back to work with Cristelli, or whatever. I don't want anything to do with him or Cristelli or any of that business. Now leave."

A dark boy of about thirteen emerged from inside the house.

"Grandma? You okay. What's going on?"

The boy was tall, skinny and sweet. He held a feather duster and a rag. His hair hung down to his shoulders. Earrings protruded from both his earlobes. He wore an apron and a red scarf wrapped around his head.

"Go back inside, Armando. This doesn't concern you."

The boy gave me a good look. "You sure, Grandma? If this guy is bothering you . . ."

"No, no. Just go on inside. I'll be right there. We're almost done."

The boy turned and walked back in the house. His steps were almost delicate. His hands fluttered when he waved the duster at the walls.

"Your grandson doesn't have school today?"

"None of your business. Anyway, we're looking for a better school for him. We . . . " She couldn't finish. Clara Villagrana's sad face turned away from me. The trembling lips were open but she didn't speak.

"I think I understand," I said. "I'll leave. You've withdrawn your complaint."

She grabbed my arm. "Look. I, uh . . . "

"I'll tell Ms. Ortega that you apologized."

I left her standing on the steps. The breeze whipped my jacket, and I turned my head away from the cold.

≫ ≫ ≫

Ana Domingo surprised me. Actually, I wasn't sure what to expect, so I guess anything would have surprised me. The woman who sat behind a very organized desk in her office at the old City and County Building oozed confidence. Nice clothes, tasteful make-up, serious attitude. She was about my age, my height. Hint of a smile but heavy emphasis on playing the cop role. A framed photo of four Mexican-looking men sat on the corner of a bookcase. Nothing out of place, nothing unnecessary to her job except for the photograph.

The city big shots who'd created her position did all they could to make it clear that she was different from the rest of the department. The first thing I noticed was that her office was not in the police building.

Positively not my type so, naturally, I was attracted—and not just because I'd been locked up for years with lowdown, mean, insane and hostile men.

Luis Móntez sat in the chair next to mine in front of her desk. He stayed out of the first part of the conversation. I did most of the talking since it was really my story. Her face told me all I needed to know. She went from curious to amused to shocked to something like disgusted.

"Let me get this right. You're on parole. You saw a murder . . . "

"No, I didn't actually."

She quickly nodded. "Correction. You saw a dead man, who died because of an apparent violent attack. But you did not report what you saw to the police or . . . "

"He's reporting it now, Ana." Móntez finally chimed in.

"Yeah, with his attorney present, I should note."

"I thought you guys were friends," I said.

She grinned while she looked at the lawyer.

"Not exactly," she said. "But, in any event, you did nothing when reporting the crime to the police might have made a difference."

"The guy was dead. Nobody could have done anything for him," I said.

"No, but maybe the murderers might have been arrested if the police were involved at the beginning?"

"What I saw was the end of something, not the beginning. And anyhow, I understand there was no body in the house, so who knows for sure what the police might have found?"

"We'll never know, will we, Mr. Corral?"

I shrugged. "Look. I just want to do the right thing." I hoped I sounded sincere, even a bit naïve. "I probably should have called you or some other cop when I saw what I saw. I didn't." I waited a long second. "My bad."

She stared at her well-manicured hands and shook her head.

"I can't undo my screw-up," I continued. "You do what you have to do. It's your job. I guess my hard-ass parole officer will yank me back in the joint, so maybe I should've just kept my mouth shut and let the police department stumble around until maybe they bumped into something that might lead them to think there was a body in that house before the fire." That last part came out slicker than I intended.

"Your story has several problems, not the least of which is that there has been no indication that anyone died in that house, either immediately before or during the fire. What am I supposed to do with that?" She glanced at Luis, then fixed her eyes on me.

The conversation wasn't going well, even I knew that. I glanced at Móntez for support.

"Ana, please," Móntez said. "You should appreciate what Gus is doing here. There's no reason for him to put himself on the line like he has, except that he wants to be cooperative, a good citizen. He could have walked away from what he saw, and no one would have ever known. And, besides, he was following my instructions, as his employer and his lawyer. I thought we, he and I, should talk over the situation, and figure out what was happening before he went to the police. It's what any attorney would want his client to do before he talks with the police."

"Maybe I should have you arrested then, Luis."

He jerked his head. "You're funny, Ana."

An angry wave flowed across her face, then, just as quickly, it was gone. "I'm not trying to be funny. I'm trying to figure out what is going on here. Your client apparently saw the results of a violent crime but he didn't report it. A man was probably murdered and Gus did nothing about it. That alone is enough to get a warrant, search his house, arrest him and, like he says, get him thrown back in jail. You know that, don't you, Gus?"

Before I could answer, Móntez reacted. "Here's what I know. It's not clear that not reporting a crime in Colorado is a crime. There may be a statute that says we have a responsibility to inform the police and that we all should do it, but I've never known what the penalty is for not doing that, and I've never heard of anyone being arrested for it. If it's a crime, it's minor, a misdemeanor. And that means it's a discretionary call by the parole board about whether it's enough to revoke parole." He leaned over and patted my shoulder. "What I also know is that Gus is willing to help. Right, Gus? That's all he can do. You should take him up on his offer."

She looked at me, then at Móntez. Her smile finally broke out completely. "Slow down, Luis. We're not in the courtroom. This is only between the three of us, for now."

"He's telling you what he knows, Ana, what he's learned," Luis said.

"How about his parole officer?"

"He's not in on this."

"Maybe we can work out something that is good for us all, including the department."

I didn't quite understand what happened, but just like that the tension in the room faded. Luis relaxed in his chair. Ana Domingo, Community Liaison Officer for the Denver Police Department, stood up and walked to a water cooler sitting in the corner of her office. She pulled a paper cup out of a holder attached to the cooler and helped herself to a drink of water.

She held my fate in her smooth-skinned hands. I think I quit breathing for a few seconds.

"You guys want a drink?"

She talked to us a few minutes more. She confirmed that Luis made the 911 call. She asked about María Contreras, but we didn't tell her anything more than that I watched the house as part of Luis' work for her. I never offered that I saw María Contreras at the house, and Domingo never asked me that question directly.

Luis drove me back to Corrine's house. We decided to call it quits for the day.

"Long night, longer day," Luis said.

"Let's hope tonight doesn't turn into another drama." As soon as I said it I knew I'd jinxed the evening.

10 [Luis]

yeah, my bad luck boy
been havin' bad luck all of my days, yes

I gave Gus a ride home. On the way, he wrapped up Jackie O's problem.

Gus believed that Cristelli's threats against Jackie were dead. "He has no witness, no complaining party. Villagrana isn't going to do anything. Without her, he has no leverage."

"You sure about that?"

"I'm sure. It's her grandson. Blood is thicker than whatever she was carrying around. She's seen the error of her ways. She's doing penance for her sins by cleaning toilets at the church. She doesn't ever want to see Cristelli again. I think Jackie can get whatever she wants out of Cristelli."

"She doesn't want anything for herself. She wants him out of business."

"Can you do that? "

"I can't. But Jackie can. I'll arrange a meeting with the district attorney, maybe the consumer fraud unit at the attorney general's. Good work, Gus."

"Hell, I didn't do anything."

"You tracked her down. That's something."

"If you say so."

≫ ≫ ≫

I'd intended to go home to recapture some of my missed sleep, but there were a dozen different things at the office that I had to finish. They wouldn't wait for me to take a nap. I felt like I had a second wind. I dropped off Gus and drove to the office.

The meeting with Ana Domingo had gone as well as could be expected. We parted apparently on good terms. That's why I worried when I walked in the office and Rosa told me she'd called and left a message that I had to get back to her as soon as possible.

"She didn't say what it was about?"

"I'd of told you if she did, Luis. But you know it's gonna involve your hoodlum pal Gus."

"You need to let go of your attitude."

"Only thing I need's a raise. When that guy finally messes up, I'll be there with my attitude and shit, just so I can say I told you so." She rotated in her chair back to her computer screen.

I called Domingo's direct number as soon as I closed my office door behind me.

She answered and waded right in.

"We got a problem, Luis," she said. "Rather, you and your guy Corral have a problem."

Kind of what I expected. "What? You know everything we know. You said it was okay."

"What I said was that we could probably work something out, since you guys were trying to do the right thing. But now, well, now, there's a hang-up. A bump in the road."

"Am I supposed to guess what it is until I get it right?"

"Be nice. I don't have to talk with you, Móntez."

"Yeah, okay, whatever."

It was obvious she had ambivalent feelings about me, with good reason. The truth was that we'd crossed paths months before because of one of my more unsavory clients. She called me in her office and let me have it about the client, a certain Clyde Williams. Seems that Clyde showed up at her office and tried to get friendly with Ms. Domingo. Apparently he was a bit aggressive about it. She told me that she had to get physical herself. Williams ended up on the floor with a swollen eye from a well-placed jab delivered by Ana. He didn't say anything to me about the incident, but I had no doubt that it happened. Somehow, Williams' crap brushed off on me and she held a grudge of some sort.

"I went over the fire and what's been found so far with Brett Montaño, the chief investigator for the fire department. He knew about the 911 call, so he had his antenna up for signs that something happened in that house before the fire. He says it looks like someone probably was killed in the house after all, but nothing definitive until the test results come back to him. Weeks from now."

"So, that gibes with what Gus said, and what we reported to you."

"You're half-right."

"What do you mean?"

"This isn't official yet, so you can't do anything with it." It was more a question than a statement.

"I get it."

"Montaño says there might have been two people killed in that house. Something about a preliminary report on blood stains that were found on bits and pieces of the wall that survived the fire. He said he was guessing since the fire destroyed almost everything that might be considered hard evidence, and that it would be weeks before the actual test results come back."

"Wow. He went from no bodies to maybe two? Gus doesn't know anything about a second body. He would've told you about it. This doesn't mean that Gus was hiding anything. Just that he didn't know."

"Maybe. I'd still like to talk to him again."

"I'll let you know when we can make it."

"Uh . . . Luis. It might be better if I meet with Gus alone. Less formal that way. I just want to confirm that he saw two live persons and one dead man in the house, and that there wasn't a fourth person or body. If it's just him and me, I don't have to go through all the hoops that are required when a lawyer gets involved. You understand that, right, Luis?"

Yeah, I understood. She wanted me out of the way. She thought she could trip up Gus, or she thought he would be more honest if I wasn't around. Or she was telling the truth. I would leave it up to Gus as far as how he wanted to play it.

"I'll see if he wants to give you a call. If he does, you can set up your meeting. But there's no reason for him to lie about any of this."

"Oh, there's a reason. More than one when you think about it. He could be more involved than he's letting on. He could be covering for what he really did. Or for someone else."

"Don't go there, Ana. We've been straight with you."

"Hope so. I checked up on your boy. He's not exactly the poster child for civic responsibility and good citizenship."

"He's done his time and he leveled with you about his record, which you knew about anyway. Give him a break. It's no secret he was just released from prison."

"True enough. But he was busted for some wild stuff. Could be that once a thug, always a thug. A lot of cops think he skated away from some very serious time."

"He almost got killed. He saved the life of an abused woman. His sister was kidnapped. He opened the door for your department and the feds on enough information to shut down a major operation of one of the cartels. I think he earned whatever skating he enjoyed."

She took a few seconds to respond. "However it went down, I need to talk with Gus Corral one more time. Make sure he gets the message. I don't want to have to track him down." She hung up.

I felt tired again. My back ached. My eyes burned and watered. I cleared my dry throat. It was nothing.

Had the guy I trusted let me down? I should believe Gus. I began to doubt my instincts. "You're too old for this, Móntez," I thought. "You lost whatever street smarts you used to have. If you ever had any."

I waited for someone to shake me, to grab me by the collar and tell me to cut the crap and get with the program.

11 [Gus]

must be the same ol' thing
that make a tom cat fight all night

I nodded off for about an hour before Móntez woke me with another phone call.

"Domingo wants to talk with you again," he said. "Something about how more than one person might have been killed in that house before the fire. She wants to clear up that you didn't know about a second dead guy."

"Of course, I didn't. Why would she think I did?"

"I doubt that she does. The fire investigator said that maybe there was more than one body in the house. She's just following the story. Pinning down the details for her report, especially about you. She has to prove her job is worthwhile, cost efficient. She's still in a test period for her funding, you know?"

"So for the sake of her budget I have to talk with her again? You sure this is the way to take care of this?"

"I'm okay with it. It's not perfect, but I doubt Domingo is hiding anything from us."

"You have anything to back up that belief?"

"A year ago. Something similar. One of my clients witnessed a shooting in LoDo, when the bars closed and all the drunken kids poured out and hassled each other. My guy saw the shooter but didn't want to get involved. Sure you can appreciate that. I thought we should try to get the killer off the streets, so my client talked with Domingo, just like you."

"And she followed through for your guy?"

"Yes. My client gave her a description of the shooter, then she talked with others on the force who put a name to the description, and when the cops looking into the shooting learned the name, they tracked down the bad guy and eventually got a confession. And my client never testified or anything else. Domingo took care of it."

I didn't like all of it but since I was already in deep, I had to play it out.

"When does she want to meet?"

"Not set yet. She wants to hear from you. Maybe you can handle it with a phone call. She made it clear she'd rather not have me around, but that's up to you."

"What do you think?"

"I always advise that you have an attorney when you talk with the cops, but, honestly, I don't see too much of a downside here. You confirm your story to her one more time, hopefully she lets it go."

"I never thought I'd be volunteering to talk to the cops. Especially about someone getting killed. Prison did a job on me, for sure."

"She's still a law enforcement officer, still a cop no matter how innocuous her job title is. Keep that in mind."

"I'll try to remember."

"Any thoughts about who the second body might be?"

"Hell no. I don't even know who the first body is. Those two, Contreras and the guy in the hoody, I don't want to mess with them. They've killed at least one guy, maybe two, maybe more, and we have no idea why."

"And they have no way of knowing that you are in any way involved. The most María Contreras knows is that you work for me and you did some investigation to help with her Richard Valdez problem. Which looks like she's resolved."

"He must be body number one. I just hope I don't end up as body number three."

"Or suspect number one. Good luck with Domingo. Call her when you feel like it."

I felt like calling her as soon as I hung up on Móntez. When Domingo and I connected, it was short and sweet and to the point. Yeah, she was anxious to meet. No, it wouldn't work to talk over the

phone. She offered to meet after she closed her office. She said she
wanted it to be informal—less paperwork, she repeated. The
woman had a big distaste for paperwork. She suggested that I come
by her apartment around eight. I agreed, wrote down her address
and hung up. The call lasted less than two minutes.

≫ ≫ ≫

That evening I explained the set-up to Corrine. We were at her
house, me with coffee and her with a glass of wine. She reminded
me that we were supposed to talk about the case I was working on
for Móntez and, of course, she had a hundred questions about the
client, my surveillance, the fire, the dead guy. I patiently explained
all of it to her. She was okay with everything until I got to the part
about meeting Domingo without Móntez. She absolutely did not
like that.

"Haven't you seen the news? Cops are killing young men of color
all across the country, and getting away with it. Never indicted. People
are rioting, burning their cities, because of bad cops. I remember
when community leaders gave speeches about how the police were an
occupying force in the hood. These days they got the weapons and
technology to back up that description. You can't trust the cops."

I said I doubted Domingo was going to kill me. Then I made
the mistake of telling her she was acting all "old school."

"Is it old school to try to keep your ass out of jail? Is it old
school to try to clue you in on the way the world really operates?"
She worked herself into a good display of emotion.

I wanted to say, yeah, that is really from the past, the way-way
past, but instead I told her that nothing serious could happen since
the meeting would be in Domingo's apartment.

She stopped in mid-hysteria. She looked me up and down,
finally smiled. "She wants you to come to her place? At eight
o'clock at night? And you don't think there's anything strange
about that?" Corrine folded her arms in front of her loose-fitting
sweatshirt and chuckled.

"Think about it. If she wants me arrested, she can have that happen anywhere. If she's trying to pry info out of me, there's nothing to find out. What kind of trap could she be setting?"

"Then why in the hell is this meeting even happening?"

"For the reason Móntez said. She's finishing up a few details. She wants me to deny for the record that I know anything about this second body, without making a big deal out of it. That's all. If Móntez isn't worried, I'm not either."

She made a show of pretending that she washed her hands of me and my problems. It was seven-thirty. Time for me to leave.

"Uh, can I borrow the car?"

She tossed the keys to me. "Good luck, little brother. I'm not bailing you out this time."

I hoped that was true.

Ana Domingo lived about twenty minutes from Corrine. The less than five-year-old building sat in the Five Points neighborhood. Once thought of as the "black" part of town, which in Denver, and everywhere else, I guess, was real estate agent code for poor and crime-ridden. Five Points had been trying to remake its image for a number of years but it hadn't quite enjoyed the same economic turnaround as other parts of Denver. Five Points had great history—jazz, food, famous and infamous residents—but that history wasn't always appreciated by city planners or the young families and hustling entrepreneurs who took a chance on a remodeled Victorian or a new condo. Duplicating a pattern I knew only too well from changes in my own neighborhood, older residents shared an uneasy mix with newcomers.

I drove east on Thirty-Eighth Avenue until it curved southward under I-25 and became Fox, then Twenty-Second—past a dark and quiet Coors Field towards downtown, where I turned on Lawrence and drove northeast until Thirtieth. I switched on the Kia's radio and listened to a nice Latin jazz number that had me shaking my head and tapping my fingers on the steering wheel. Corrine's favorite station was the public jazz outlet, KUVO, an iconic enterprise that had been part of the Five Points neighborhood for decades. Southeast, more or less, past Curtis Park, and I arrived at Domingo's building. Further east a few blocks sat the Five Points Media Center, where public and community television stations shared space with KUVO.

The walk to the front entrance of the building was unevenly lit, and I couldn't see whether anyone waited. I thought over why I'd agreed to meet with Domingo. Móntez seemed okay with the idea, so there was that. But usually the word of an attorney wouldn't have been enough for me to cooperate with the police to the length I'd already gone. Corrine saw through my posing and acted as though she'd figured out what was going on with me. But since I didn't know what that was, she could only be guessing.

I walked slowly and made sure I was alone. The door to the complex was an impressive solid hunk of dark wood with several wrought-iron fixtures that made it look like the entrance to an old castle. With the help of an overhead light I searched through the directory and pressed the button next to the name plate that read "364 A. Domingo."

"Gus?"

"Yeah, I'm here."

The lock clicked and I opened the door. I took the elevator to the third floor. When the elevator doors opened she surprised me by standing in the hallway, waiting.

"Right on time," she said.

"Not hard to find. Especially with GPS."

She turned and walked down the hall to her apartment. She was dressed in jeans and a V-necked shirt that looked like it was made for working out—shiny, tight, colorful and red. She may have tried to look relaxed but her hair was still tied up on the top of her head.

Her apartment reminded me of her office. Clean, neat, nothing frivolous. A half-dozen photographs hung on one wall. They looked like family pictures. She was in all of them, usually surrounded by three or four men I took to be her brothers, maybe a father. They were the same men from the picture in her office. No other women, not even someone who could pass for the mother.

She waved her hand at the couch signaling me to sit down. When I did, she disappeared into the next room.

"You want something to drink?" she hollered from around the corner of the wall. "A beer? Maybe some wine? I have an awesome Malbec."

"You serious?"

She came back to the room, a bottle of red wine in her left hand.

"Why not? I told you and Móntez this was informal. I've had a rough day. I need a drink. You can join or not. Up to you."

"I'm not much of a drinker anymore. But I'll take a beer."

When she finally sat down to take care of business, half of her glass of wine was gone and I'd taken a few healthy swigs of beer. Somehow, it slid down my throat easy and I remembered that at one time I'd actually enjoyed beer.

"I assume Luis told you about the second body that was probably in the house?"

"Yes. But I never saw a second dead person. I saw three people in that house. The woman, a tall guy in a hoody sweatshirt who drove a pickup truck and a man on the floor, bleeding from his head, probably dead."

She nodded.

"Are you recording this, or taking notes, or what? How does this help me?"

She laughed. "Easy, Gus. I'll put your responses in my report. The report goes to my supervisor, who talks to the detectives looking into the fire, which is now confirmed as arson by the way, and maybe they'll want to talk to you."

"What? I thought this was gonna end it."

"If I put your name in the report, you know the officers on the case will follow-up. You know that."

"Shit. Of course there was a catch."

She finished her drink and poured another.

"Well, wait. Don't get all heated up. I doubt there was a second body. The fire report says something like 'indications of a second body?' Could be anything. Don't worry about it. These fire investigators tend to over-include, if you know what I mean. If I'm convinced that you don't have any more involvement than what you've told me, maybe I can help. So far, I'm the only one who knows about what you saw and what you reported."

She swirled her wine. She slipped out of her sandals, curled her feet under her butt and leaned forward. I thought she might fall off her oversized chair but she maintained her balance.

"What does the investigator, Montaño, know about me?"

She shook her head and set down the glass. "I didn't tell him about you. I only went over what he's found out so far. He's the one who told me that there might've been two people killed in the house before the fire, but he's just dotting i's and crossing t's. He doesn't know about you."

"Why would you do that?" The meeting with Domingo was looking more and more like a big waste of my time.

She smiled. "If you're telling the truth, maybe there's no reason to drag you into the full investigation."

"I'm trying to understand." I finished the beer. "What else do you need to know?"

She sat back and gave me a look I hadn't seen in a long time. I calculated the risk of any involvement with the human relations cop. She gave off a vibe that in the past would've been all I needed to make a move. But I didn't live in the past anymore.

"You didn't really have to see me about this, right? I could've given you whatever you need on the phone."

"Truth is, I want to get to know you better. Is that a mistake?"

That was a big mistake, I thought, especially with the old Gus Corral.

By the time she raised her arms and pulled the T-shirt over her head and her hair tumbled around her shoulders and a red blur flashed as she tossed the shirt against the wall, I was won over to the idea that no mistake had been made, and the old Gus Corral was gone. Not forgotten, but gone.

12 [Luis]

well I know, know my time ain't long

The morning after Gus was supposed to meet with Ana Domingo, I arrived at my office early, not quite eight. I made coffee and opened a computer file for a client who had been especially needy. I hoped Gus also would come in early to review everything that he and Domingo talked about, and how she reacted. I hadn't let on to Gus but I shared his anxiety about the meeting. I'd spent a fitful night regretting that I talked Gus into the second appointment with Domingo. I wanted things to work out—wishful thinking I guess—but deep down I doubted that I would be able to close the file on María Contreras.

I drank a quick cup of black coffee. I poured a second cup before I sat on the carpet and stretched my legs, twisted my torso and did a few other moves and poses designed to keep me limber. So far they hadn't worked. I used the office restroom sink to splash water in my face, then dried with paper towels as vigorously as I could manage. Somewhere along the line, waking up had turned into a major endeavor.

I returned to my computer and forced myself to focus on the marital problems of Mrs. Viola Atencio, whose file lit up the screen.

In a few minutes I was deep into a divorce settlement agreement that no one, including my client, was happy about, trying to tweak the document so that it would be more palatable. I focused on the minutiae of a wrecked relationship that had become important, even vital, to Mrs. Atencio and her soon-to-be ex: holiday visits with the dogs, the outstanding balance of a joint wine-of-the-month club, a motorcycle that hadn't been started in three years. For the thousandth time I said to myself that after retirement I would not miss divorces and divorce clients. Then I thought about it and accepted that, most likely, I would fondly remember these clients and cases. They'd been part of my identity for years, burned into my consciousness with the same intensity as any of the rocky memories and nostalgia I could dredge from any other part of my life.

A yellow note from Rosa stuck to my desk near the phone charger cord. "Your bar dues are past due. You get a reduced rate now because of your age, Mr. Senior Citizen. Should I cut a check?"

I whispered to no one in particular, "I'll write the damn check myself."

I didn't expect to see María again. As far as I was concerned she was my ex-client, most likely a killer and a con artist on top of everything else. I was the guy she'd conned. I couldn't escape that basic fact, and neither could the cops once their involvement turned into a murder investigation.

Several minutes passed with me alternating between hard work on language for the Atencio agreement and worry about Gus and my vanished client, María Contreras.

I was still alone in the office when I heard the main door open. I assumed it was Rosa, although she never showed up before nine.

"Mr. Móntez. Luis?"

I looked up into the tired and much older face of María Contreras.

I jumped up from my chair. She jerked back. I showed her my hands to let her know that I meant no harm.

"What are you doing here?" I asked.

"I need to talk to . . . you, you." I had a hard time hearing her. Her breath caught in her throat and she repeated thin words. "I think . . . think, I'm in trouble."

"I think I'm in trouble." How many times had I heard that sentence uttered by a client? The words usually meant business for me, another retainer and billable hours. Unlike most attorneys, sometimes—actually more often than I cared to remember—they meant a wild ride into a dark pit, for the client, me and anyone else unlucky enough to be involved in whatever the "trouble" turned out to be. This looked like one of those times.

She collapsed onto the leather chair. The woman was in bad shape. She slumped like a soggy clump of mud. Tangled and dingy hair framed bloodshot eyes that jumped from me to the door to the ceiling, back to me. Her hands and arms shook. I smelled urine and sweat.

Bruises circled her wrists and forearms. Jagged cuts and scrapes framed her eyes. Scabs dotted her fingers and neck.

"You want some coffee, or water?"

She nodded. "Coffee would be good. Yes . . . yes, please." She grimaced as though speaking was painful.

I fetched the pot and a cup from our break room. When I returned I thought she was asleep. Her eyes were closed and her chin rested in the palm of her right hand, which was propped on the side arm of the chair.

She stirred as I poured the coffee.

"You need a doctor. I can take you to an emergency room. You don't look good at all."

She shook her head. "No. I have to . . . tell . . . " Her lips quivered.

"Where have you been? What happened to you?"

She drank her coffee but most of it dribbled out the side of her mouth. "You won't believe. I don't . . . myself."

"Try me. I need an explanation. You disappeared. I've been trying to find you since I last saw you. A lot has happened."

She appeared to nod but she didn't say anything.

"And you know about the fire at Valdez's house? The police are looking into that. It's not good for you."

Still nothing from her.

"What's going on? What are you mixed up in?"

She held the cup in both hands, resting on her lap. "I don't know . . . where to . . . start."

I breathed easier. She was going to talk. "Start with what happened after I told you the address for Richard Valdez. You remember that? What did you do? Where did you go?"

"'Uh . . . that address. That was . . . uh, Sam's."

"Right. That house was your husband's. Valdez was living in Sam Contreras' house. And you didn't know that? You were there the night he was killed. How do you explain that?"

I reached for the phone to call an ambulance.

Fear opened her half-closed eyes. "I . . . uh . . . "

She hyperventilated and groaned with each labored breath. She clutched her throat. The cup dropped in her lap and then bounced on the carpet. Coffee spread across her jeans and the floor. She slumped forward and fell on the spilled coffee. I rushed to her and felt for a pulse, checked for breathing. A thin line of white foam stretched from the corner of her mouth to her chin.

It happened so fast I couldn't react. I heard the outer door open again.

"What the . . . ?" Rosa rushed in, dropped her purse and immediately tried CPR on Contreras. She worked intensely for several minutes but it was futile.

I punched 911 on my phone. "We have a medical emergency. Send an ambulance. We think the woman is dying. As quick as you can." I kept talking until the dispatcher had all the information she needed.

When Rosa gave up she sat on the floor, leaning against my desk, a few feet from the dead woman.

"What happened, Luis?"

I looked around my office. Nothing about it had changed and yet it felt completely different. A dead client sprawled on the carpet. My overwhelmed secretary, also on the carpet, looked at me as though I finally had surprised her one too many times. I offered her my hand and helped her stand.

"I don't know. She stumbled in here, looking like a ghost. We were talking when she collapsed. Then you walked in. You know the rest."

We waited for the ambulance and the police. Gus never made it.

Part Two

Days of the Dead

13 [Gus] *Six months later*

I'm dead and buried
somebody said that I was lost

Corrine arranged the final sugar calavera on her altar. The red skull had "Gus" written across its forehead in black letters. It joined a dozen other skulls, life-size to miniature, Katrina figurines, muertos and mementos of dead people we knew or wanted to know—parents, uncles, aunts, abuelos, friends, coworkers and our own heroes. Corrine included photographs and trinkets that were supposed to remind us of something about the particular person's personality. That explained the unopened cigarette packs, empty candy bar wrappers, laminated cover of *People* magazine and several other things that looked more like litter than altar decorations.

Corrine strategically set up a glossy of Ricardo Montalbán and Katy Jurado, the "all-time" Mexican actors according to her. Max contributed a signed photo of Chavela Vargas, Frida Kahlo's girlfriend and idolized singer who had died recently at age ninety-three. After much nagging from Corrine to "do something for Day of the Dead," I placed a magazine pic of Freddy Fender on the altar. She clicked her teeth and shook her head.

"Is the policewoman coming to dinner, after all?" she said. "Be nice if I could plan for the number of guests."

I had no doubt that a dozen uninvited guests could drop in and they would end up fed to complete satisfaction. Corrine cooked enough food for her annual Día de los Muertos dinner to feed all the soldiers on one of Pancho Villa's troop trains. The feast had great-party status among her circle of friends. For the meal, she rolled out platter after platter of enchiladas and tamales, and bowl after bowl of pozole, green chile, arroz and beans. The table included stacks of tortillas (maíz and harina), side dishes of roasted jalapeños, olives, chiles güeritos and serranos, lemons and limes, walnuts and almonds, pink and white sea salt, oregano, onion and cilantro. Bottles of beer, wine, tequila—the liquor usually carried skull labels—and a jug or two of fruit-infused water and Mexican hot chocolate. Pan de muerto, dead man's bread, of course.

The diners brought dishes, too. The one dish that Max boasted about was her fideo, and there was always a bowl of the Mexican pasta, with tomato sauce and onions, on the table. Corrine's dining table quickly maxed out and the guests followed a trail of serving dishes back to the kitchen if they wanted to sample everything. When we finished the main courses, desserts took center stage. Pies, empanadas, cakes, cookies, chocolate covered pretzels, Jell-O, leftover Halloween candy, biscochitos. All to honor the dead.

"I can't say yet. I told you, she doesn't know if she has to work. That's all I got."

Corrine didn't exactly approve of my ongoing relationship with the policewoman, as Corrine called her. Nothing surprising about that.

She set the time for the party at 4:00 p.m. That gave the guests about an hour and a half of talking, drinking and remembering before she began serving. The late afternoon start also meant that she had time to visit our parents' graves in the Crown Hill Cemetery, where she left a vase of flowers, a few cookies for my father's sweet tooth and a shot of tequila in a paper cup for my mother.

"Luis is coming, right?"

"Yeah, he's for sure. When I gave him your invitation he went on about how no one used to know what Day of the Dead was all about, and now it's practically as popular as Christmas."

"Wh-a-a-t? Mexicans knew about it. Mom always put up a little altar when we were kids. What's the lawyer talking about?"

"I think he meant in general. You know Móntez. He's always going back to the days when things were different. He's more and more like an old man every week."

"I hope when I'm his age I'm as sharp as he is."

"His mind's okay, I think. His body, not so much."

"Happens to us all."

She rushed to the kitchen and her food. I went downstairs to my cave in the basement.

I called Ana.

"What's up?"

"Still at the office," she said. "But with a little luck I'll get out of here in time for your sister's dinner. Around six, you said?"

"Be better at five-thirty, even earlier if possible. We'll be almost done eating by six."

"Okay. I'll do what I can."

"Be nice to see you."

"If I don't make it, we can get together later, right? You coming over?"

"I think so." I hadn't figured out what our relationship was all about, other than we were both having a good time. She rushed through the next few seconds and hung up before I said much more. Our relationship, or whatever we had, was stuck on fast forward.

By the time Móntez arrived for the dinner I'd popped open and finished a couple of Mexican beers. My taste for booze was slowly returning. He sat down next to me on Corrine's couch, where we listened to her homemade mix of Mexican oldies, watched a silent TV game show on her big screen and munched nachos.

"I need to talk to you," he said. "It's about the Contreras thing."

I hadn't heard that name for a few months. After her heart attack in our office and the official conclusion that she died of natural causes, Luis and I passively let her case close. I didn't think there was anything we could do to find out more about what she'd experienced, and nothing came of the investigation into the Westwood arson. Other than Ana and Luis, no one knew what I'd seen in the house before the fire.

My own investigation of María Contreras had hit the pause button. I looked into her background again, and learned a little more about Valdez. Nothing new. As a last step before I shut the file for the final time, I figured out where she actually lived. Her driver's license address was a dead end and the fake address she gave Luis stalled me for about an hour before I dug up her real address online. It wasn't that hard. I scoped out her house for three days, off and on, but I didn't see anyone enter or leave. Finally, I visited María's home late one night. Very late. I used some tricks I'd picked up in prison to open her back door and spent about twenty minutes looking for anything that might explain what she had going on in her life that involved Luis or me. The place felt damp and smelled musty. I hurried my search because of the uncomfortable feeling the place wrapped around me. I took a folder of papers related to the import business, a key that looked out of place in the folder, a few business cards from artisan shops and distributors in Mexico, and the insurance policy for Sam's bar. The visit wasn't a complete waste of time, but we didn't end up with any more of an explanation.

"The police and the fire investigators know the fire was intentionally set, and a few think someone died in the house, maybe more than one person. But there's no evidence, no proof. Nothing verifiable, at least."

"I know all that, Luis. What's new?"

"How'd you like to take a quick trip to Mexico? A vacation, more or less?"

I stopped in mid-dip of a tortilla chip into a dish of salsa.

I made a wild guess. "La Paz?"

"I got a call from the cop that María Contreras talked to about Sam's death down there. Apparently she contacted him just before she disappeared. She gave him my name and number."

"This cop has news?"

"His name's Fulgencio Batista."

"Where do I know that name?"

"The original was the dictator of Cuba before Castro threw him off the island."

"Sounds phony."

"Maybe his father was an anti-communist. Maybe he had a sense of humor, seeing as how the family already had the last name. Maybe it's just a name. I don't know."

"Whatever. You sure he's a cop?"

"I checked up on him. Talked with some of the local feds who work with the Mexican police. According to them, Mr. Batista is part of the Policía Federal Ministerial, the PFM. What we used to call Federales. He was pulled in on the case because Sam was a U.S. citizen and his death involved what looked like pirates, maybe drug-smuggling. They wanted a high-profile cop to work the case."

"He team up with U.S. cops?"

"He has. That one fed that interrogated you when you were arrested. Collins? From the DEA?"

"I remember him. Hard ass. Big ego."

"That's the guy. I've run into him a few more times. We developed a certain level of trust, especially after the way your case turned out. Anyhow, Collins said that Batista has been involved in dozens of high-profile arrests. And I mean involved. He once was captured by some cartel guys. They tortured him for a couple of hours before he managed to escape. He killed four of the gangsters getting away."

"Sounds like he can take care of himself."

"That same cartel has issued a death notice for him, and a five hundred thousand dollar reward."

"He must be doing something right."

I sauntered to the kitchen and dug out two more beers from the ice chest set up in the corner. I asked Corrine if she needed any help. She shook a large serving spoon at me and uttered a Mexican curse, which I took to mean she didn't require my assistance right then. When I got back to the couch the nachos were finished.

"All this action from a run-of-the-mill case. What Batista want? They finally figure out what happened to Sam? They find a body?"

"Something like that."

I waited.

"The case is cold. Almost four years and no developments. But Batista called me because he was trying to find my client, María. He had news for her that he thought she would want to know."

"So something did turn up?"

"Yeah." He waited one beat. "They found the guide that Sam hired for his fishing trip."

"After all this time? I thought he was dead, too."

"Exactly." He nodded his head. "Batista said he turned up about a month ago in a sweep of drug traffickers off the Southern Baja coast. The guide, a certain Francisco Paco Abarca, was arrested when officers in the PFM and a dozen Mexican marines captured four fishing boats heading north that were empty of any fish but were well-stocked with kilos of heroin. Needless to say, Batista was a little surprised that Abarca was alive."

The doorbell rang.

"Hold that thought, Luis."

I opened the door to more guests. It was close to five-thirty so I figured Corrine was ready to start serving. There was no denying that I was hungry.

"Let's eat," I said to Luis. "Then you can finish telling me why I should go to Mexico and have a heart-to-heart with Fulgencio Batista."

14 [Luis]

don't start me talking, I'll tell everything I know

María's death fortified my decision to retire. Gus and Rosa rolled with it and eventually they traded ghoulish jokes about what happened, but I couldn't let go of the image of the dying woman in my office, desperately trying to tell me something. I saw her gaunt, exhausted face in my dreams. I heard her sickly voice in the early autumn breeze that whipped leaves around my house. A client dying in my office was extreme, even for me, and when the police concluded that they had nowhere to go because the death was from natural causes and they had no suspects, I came to terms with closing the shop and getting on with the rest of my life. I didn't believe in signs or omens or fortune tellers but the ominous demise of Ms. Contreras was an unwelcome reminder that I was on the down side of my own existence. It made me think long and hard about how I wanted to spend the next fifteen or twenty years, if I was lucky.

I instructed Rosa to line up a few attorneys who'd take referrals from us. She had numerous friends in the Latino legal community of Denver, and I had no doubt that she could find trustworthy alternatives for my clients. I gave her a few names of old pals who might take a client or two, but most of my attorney acquaintances were either retired themselves or close to it, or dead.

I met with the office landlord and we worked out a timetable that would get me out of the lease by the end of the year, more or less. By the beginning of November and the Day of the Dead, Rosa and I were well on our way to retiring my law practice.

Of course, the one thing I knew for sure that I wanted to wrap up before I locked the office door for the last time was the Contreras matter. There was just too much left undone for that client. She'd come to me with her story about Richard Valdez and the missing money and seemed sincere when she asked for my legal assistance. She used me and my office to find out where Valdez was staying, but she should have known that already. Was she really that out of touch with her dead husband's affairs? Why me? According to Gus she was on the scene when someone, most likely Valdez, was killed. The unknown second man in the house— who was he? Where had she disappeared to for those crucial days after the fire? What happened to her that destroyed her health, and why did she come to me on the day she died? She looked like she wanted me to help her, but with what?

The images and memories would remain until they were satisfied or I lost them because of old age. Any chance for a peaceful retirement hinged on my finding out the answers, the truth about María Contreras. I had to put that ghost to sleep.

The contact from Batista of the Mexican federal police came out of the blue, and at first I had a difficult time believing anything he told me. He spoke without much of an accent. In fact, he was very polite, too polite, I concluded. But all he asked for was how to contact Ms. Contreras. "I promised I would call her if we uncovered something new but the numbers I have for her don't work."

"She's dead, months ago," I said.

"I'm sorry to hear that. How did she die?"

"Heart attack."

"Anything suspicious about her death?"

"She was in miserable shape when she died. She disappeared for a few days. I think something very bad happened to her. She came to me for help, but she died before I could learn much from her, or help her in any way. So, I am suspicious, yes."

"That's troubling. What do you mean she disappeared?"

"I lost touch with her. She went missing. She was my client but I didn't know where she was. I heard nothing from her, had no way to contact her and then one day she walked in on me here at work. She looked terrible. She actually died in my office before she could explain what happened to her."

"Was she ill or injured?"

"Both, in my opinion. She had a heart attack but it was obvious she'd also been through some physical abuse. But the official verdict here is that she died from consequences of unknown trauma. In other words, they can't say for sure."

"I feel badly about this. I wanted to talk with her because I have some news. I'm too late, it appears. When she asked me about the investigation into her husband's death, I had to admit that nothing had been done for years. We lost momentum because we had no leads at all. The men who attacked the fishing boat and who we thought killed Contreras and his guide vanished. There was a time when the pirates were extremely active in the Sea of Cortez. Attacks on fishermen, tourists, cruise ships, every day. That slowed down and now it rarely happens. So there was nothing for me to tell her when she asked. Now, al fin, there is a development."

"Thanks for following up," I said. "It's more than I would have expected. I know only some of the facts surrounding her disappearance and then her death. There are many unanswered questions." Like why was she involved in the killing of a man in her dead husband's old house?

"I wonder if Francisco Abarca can shed any light on all this," he stated.

When I asked for more details he didn't hesitate to tell me.

"Where is Abarca now?" I asked after he finished his account of the arrest of the fishing guide.

"Sitting in La Mesa prison in Tijuana. He'll be there for a few more years. We have him on several charges. We, meaning me, control where he sits out his sentence since he's facing federal charges. We put him in La Mesa and will keep him there until we come up with a better place." He sounded sure and pleased with himself. "I thought the widow would want to know that we will be asking him about Señor Contreras and the incident on the boat. So far, he has not said anything about anything, but a few months in our custody should soften him up and persuade him to be more cooperative. Eventually, he will tell us all we want to know."

The man's words made me uneasy. I hoped he never arrested me.

"The questioning will now include this new information you have given me."

"I'd like to talk with him myself," I said. "Do you think that would be possible?"

"Highly unusual, señor. There would have to be an overwhelming reason."

"I'd be asking as an officer of a court of the United States. That may not mean much in Mexico. My client died under strange circumstances. This man has a connection to the death of her husband. He's a witness that could be very useful in resolving my client's interests, even if she is dead. Maybe I can visit him in prison?"

"I can't promise anything, but I'm not opposed. He's not allowed visitors. We have him in what your prison wardens call solitary confinement. I won't forbid you speaking with him. It might help us finish the investigation. It may take some time, and I can't make this decision on my own. Mostly, it's a matter of processing the papers and getting the right signatures."

When the call was over I summarized it for Rosa, who typed up a memo for the file.

"I never liked this case, from the jump," she said. "Stranger and stranger, like Alice falling in the hole with the white rabbit."

❯❯ ❯❯ ❯❯

After we finished gorging ourselves at Corrine's Day of the Dead dinner, I tried to bring Gus in the loop. We sat in Corrine's basement surrounded by someone's meager possessions: a few shirts and pants hanging in a portable closet, dozens of records and CDs, a handful of paperbacks with lurid covers and a framed painting of Our Lady of Guadalupe. A pair of stuffed black trash bags huddled in a corner.

"This all yours?" I asked.

He looked around the room. "Not really. The clothes and books, yeah. Everything else is Corrine's."

I picked up a worn record album cover. B.B. King. *Live and Well.* "You listen to this stuff? Not too old for you? These are from my day, what I listened to as a student. This one's 1969, more or less."

"The music belonged to my father, and now Corrine. I like it."

I set down the album and gave Gus a quick update.

"Batista called you today?" Gus asked.

"Yeah. I just found out about this Paco Abarca."

"He knows what happened to Sam, might even have killed him. And he may know why María disappeared and then died."

"That's what I think. I need to find out for sure." Paco Abarca suddenly had become a very important man. He was a man I had to see.

Gus looked at me in that way he'd developed that said he had a difficult time with my logic. "Why? Who cares? The woman is dead. It's not the money, is it?"

That surprised me. "No, of course not. I doubt the money will ever turn up. Its location died with María and Valdez. No, it's not the money."

"Then what?"

"I, I . . ."

"What? You owe it to her? You must be joking."

"I know, it's hard to explain. But, at the end, the morning she died, she came to me, for something, for help. We don't really know what happened in the house, who set the fire or why she tricked us to get at Valdez. We don't even know what happened to Valdez. I guess I need to find out. That's all I can say."

"I thought you were retiring. I'm already looking for another job. I've told Dirty Harry. He's not happy, but he figures I'm on a short leash and so far I've been a real good boy. So he's looking for a job for me. I've made plans to move on. But it sounds like you're not there. Like you're ready to invest some serious time in tracking down these answers you say you need. Is that it?"

"All I'm planning, so far, is to meet with Batista so he can set up a visit with Abarca. I'm betting the guide knows something that may help me get to the bottom of some of this."

"Or he may not know anything that will help you understand the woman. More likely, he won't talk to you. Why should he? Especially if it means you want to know about his role in the killing of Sam Contreras."

"Yeah. It's a long shot. But, I'm gonna do it." I didn't know what else to say.

"And you want me to come along on this wild goose chase?"

I put on the leather jacket I'd draped across a large cardboard box marked "Christmas."

"No. I didn't mean that. I only wanted to talk with you about it. I can't ask you to get any more involved. In any case, you can't leave the state. No, this is something I have to do." I zipped the jacket and readied myself for the breezy November night air.

Gus stood up and walked over to me.

"I can't let you do this on your own. I owe you that much. I may not like it, but I'll help. Bringing me in to work in your office. The deal you worked out when I got arrested. There's a lot there between us."

"Not that it wasn't important, Gus, but I was just doing my job. You don't owe me."

"We see things differently. Besides, I think I can really help. I've got some skills I've developed over the past few months."

I paused, thought for a few seconds. "There's still the problem with you being on parole."

"I have a few ideas about that. You forget. I have a connection in the Denver Police Department. And Dirty Harry? I think he's starting to like me. If we tell him you need me to work on a case, he might approve a temporary absence from Colorado. It's been done."

I must have smiled because he smiled at me.

"Ever wonder what the Baja coast is like in November?" he said.

"And then Tijuana, and the prison," I said.

"Sounds like fun."

15 [Gus]

it's a thin line between love and hate

"No way. No fuckin' way."

"It's work. Móntez needs my help. I told you about the Contreras case. There's finally a break in the story."

I tried not to sound pitiful. I presented the idea to Dirty Harry during my regular sit-down meeting with the parole officer. He immediately hated it.

"This smells. You know it, I know it and Móntez knows it. The whole damn state knows it. These types of requests are never granted. Never. Somebody closer than your mother has to die in another state, and even then it's unlikely you could leave Colorado. You get down to Mexico, decide you like the idea of not having to report in any more and you never come back. Or, you slip back and end up somewhere else in the States. Where does that leave me? Dillings will have my ass for letting any of that happen."

"What if I get something official from the Mexican police? What if they agree to watch me, or report to you, or whatever the hell you want?"

He snorted through his nose. "Is that supposed to make me feel better? Mexican cops don't exactly have a reputation for honesty. Or for cooperating with Americans who work in criminal justice enforcement, like me."

He was pissing me off but I called on the patience I'd discovered in prison and kept myself in check.

"Harry, look." I tried to sound sincere. "Let's quit the bullshit. What's it gonna take to make this happen?"

"You're somethin', you know that?" He snorted again.

I hated the guy. "Yeah, I know that. I'm a pain. It's only that I got something good going with Móntez. Why mess with it? It's what you want. Gainful employment." He cocked his neck to the right and stared through me with milky blue eyes. "What has to go down for me to keep my job by doing what Móntez wants? It's probably the last big thing we work on together before he retires. This is important to me. You know that."

"It ain't gonna happen, Gus."

He glanced over his shoulders as he said the words. He cracked his knuckles. He looked bored. He let the breath out of his lungs and his lips shook. Then he stood up and shut his office door. He clicked the lock.

"What now?" I asked. I stretched forward in the hard wooden chair and put most of my weight on the balls of my feet.

I felt like I was back on the streets standing up to the latest jackass who'd decided that the Corral family would be his target for the week. Sometimes they fooled around, bluffing, and I didn't have to do anything. More often, they hassled Corrine or Max, or me, and then I had to escalate to protect our good name, or my sisters' safety, or whatever was the object of the jerk's particular obsession. I grew up on defense, and that's where I found myself that day with Dirty Harry.

"Look. Between you and me. Right?" Harry almost whispered. I eased up on my feet. "I could use a favor. Maybe we should talk. Uh . . . how bad you want to go to Mexico?"

Finally. He asked a damn good question.

"Bad enough. If it's something you need that I can help with, be happy to." Not exactly happy. I wanted to see where he was headed with his little game.

"You screw with me and you're going back to prison. You get that, right?"

The guy was a fan of the obvious. "You don't have to remind me that you have me by the nuts."

"Remember that, and we'll be okay."

"Jesus." I tensed up again. "What is it?"

He circled his desk and stood in front of me.

"It's not that much, when you think about it. Maybe take you a couple of hours."

"Yeah?"

"You met Ed Dillings." He waited a beat. "No secret that we don't get along. He's a weak man, inside, but he has the power in this office. He's worked as a bureaucrat for the state too long and it's gone to his head."

I guessed I was supposed to agree. I nodded.

"He's been out sick for two days now. It's a pattern with him. About every four months."

"You think he's not sick?"

"He's sick, but not like with the flu or anything."

"What are you talking about?"

"I've been here in this crummy office for five years, almost six. He won't promote me, says I still have a lot to learn. Meanwhile, the son of one of his pals has moved up, out of the trenches. He was hired two years after me. Got a nice office over in the new court-house. Pushes paper, talks to politicians. Doesn't have to interact with lowlifes directly."

Lowlifes like me.

"Dillings doesn't appreciate you?"

"You could say that. I dated his daughter for about a year. He was my friend then. Promised me more responsibilities and more pay."

"Good to have the man's daughter for a girlfriend, right?"

"Good and bad. He never let me forget that Barbara was his daughter."

"What happened?"

"We were engaged when I screwed it up, bad. All my fault. I accept that. I tried to make it right but it didn't end well. She went from love to hate overnight. I tried to get her back but there was no changing her mind. It's not like she was the great love of my life or anything like that. But the bitch has no compassion."

I didn't feel sorry for him. "Must have made it awkward around the office."

"Dillings told me that he wouldn't let the personal interfere with our professional relationship. That was a bunch of shit." A thin spot of sweat appeared at his temples and along his upper lip. "He started payback and hasn't eased up yet."

"I don't see how I can do anything about any of what you've told me." I wanted him to sweat even more.

"When Barbara and I dated, one of the things she talked about was her relationship with her father. She went through some rocky times as a teenager. Her mother died in a car accident that Barbara blames on Dillings. She was a real wild child for a few years, in and out of trouble. The way she explained, her old man worried that her troubles would interfere with his career. They had some mighty blow-outs. She ran away like a half-dozen times, spent time on the streets. So she and her father aren't exactly close. She'd get real wound up talking about her daddy. She told me things she probably regrets now."

"Love, or hate, will loosen lips in more than one way."

"Yeah, I guess." He picked up a pen from his desk and chewed on it for a few seconds. "Looks like Dillings has a booze habit. He likes to drink all alone in his house. That's nothing. But according to her, when he gets too deep into the booze, he'll disappear for days. During those times, he often calls up an escort service. He's a regular customer. Gets special treatment for special performances. That's what Barbara called them."

"Kinky stuff?"

"Oh yeah. Weird."

"How's the daughter know this?"

"She busted him one night. She stopped by because he hadn't been seen for a few days. Called in sick here at work. Apparently he was on a genuine bender. She let herself in to check on him, make sure he hadn't croaked. Turns out, Dillings was enjoying one of his kinkier episodes."

"Because he's out sick now, you're thinking you can use that against Dillings? Give you some leverage for a promotion?"

"What do you think?"

I looked around his office, checked that the door was still closed. "You know, most of that kind of stuff doesn't raise too many eyebrows these days. Everybody has their kinks. Nothing illegal or underage, right? If he's in his own home, not out in public exposing himself, there's not much to help you."

He shook his head. "It's not the legality of what he does. It's that he's such a power figure around here that anything that could tarnish that view would at least embarrass him. He's the man, the main horse. Knocking him down a peg or two would be okay with me."

"Again, not sure I can help with that."

He threw the pen in a wastebasket. "From what Barbara told me, her father was in some humiliating situations when she walked in. Freaky stuff involving bodily functions and fluids. Just Dillings knowing that I know about those things might be enough for him to cut me some slack. That's all I want."

"But you don't have any proof?"

"Right. Barbara will never back me up. She's my only source but she hates me almost worse than her father."

"You sure she told you the truth? If she doesn't like her father, she could have lied about him to you."

"Nah. The way she talked about him, the way she described what he did, what she saw, she was telling the truth. But I need something tangible that I can hold over his head."

The guy had certainly opened up to me.

"Like what?"

"Photographs. Video. Recording."

"You mean of him doing whatever it is that you think is humiliating?"

"You got it, Gus."

I acted like I was thinking it over.

"Let's assume I can get this proof you want," I said. I placed my bet. "Then you'll approve my request for temporary absence from the state?"

"Let's say that I would be more amenable to such a request if I knew that I had a better chance of getting out of this hole. You help me, I'll help you."

"Just like that?"

"Yeah. But you gotta take care of it tonight. He won't do this again for another four months, at least. You miss out tonight and we don't have a deal."

I quit acting.

"Give me his address. I'll see what I can do."

≫ ≫ ≫

I called Harry first thing the next morning. No one else was in the office.

"You got what I need?" he asked. "What happened?"

"You're set. I'll tell you all about it tonight. I think you'll like it."

"He was up to his tricks, right? Great. He's out sick again today. Must have been quite a party."

"I can't even talk about it."

He laughed. "Yeah, the perv. Makes me want to puke. I got him now. Come to my place after work. We can talk there."

"Uh, no thanks. I'd rather be somewhere I know. Let's meet here at Móntez's office about nine. Can you do that?"

"Strange place for this kind of meeting."

"I have a key and a good reason to be here. It's where I spend most of my time. We'll be alone. No one will bother us, but if anyone does come by, you can say you were looking over some of the work I've done for Luis. If anyone saw me at your house, it might raise questions."

"Yeah, maybe. Okay. Who cares? I'll see you at the lawyer's office at nine. Don't be late."

"Don't worry about that. Remember our deal."

I made coffee, fired up my computer and kept busy while I waited for Rosa by entering my notes into a couple of files where I'd done basic grunt work.

I trudged on through the morning helping Rosa close out files and finish up final billings for many of Luis' long-term clients. At noon I left the office and walked several blocks to a hamburger joint that recently opened on the Sixteenth Street Mall. Maxine waited for me in one of the wooden booths.

"Hey, bro. About time."

"Sorry. The walk took longer than I thought. Good to see you. You look good."

Maxine was beautiful and, since she had fallen in love, she looked better than ever. She had the dark features of my mother—hair and eyes—and the healthy look of my father, who at the end of his life was heavy into exercise and eating the right food. Maybe the fact that she reminded me of our parents was why I thought she was beautiful.

"How's the wedding plans? Everything still a go?"

"So far so good. I'm waiting for Sandra to come to her senses and tell me, 'See ya, sucker.'"

Max insisted on downplaying the emotional attachments she created in her life, although she had several over the years.

"You and I both know that ain't gonna happen. Still set for the summer?"

"Yeah. That's why I wanted to see you today. But let's get something to eat. I'm starved."

We waited in line to order our burgers. The mall was packed with the typical downtown lunchtime crowd of young men in suits, young women in suits, construction workers in hardhats and muddy pants, homeless guys panhandling, kids dressed in black hoodies and boots sitting on the sidewalk leaning against the building, and an older man strumming a guitar while he tried to find a song that would catch someone's attention.

When we finally made it to the counter, I went all out and had something called a California Whirl, which turned out to be a thick slab of ground beef smothered with avocado, bacon and sprouts on a toasted multigrain roll. I picked off the sprouts. Maxine demolished her turkey burger in about a minute. The girl never lacked for appetite.

"You're sure about this?" I asked between bites. "No doubt that Sandra is the one?"

"I'm as sure as anything I've ever done. Sandra and I are good together, and I don't mean just in our music or the band or the other projects we have going. We're good in everything. It's wonderful to be in love. I hope it happens for you soon, Gus."

The way she emphasized "everything" said it all.

"Sandra and I are going to have a full-blown wedding, Gus," she continued. "A good friend is going to be the official—she's done it for many of our other friends—and we want to keep as many of the traditions we can, that we feel comfortable with, of course. We are pretty untraditional, after all. But there's going to be a dance, for sure."

"With the Rakers playing?"

She laughed. "I think so. My band's gonna rock the house."

"Food, presents, champagne, all that?"

"Yeah, food, what do you think? Plenty of food. Corrine's coordinating. Who else, right?"

I nodded at that.

"So I want you to be a part of my wedding, too, Gus. I hope you can. It would mean a lot."

Maxine had gone through issues with our father when she came out, and that had carried over to how much she wanted to talk to me about her personal life and the tumult of what she lived through when she was younger. She figured that my father and I were similar in so many ways that she was skittish about confiding in me. That had changed in the past few years, and I hoped that she was as comfortable with me as I was with her.

"Whatever you need, Max. Eager to help. Very happy that you want to include me."

She reached across the greasy table and covered my hand. "I want you to give me away, Gus. Walk me down the aisle and hand me off to Sandra. Can you do that?"

I squeezed her fingers. "No problem, Max. You can count on me."

"Thank you. Its means so much."

"Who's the minister or judge, or whatever you're gonna have to make it official?"

"Our old friend Jackie O."

I laughed. "Really?"

She leaned back in the booth. "What's so funny? She's been great at many of our friends' weddings. And she always brings color and, uh, panache to the celebration. Choosing her was obvs."

"Jackie is fine with me. Can't wait to see what outfit she chooses for this."

"Me, too. Just hope she doesn't outshine the bride."

We finished our lunch telling stories about Jackie O. We ended up remembering how Javier Ortega had become Jackie O and the heartache that process had caused in her family until finally the chaos, fighting and tears had settled and only Jackie's laughter and good humor remained. Jackie had proven that she was a good friend, and I couldn't think of a better person to preside over my sister's wedding.

≫ ≫ ≫

I turned on only a few lights in the office. For what I was about to do I didn't want too much exposure. I sat at my desk where I had a view of the main door but not much else.

I hadn't told Luis anything about what I was doing with Dirty Harry. The less he knew, the better for him, I calculated.

Harry showed up right at nine. He walked in the office and took his bearings in the dim light. Then he swaggered over to my desk.

"What you got for me?" he asked.

"Not even a hello, or how did it go, or was there any problem or trouble?"

"I don't really care about that. I just want the dope on Dillings."

"Are you sure about this? What you're talking about is coercion, blackmail. Dillings could go to the cops."

"If you have what I want, there's no way he's talking to anybody about this. You did get something, right?" He paced across the room. His right fist slammed into the palm of his left hand.

"You told me to find some concrete evidence about Dillings' sexual hang-ups. According to the deal we made, if I did that, you would do what you could to get me a pass out of state. And it gives you the upper hand with Dillings."

"I know all that. Get with it. What's the delay? Why are you stalling?"

"No stall, Harry. I'm only making sure that I understand you and everything you intend."

"Yeah, yeah. That's it. Let's see the pictures, or whatever you got."

Someone moved a chair in the dark. Harry and I turned to the noise.

"How about me in person? Will that do for proof, Harry?" Ed Dillings walked out from the shadows at the back of the office. He stopped at my desk about three feet from Harry.

The smell of stale booze leaked off his skin. His hands shook.

"What is this?" Harry said. He backed away from Dillings into the semi-darkness.

"The end of your scam, Harry. That's what this is." Dillings pulled a gun from inside his jacket.

I should have searched him before I let him in the office. "Oh no," I shouted. "That's not what's happening here."

I jumped to my feet and grabbed Dillings' wrist. He turned in surprise towards me and that's when I wrenched the gun from him. Sweat glistened from the large white spot of his forehead. His breath reeked like a bar at closing time.

"Goddamn you," he said. "Give me that gun. I'm gonna kill this son-of-a-bitch."

Harry bent over. It looked like he was trying to hide behind my desk. His head dangled only six inches from the floor. "You double-crossing motherfucker."

I barely heard the words.

"Dillings has the power, Harry," I said. "Direct quote from you. Can't go wrong with that."

Harry acted like he wanted to jump me. His half-hearted movements stalled. Dillings clenched his fists and held them rigidly at his sides. I pointed the gun at Harry and Dillings.

"Both of you relax. No one's gonna get killed tonight. But we are ending this."

Harry looked up. "You screwed yourself, Corral. You think Dillings won't use this? You were part of the plan. The most important part. He's got you now."

"You're the only one he's got, Harry. I told him about your scheme last night. He sobered up enough to understand what you were trying to do. And now that we have your admission on tape, I don't think Ed or I have anything to worry about from you." I showed him the recorder hidden in my pocket. He collapsed completely to the carpet.

"You're done, Harry. Can't say I'm sorry." A woman's voice whispered from the front of the office. I jerked the gun in her direction.

"What are you doing here?" I assumed it was Dillings' daughter, Barbara.

"I told her everything," Dillings said. "I didn't think she'd show up. But it's good she's here."

"Ain't no way there's anything good about any of this," I said.

Barbara's pale face contrasted with the darkness of her clothes. Everything she had on was black, including a purse that dangled from her shoulder. She constantly moved her trembling hands.

My anxiety lurched upward. I was outnumbered by a trio of whacked-out, nervous people who hated each other.

"Everyone take it easy. What the three of you do to one another is not my concern. Just don't do it here. I'm done with you all. I got the tape. That takes care of Harry. I know what you're up to when you call in sick, Dillings. That takes care of you and my future obligations to your office."

"And what about me?" Barbara asked.

"You're not really part of this, as I see it. You shouldn't even be here." She didn't look like she'd heard any of my words.

"But I am. And now I get what I want." She casually opened her purse and pulled out a small pistol.

"Drop that, Barbara." I held Dillings' gun on her but I didn't intend to use it. If she wanted to waste either of the two assholes, I wasn't going to stop her.

"Barbara! What are you doing?" Dillings hollered his words.

"You're a sick man, father. We both know that. You showed me how sick many years ago. You ruined my life, you ruined me. You killed mother. You killed me. And him . . . " She pointed the gun at Harry. "Another worthless piece of garbage."

"Don't do anything crazy, Barbara." Dillings interrupted but she continued to mumble. "Be careful with that gun. You can't shoot me. I'm your father."

"Worthless, both of you." Barbara stretched her hand holding the gun in Dillings' direction. "But still I couldn't keep him. Because of you, father. You. You."

The gun went off and she screamed. The bullet tore out a chunk of paneling near Dillings' shoulder. He whirled and dropped to his knees.

"Don't do it, Barbara," I yelled. "He's not worth it. None of them are." For her own good I had to stop her. "Drop your gun and everyone calm down. We can take care of these two, Barbara. You don't have to do anything."

She held the gun with both hands and moved it in a wide arc that covered Harry and Dillings.

Harry cringed on the floor. He clasped his hands around his head. He rocked back and forth on his heels. Dillings looked up at his daughter from his knees. Drool and tears streamed down his face and off his chin. His lips were moving but I didn't hear him say anything.

Barbara jammed the gun barrel in her mouth and pulled the trigger.

16 [Luis]

somebody done hoodooed the hoodoo man

One of the last official acts of Ed Dillings was to approve Gus' request for a temporary out-of-state travel permit. Gus had him sign the form when he told him about Harry's scheme and the meeting at my office. Later, after the parole chief had been disgraced, nothing mattered to him. Gus' request slid through the grease of the bureaucratic machine. He could come and go as he pleased.

Dillings resigned because he had no choice. His daughter's suicide opened up too many cans of worms. Ugly secrets were revealed from the journals that Barbara kept neatly stacked in her closet. They were found by the girl's aunt after the funeral. The aunt immediately turned them over to the police. Dillings not only abused his daughter when she was a child but he'd continued to manipulate her and basically destroyed any chance she had for a normal, happy life. Whatever that may be.

The governor made quick work of removing him from office. Dillings was charged with a wide variety of crimes based on his daughter's journals, but the state never had the opportunity to prosecute. The end came with efficient finality. His sordid, perverse life was spread out in public for anyone to pick over, and it turned as foul as it deserved. It was too much for Dillings. He followed in his daughter's footsteps and ended his own life. He laid down in the back seat of his running car in his closed-up garage until he died from the carbon monoxide flowing from a hose connected to the car's exhaust. The cops found him the next day when they came to arrest him for not showing up in court at his arraignment.

Dirty Harry? The district attorney filed charges based on what Gus knew, his tape of the fateful night and what Dillings told them before he offed himself. Harry copped a plea to criminal intimidation and was given probation. Everyone assumed that sending him to prison would have been a death sentence, so I guess that's why he slithered away relatively clean even though the D.A. had him cold because of Gus' recording. The last I heard he was looking for a job.

And Gus and me? Naturally we caught a raft of crap because Barbara ended her life in my office—the second death of a woman in my office in less than a year. That looked suspicious to more than one policeman who didn't like the idea of coincidence. The cops cordoned off my office and kept it closed for days, making my retirement almost a done deal without any fanfare.

Rosa and I were questioned more than once about any connection to Dillings or his daughter. Eventually they understood we had none.

Gus took the brunt of the heat. His recording of the event went a long way to clearing up any confusion the cops had about what had happened, but still they grilled him hard when they had the chance. They didn't like it that he had possessed a gun, even though it wasn't his and he had taken it from a man who was about to use it. They didn't appreciate that he was involved in an extortion scheme, no matter that he stopped the scheme cold. And for sure they didn't like it that he was on the scene when bullets were fired and a person died. It took a while and I had to go toe-to-toe with an ambitious assistant D.A., but finally even the police agreed that Gus was the good guy in the wretched drama, and that Dirty Harry and Dillings were the outlaws.

The shutdown hit my bottom line hard. No new clients came in and I had to cancel several appointments I'd already scheduled. The little bit of business I was able to conduct had to be done on the run, in my car or at the offices of a few attorneys who were willing to help me out. Rosa took a leave of absence since there wasn't much for her to do.

Instead of getting ready to celebrate the triumphant end of my legal career, I felt like Luis Móntez at the beginning of his lawyer life: no prospects, no money and no clue.

When I got the call from Gus about the shooting and I rushed to the office the night it happened, I thought I'd reached the end of my joint venture with the ex-con. To be honest, I figured he was up to his old bad-boy tricks and Barbara Dillings had paid the price. His scheme to finagle out-of-state travel had imploded. The parole chief's daughter died as a result. I was not feeling any love for Gus Corral. I stayed that way for several days until Gus and I met to iron out the details of what happened.

"You should have told me what you were doing, Gus." I was angry and uncertain and my voice reflected both feelings.

We talked in the office when we were allowed back in after the cops finished their work and the cleaning crew clocked out. The landlord had demanded that I invest in a service to remove all traces of Barbara's sad end. The place smelled like bleach and ammonia. The carpet had been replaced and the walls repainted. The office never looked better.

"I didn't want to drag you into something that could have gone off the tracks. Which is what happened, right?"

"And yet I was dragged into it. Funny how that worked out."

"You firing me?"

That stopped me. I couldn't do it. I shook my head.

"You and me, Luis," he said. "We're meant to get the short end, no matter what we do. That's what it's all about."

It didn't sound like he was serious enough about his responsibility. "Don't say that. I still have hope."

"Good for you."

He laughed.

"Seriously. Playing Dillings against Harry was a dangerous game." I wanted him to admit he might have made a mistake.

"For those two jerks," he said. "Nothing about Dillings or Harry worried me. Barbara was the wild card. After all these years she finally broke."

"She could've shot all of you as well as herself. You literally dodged a bullet. You see that, don't you?"

"She must have lost it completely when her father told her what Harry had done, how Harry revealed what she told him, and that he was trying to use it against Dillings. She had to feel used by both."

"She was." The conversation stopped for a few seconds.

"I'm sorry about what happened, Luis, if that's what's bothering you. But these people are all damaged goods. Barbara was broken a long time ago. She would have ended her life sooner or later unless she got help, and that wasn't in the cards. I just happened to be around when she pulled the trigger. If there was anything I could have done to stop her, I would have tried."

"That's the thing about unintended consequences," I said. "Maybe they're foreseeable, maybe not. We have to be very careful when we play around with people's lives, Gus. I think you know that. I'm not lecturing you. Hope I don't sound like I am. But if we're going to work together, we have to communicate, to make sure we're on the same page. That's all I'm asking."

"I got it. I'm with you, Luis."

That had to be enough for me.

"So, you still up for Mexico?" I asked.

"You must be kidding."

"What could be better than Christmas in Baja? Fishing, drinking beer on the beach, just laying out in the sun. What's not to be up for?" It sounded phony even to me.

"What do you hope to accomplish? The fact that there's no more case doesn't bother you? How about that little detail?"

"I want to talk to the Mexican cop, and, with some luck, the fishing guide who sits in prison and who we hope will spill his guts to us about Sam Contreras and whatever he may know about María or the missing money."

"You still want to get into that? Everyone's dead who was involved, but Luis Móntez won't stop."

I shrugged. "Bad habit. I like closure. I don't like loose ends, especially about my clients."

"To repeat. She's dead. And so is her husband. And so is the guy who opened all this, Valdez."

"Too many unanswered questions, Gus. I'm almost done with this lawyer game. I don't want any of María Contreras' life and death hanging over me when I finally lock up everything. I hope you can understand that. But, even if you don't, you know I'm going to find Batista and try to get to Paco. That may be a blind alley, but it's a step I think I have to take."

I tried to lay it out for Gus, as clean and clear as I could make it, but the truth was that I didn't understand all my motivation. I'd acted the same in the past and often it cost me. I kept promises I'd made in moments of weakness, or paid off a debt that only I remembered, sometimes risking my life. But I was too old to change. At least, that's what everyone told me since I reached forty.

Gus' face relaxed. "I went to a lot of trouble to get the travel pass," he said. "I'm not quitting now. Besides, I could use a vacation."

"Glad to hear it, although we won't be on vacation until after we get to a dead end, either with Batista or this guy Paco. But that shouldn't take too long."

"Then Ana can join me? You think maybe a couple of days?"

"We talk to one cop and one convict. First, La Paz. Then the Tijuana prison. Two, three days ought to be enough. Then I come back here and pack up my office, and you can enjoy your time off. We get ready for the new year." I realized that my retirement meant that Rosa and Gus would be out of work. "And we see about a new job for you and Rosa. I can help with that."

Gus rubbed his hands together. "Let's go, then."

"I'll call Rosa to come in and help with the travel and hotel."

"If she hasn't found something else already," Gus said. He went off to his desk to finish whatever it was he'd been working on when he figured out his trap for Dirty Harry. I called Rosa.

She was more than eager to get back to work. "Christmas!" she shouted when I asked whether she wanted to do any work. She walked in the office a half-hour later and immediately searched the Internet for tickets to La Paz. It turned out that there was no way we could travel to Mexico in the next few days. Christmas was only two weeks away. There were no direct flights from Denver to La Paz; everything was routed through Mexico City and the tickets were running more than a thousand dollars each, roundtrip. My business account couldn't take that kind of beating. I didn't even bother to check my personal account.

"La Paz is packed with tourists and college students," Rosa said when she looked up from her computer. "I can get you two a room in a hotel about three miles from the beach. But it looks real shady, even on its web page. I wouldn't stay there. It's not cheap either."

"We should hold off," Gus said. "I was ready to go tomorrow, if we had to. But now . . . We wait until after the New Year. Take our time, come up with a good plan about what to do if Paco gives us anything. We can avoid the turistas and set our schedule."

"I hate to put this off. What if Paco disappears?" I asked.

"I thought he was in prison?" Rosa said.

"What if he gets killed?"

"Luis, he hasn't been killed yet," Gus said. "What are the odds, eh? I think we'll be okay."

I had to agree. "Guess we take a long break. Stall my retirement until February, something like that."

"You weren't ready, anyhow," Rosa said. "There's like a thousand things we have to do yet."

"All right, all right. I get it. The Contreras case is on hold. Meanwhile, Rosa and I get serious about closing up. Take some time off, Gus. I can't pay you anyway."

"I'll manage," he said. "Don't worry about it."

Gus and Rosa disappeared to the back room.

It took several minutes and a couple of phone restarts but eventually I contacted Batista and told him our plan. He complained about the delay but there wasn't anything he could do about it, and I don't think it really mattered to him anyway.

"Your passport still good?" Rosa asked when she brought out a bottle of tequila to celebrate whatever it was she felt like celebrating. Gus carried paper plates, a bag of lemons, a knife and a salt shaker.

"Yeah. Another three years." I turned to my investigator. "Gus?"

"I'm okay, I think. At least I had one before I started my sentence."

"It should still be good. Look at the date when you get home. They don't automatically revoke passports for felons. As long as Batista clears the way, you shouldn't have a problem crossing the border."

Rosa sliced lemons. Then she spread salt on a paper plate and rubbed lemon juice on the rims of the shot glasses. She salted the glasses and poured the liquor.

"That tequila's been sitting in the back for years," I said. "It's cheap stuff. Be ready for a jolt."

I scanned the view from the windows of my office. Several lights were on in the building across the street. A medium-sized law firm occupied the first floor and the arched entrance evoked security and success. Large snowflakes glistened in the fading light and the world turned gray as clouds rolled across the skyline.

Gus reached for his drink. "Even if Batista doesn't get me a visa," he said, "I can sneak into the country, can't I? Shouldn't be a problem."

Rosa and I stared at him.

"I'm joking." He said. "Relax."

We raised our glasses. "Merry Christmas and próspero Año Nuevo," I said.

We chugged the tequila, everyone's eyes teared up, and Rosa shouted, "Ay-yay-yay!"

Just like old times.

17 [Gus]

*you know it's nine below zero people
and my love don't mean a thing*

The Colorado winter blew into town with the solstice, but not with any goodwill. Denver was hit with a December cold snap that sent the temperatures below zero for a week. In the middle of that week, the snow started and didn't quit for another day and a half. The residential streets were snow-packed, ice fingers hung from tree branches and roof eaves, schools began the holiday vacation early, snowdrifts muffled all sounds, and the world seemed to have stopped.

"I love it when it gets like this," Corrine said. We ate oatmeal, toast and coffee in her yellow kitchen. There was little else left in the refrigerator or pantry. "No one's going to work, no one's hassling anyone about anything. It's like peace has finally broke out."

"It's like Ebola wiped out the city and you and I are the only ones left alive, and to tell you the truth, I'm not feeling all that good."

She punched my arm and a sliver of pain arched through my bicep and across my shoulders.

"Damn. That hurt, Corrine."

"You're such a drudge sometimes. Can't you enjoy the moment?"

My older sister had developed a sense of Zen awareness, or something, which had me stumped about how I should act around her.

I rubbed my arm with more enthusiasm than called for. "Christ, I think you gave me a bruise."

"Quit crying. For a guy, you sure fold up easy."

I shook my head. "You're too much, but you know that."

It'd been three days since we'd left the house for anything more than shoveling the sidewalk or retrieving the newspaper. Although Corrine rattled on about winter's serenity, cabin fever made us delirious and crabby.

"You should've gone to Mexico. At least you'd be out of my hair."

"First chance I get, I'm out of here."

She ignored me and rifled the pages of her newspaper as though it actually had something important to report. I poured a third cup of coffee for both of us.

"God, what next?" she said.

"What's up?"

"¡Ay, mi México! Won't that shit ever stop? All the killings. The innocent pay the price for the drug dealers and the politicians."

"Don't forget the U.S. druggies and their addictions."

She showed me the article in the paper that caused her anger. A newsprint photo of a smoking building with bars on the windows included several bodies scattered around the walls. The headline read, "Riot in Mexican Prison Spreads to Tijuana—Dozens Killed."

"The inmates took over the prison," she said. "Before the federal troops regained control, a mob of convicts ran through the streets of the city, killing, raping. They were eventually gunned down but several blocks were torched. I can't believe it. It gets worse every damn day. Mexico's on fire and no one cares enough to turn on the water hose." She read more. "Now I'm glad you didn't go down there. What a mess."

"I should talk to Luis. We were supposed to meet with the guy, Paco Abarca, in La Mesa, that prison."

"You're kidding me?"

"Wish I was. This probably screws up everything."

My cell buzzed. I assumed it was Luis.

"You heard the news?" Ana's voice surprised me.

"About the Mexican prison riot?"

"Yeah, of course. Homeland Security sent out an alert early this morning that more than a hundred people were killed."

"But it's over, right? That's what the paper said."

"Some fighting continues in Tijuana, but it's not clear that any of it involves escapees. In Mexico sometimes you can't tell the difference between so-called convicts and gangsters on the street."

"Our guy Paco could've been killed. He's the only link we had to the mystery of María Contreras, and that was a very weak link."

"Too bad for Móntez and his need for closure."

"Yeah. Is there a list somewhere of all the dead?"

"I'm sure there is but I haven't seen it. Those lists are always wrong anyway, initially. Especially if they deal with violence across the border. Give it a week or two and the data will be more accurate, if not completely reliable."

"I guess we wait until it settles down in the prison, then check with Batista again."

"There's something you should know."

"What's that?"

"A handful of prisoners are still on the run. The news is saying that the Federales and marines have regained control of the situation, but that comes from the Mexican government. Our sources—Homeland Security, really—say that six of the prisoners are unaccounted for. We've got one report that at least two of them headed north across the border into the States."

"You think one of them is Paco?"

"No, I'm not saying that. These reports have to be verified and they're sketchy on details. I'm just saying you should know. Paco could be alive but not in custody."

"And he could be headed for the States?"

"That's quite a jump. I highly doubt that. Odds are that he's either dead or back in lock-up. That's most likely."

"But not necessarily the only outcome, right?"

"Well, no. That's why I mentioned it. Still, it has nothing to do with you."

I thought about that for a few seconds.

"Gus? What's wrong?" She didn't sound worried, only curious. Ana never appeared to lose her self-control.

"Paco doesn't have any reason to come to Denver, as far as we know. So, it doesn't matter. Nothing to do with me, as you say. But . . ."

"What?"

"What if he knows something about Sam's missing money? Might be motivation to run to Denver. Nothing to lose by trying to come up here."

"Now you really are jumping to conclusions and getting all bothered about nothing."

"Maybe. But we thought Paco was dead. Wrong. He rose from the bottom of the ocean. Now, anything's possible."

"Don't let your imagination run wild. Even if he knows about the money, what's that have to do with you? He wouldn't know anything about you."

"Maybe, maybe not. If not me, then how about Luis?"

"The guy's been on the run, or smuggling drugs, and then in a Mexican prison. I can't see how he would know anything about either of you guys." If I believed such stuff, I would have sworn that I could feel my blood pressure rising. "Come on over," she said. "We can talk about this. You're tripping. I'll calm you down. We haven't been together in days."

Her offer was tempting.

"Save that thought. I should call Luis. Get his angle on this. I'll get back to you."

When I hung up, Corrine grabbed my wrist.

"How serious is this thing with this person from Mexico . . . Paco?"

"To tell you the truth, I don't think it's anything at all." I shook off her grip. "I'm thinking out loud, mostly. Luis wanted to talk to him because he was with Sam Contreras when Sam died. He thought Paco might be able to shed some light on what happened to María Contreras when she disappeared. It was a long shot. Now, it's a no shot."

Corrine leaned against her stove and stirred her cup of coffee. "You don't sound too sure. Maybe your friend Ana should have a few cops talk with you, figure out some security. Couldn't hurt."

"You may be right. I'm gonna see her later. I'll bring it up."

18 [Luis]

he's a real nowhere man

Gus called about the prison riot and the possibility that Francisco Abarca was on his way to Denver. At the time, I didn't give Gus' concern a second thought.

"The guy's running for his life," I said to Gus. "He'll disappear into the Southern California freeway maze of immigrants and wannabe actors. Denver isn't even on his radar. No reason it should be."

"What if he knows about Sam's money? What if he had something to do with María's disappearance? Maybe she clued him in to where the money might be. You wanted to talk to him about all that, remember?"

"I wanted to ask him questions about some of that. You're worse than a law school exam with all your what-ifs. He's been in Mexico smuggling drugs. Then in jail, apparently. When would he have had any contact with María? It's not logical."

He sighed over the phone. "Yeah, you're right. You and Ana. I'm just leery. Things don't always go logical for me."

"Given your history, I can't blame you. And we'll be careful. But, really, what else can we do? I'll talk with Batista and find out what he knows about where Paco might be, and whether he's any kind of threat to you or me."

I added that he should try to relax until I had concrete info I could pass on to him. He said something about visiting Ana Domingo.

We basically closed the office because of the storm, but Rosa and I continued to slog through retirement issues. We were at our desks dressed in jeans and sweaters, drinking too much coffee and scarfing down more doughnuts and empanadas than I'd eaten in years.

Rosa efficiently mopped up the finish work for the files I knew I would never get back to. She called the clients, told them that I'd done all I could, and diplomatically terminated the relationships, usually with a cheery statement about how the final bill for services was in the mail. If needed, she offered a referral.

"That Mrs. Trujillo is a trip," she said at one point. "She absolutely refuses to believe that you are retiring. I repeated like a dozen times that you weren't going to advise her anymore, and she just kept asking about when she could see you again to go over some business things about her grandchildren. By business, she means trying to keep them in school and out of jail. I think that woman is in love with you, Luis."

"Sounds right. She's only about eighty-five."

"Closer to you in age than that miniskirt you escorted around town for a few weeks last summer."

"Olivia? You talking about her? She wasn't that young."

"I'm older than her, and I think you're too old for me, so what does that tell you?"

"It tells me you should get back to the phones."

I dictated several letters to various clients advising them of my retirement and giving them suggestions about who could now handle their legal affairs. The files triggered images from across the decades. The office clutter stimulated memories that picked at my sentimentality. A dim face associated with a name and I recalled a particular incident that meant something to only me. Or a formal pleading transported me to a courtroom and a hard-fought trial. I flashed on bits and pieces of my attorney life: a question I asked during cross-examination that cinched a ruling in my client's favor; a point I pressed in the oral argument of an appeal that ended up in the judges' written opinion; a bottle of cheap cologne from a grateful elderly client who worried that I wasn't married.

The idealistic reasons I had for becoming an attorney rolled over me like the marijuana cloud at the annual 4/20 rally, and for a brief second I worried that I'd never succeeded at my own ambition. I'd wanted to be the Chicano attorney of and for the people, the fast-talking, clever abogado who could go mano-a-mano with the best legal minds in the state but who never forgot his roots in the housing projects of Denver's Westside. I'd wanted to create change, change for the better.

"But not much has really changed," I muttered.

I was slipping into reminiscences that had nowhere to go except regret.

My imagination left me and the letters turned into rote and depressing exercises. I paused and surveyed my office. Forty years was a long time—for anything. Now what? The wave of nostalgia felt colder than the gusts of icy wind that cracked against the office windows.

And where in hell was I going to put all the stuff?

Rosa walked in and interrupted just in time.

"The Mexican cop, Batista. Sent an email to our office mail box. He says he has something very important to talk over with you, and that he hopes you can use Skype to do the call today."

I'd rarely used that technology and I needed Rosa's help to make sure everything was working on our end. Turned out to be simple, but I told her to stay in the room in case anything happened. The face-to-face format of a video call had to mean that the Mexican cop was very serious about his message. I worried before he said a word.

When Batista flashed on my computer screen, I could almost hear Gus say, "I told you."

I saw only Batista's face for most of the call, but somehow he gave the impression that he was a muscular, wiry man. He had a coarse moustache and wavy hair that gleamed in the florescent light of the office from where he made the call. That same light made the scar on his left cheek shine. His deep voice had the singsong quality that many native Spanish speakers carry, even when they're speaking something other than Spanish.

We got around the small talk quickly. Batista obviously wanted to deal with our business as soon as possible.

"Esto es un poco raro. Very strange."

"That's not what I wanted to hear," I said.

"Well, here's the deal. The riot, to begin with. A massacre of guards and prisoners by members of a faction of the Sinaloa cartel. Most of the men who participated in the butchery are dead. The odds were always against them. They had little chance to survive, so we believe this was primarily a suicide mission. Only God knows why."

"Or the devil," I said.

"Sí, el diablo."

"Paco? Is he dead?"

"This tipo, Abarca, is still on the run. He beat the odds and escaped. We are fairly sure that he connected with someone who helped him across the border, probablemente un coyote who does that for a living. He slipped through the roadblocks we set up around Tijuana. I've seen video of a man who looks like him jumping off the back of a pickup truck at a bus station in Chula Vista, in the States. After that? ¿Quién sabe? To be frank, we don't know where he is now."

"Is there any reason to think he would be on his way to Denver?"

"That's an unusual question, señor."

"I'm sure you understand why I ask."

He scratched his scar, then ran his fingers through his thick hair. "You wanted to talk with him about your client, la señora Contreras. Which means you think he may have an interest in your city, or an association that would make it a good place for him to run to."

"Yes, exactly. Do you have any information about him that would indicate something like that?"

"I said this was a strange situation. He resisted our interrogations while we had him in jail. We thought eventually he would yield, but that didn't happen. We didn't learn anything from him about his involvement with the death of Anselmo Contreras, or why he was reported as killed by the local police in La Paz, or where he's been for the past several years. And now he's gone. When I tried to find out more about this Abarca person, I ran into dead ends, as you say."

"What does that mean?"

"There is documentation about his killing by pirates in the raid on the fishing boat. Police reports, newspaper stories, even tape of a television news broadcast showing a few pieces of the hull of the wrecked boat. Pero, I can't find anything about him before that. No school, military or prison records. There's no history of this man before he was thought to have been killed in the attack that also killed señor Contreras. That makes it difficult, impossible really, to look for leads to find him since we have no idea who his family or friends might be, who he might have worked for, where he might have lived. Nada, nothing."

"How could that happen? He's been incarcerated. Didn't anyone try to run a background check on him when he was arrested? Or when he was sentenced?"

"These things sometimes happen, I'm embarrassed to concede. It's actually not that difficult to get lost or forgotten or overlooked in the Mexican criminal justice system. Most often, a man, what do you say . . . slips through the cracks, when he's a friend or relative of a powerful person, a politician or banker . . . someone with influence. I've come across a few in my experience who have no history, como Abarca. They were important men. I never would have thought Francisco Abarca fit that profile."

"If he's important, is he also dangerous?"

"Often there is no difference between the two. I can tell you this about Abarca. He deceived everyone for years, so he is no fool. For his disappearance he needed help in high places. He adapted to prison without any problems. If he was an unknown, his life would have been hell, at least at the beginning. Obviously, he had friends en la cárcel who were willing to help him."

"He's one of the few who survived the riot and escaped," I said.

"Yes, you see what I mean. If indeed he is making his way to Denver, and he's looking for people who knew Anselmo or la señora Contreras, then I would tell those people to be careful and to watch for this man."

My concern turned into an awkward pause on the computer screen. He tried to reassure me.

"But, señor Móntez, we don't know that he's on his way to Denver. Nor that he knows about your connection to señora Contreras. I'll talk with the Denver authorities and alert them to the possibility of Abarca ending up in your city. They will take all the necessary steps. If you let them know your worry, perhaps they can help you. Meanwhile, I'll send you a photograph of Abarca, by email. You and your office staff may have the advantage on him if he does show up. You can be waiting for him, while he will have to work to find you."

Shouldn't be too hard, I thought. I'm in the yellow pages, paper and online. I asked him to send me all he could on Abarca. He said he would but he reminded me that there wasn't that much.

19 [Gus]

oh mercy, mercy me
things ain't what they used to be

Ana picked me up from Corrine's house at two o'clock in the afternoon. She drove an all-wheel drive SUV that she borrowed from one of her brothers out of an excess of caution. The snow had stopped falling but driving was still an iffy proposition. Ana drove the vehicle over our usual route. Slow and easy on the snowy side streets, and then she let the SUV rip on Twenty-Second, then Lawrence, which had been cleared by the city crews. She had to slow down again when she turned onto Thirtieth, near her place.

She wore a pink down jacket, pink gloves and a purple hat that covered her ears. She didn't look like a policewoman, or, at least, like the image that I tied to the concept of a woman who works for the police department.

I had no doubt, though, that Ana could take care of herself. I'd seen her physical strength, in more ways than one. We worked out a few times together at the rec center. She lifted weights and stretched muscles like a pro, and I sweated trying to keep up with her. She'd grown up with a quartet of brothers who didn't spare her from their macho games. At an early age she learned how to box, play football and shoot a gun. At my early age I learned how to fight without the discipline of boxing, how to play games on the unsuspecting and how to run when the guns were drawn.

She told me that her brothers—Tony (Junior), Chris, Paul and Gabe (Baby Gaby)—were the most important people in her life. They'd watched over their sister her entire life. She was the second youngest and she didn't argue with the idea that they spoiled her rotten. "Anything I want," she said, "they try to get for me."

I took that to mean that if she couldn't handle a problem, her brothers were ready, willing and able to jump in if needed.

I had no doubt, either, that she was smart. She graduated with honors from the University of Colorado in Criminal Justice. She told me early in our relationship that she wanted to be a police officer since she was a child. Her father was killed in a robbery at the auto repair shop he'd created out of doing fix-ups for his neighbors.

"Of course, my father's death changed my life," she said. "The police did all they could to help our family, and when they finally arrested someone, they made sure we had a voice with the district attorney about what should happen to the killer. I've wanted to do police work ever since. That must sound silly to you, Gus."

"Not silly, just unreal. I come from a whole different experience. My point of view is the opposite of yours. No surprise, right?"

"And yet, here you are, getting next to a cop. Aren't you afraid you'll pay a price for being with me? Lose your cred on the streets?" She half-laughed when she talked but the laugh didn't hide the thin line of tension under her words.

"It's not my cred that's at risk," I said. "The Denver Police-Community Liaison Officer has more to lose, way more, than an ex-con who doesn't answer to anyone except his parole officer and his big sister."

That made her laugh even more.

"Let me worry about what I got to lose or not lose. I can deal with it, all of it."

A big chunk of what she had to deal with was the reaction from her family. According to Ana, her brothers thought she'd blown a brain fuse because of me. They didn't appreciate their little sister cuddling up to a convicted felon. When I asked if there was anything I could do about the brothers, she said only that I should stay away from them. So far, I'd managed to do just that.

"It's madness in Mexico," she said as she guided the SUV through an icy intersection.

"I think some of that is heading our way," I said. "There's a pot of money waiting for someone like this Paco. He needs the cash. He's the last one to have any dealing with Contreras. It makes sense that he's running to Denver. He wants what Valdez wanted. The missing body and the fire tell me that there's somebody else willing to kill for it. I don't doubt that Paco would, too."

"You don't know that. You're speculating, and that's foolish. You should deal with what you really know."

"I need to prepare for the worst, don't you think? I'm trying to be realistic."

"You said you thought Móntez was overreacting, but to me it sounds like both of you are amping up the stress levels."

I didn't want to throw my anxieties at her, so I cooled it and hoped I sounded genuine. "Nothing I can do about any of this now, anyway."

"That's right, Gus. Let's try to relax."

For Ana Domingo "relax" often meant drinking an amazing amount of wine, crawling into bed and making love until we passed out from exhaustion. She chilled with sexual euphoria followed by a deep satisfying sleep. I had no problem with her definition.

I spent almost three hours in her bed, and near the end, I did drift away for a few minutes. We did outstanding things as we explored our bodies, as she put it, and my little cop friend certainly did her best to put me at ease. But I didn't really relax. When we finished, Ana sprawled on the bed naked, and snored peacefully. I covered her with a blanket, put on my clothes and then helped myself to a beer from her refrigerator.

Paco and the missing money, as well as the nightmare scene from the Westwood house that had attached itself to my brain, had me going over as many scenarios as I could dream up, none of them resolved to my satisfaction. They all ended with me facing off against a killer over money that I didn't give a damn about, for people I didn't know. The only clear thing was my obligation to Luis Móntez. I would stick with him through this. It, whatever "it"

was, had assumed an importance in his life that I didn't understand, but I didn't care about that. The guy stood by me when I
needed help, and now I would stand by him. Thinking about it that
way made me feel better. I woke up Ana so she could take me
home.

On the way to Corrine's I called Luis. We had the same idea:
talk out the situation. Batista had filled him in on what was happening with our man Paco. That information, combined with the
news coming from Mexico that Ana fed me, firmed up that we
should prepare. Only thing was that Luis wanted me to prepare for
war. At least, that's the way he made me feel. This guy Paco had
spooked him big time. We agreed to meet that night at his house.

Ana and I said our goodbyes in front of Corrine's house while
the SUV idled and the heater kept us warm. In a few minutes we
didn't need the heater. I pulled myself away when she started to
play with my zipper.

"Baby," I said, "you wore me out. I need to recharge."

She disentangled herself from me and sat upright. "I hope you
feel better, Gus. Don't worry so much. It will be all right."

"You bet," I said. She drove away. As I trudged through the
snow to the front door, I thought that it might be a good thing to
have a cop as a friend. A very close friend.

For the next hour I watched a cop show on television. The
detectives were silly asses, non-threatening men and women who
joked around the office, or when they examined a crime scene and
found a dead body. They solved the murder mystery with the help
of a female tough-talking medical examiner, who in a matter of
minutes, figured out time and cause of death, where the dead person had eaten his last meal and a possible motive for the crime.
The lead actor employed clever use of Internet databases that
apparently only police could access, and then relied on the coinci-
dental good luck of a major reveal just before the final round of
commercials.

Cops, cops, cops. Everywhere I turned, cops. I talked myself into thinking that a dark walk to the lawyer's house would be invigorating, or at least a diversion. The stalled storm left drifts, ice and cold. I wore a heavy parka that I scrounged from Corrine's basement. One sleeve had a nasty rip and the zipper stuck halfway up, but it beat anything I had in the way of winter clothes. I also found scuffed boots and one of Corrine's scarves. Double socks and gloves topped off my wardrobe. They weren't enough. Five minutes into the walk and the cold reduced my fingers to painful, iced stubs. Fog from my raspy breathing lingered in front of my face. The parka's hood held out hope, but I discovered that it had a hole near my left ear that conveniently allowed a cold stream of air to knife around my neck and down my back. By the time I reached Luis' house I deeply regretted my hasty refusal of Corrine's offer to use her car.

We talked in the warmth of his brick home. In the living room, hardwood floors gleamed around a colorful oval rug. A black leather couch sat in the middle of the rug, and a small mahogany coffee table squatted in front of the couch. A combination CD and record player sat in one corner, a television in another. There wasn't much else. Apparently, he preferred clutter to accumulate in his office rather than his home. His gas fireplace gave off too much heat, but I didn't complain. In fact, I stood as close as I could to the artificial fire.

He offered me a drink.

"You got any hot chocolate? Coffee?"

"I can make some coffee. You don't want a real drink?"

"I'm good. I just need to warm up." He didn't move. "Okay. Put a shot of whiskey in the coffee, if you got it. The cold's in my bones."

He disappeared back to his kitchen. I thumbed through a pile of vinyl albums near the record player. His records were older than the ones in Corrine's basement.

"Rosa put together a file on Abarca," Luis said when he returned. He handed me a cup of coffee and sat down. He pointed at an expanding file sitting next to him on the couch. "It's got all the attachments Batista sent us, plus she typed my notes. I've had it for a few hours but I haven't looked at it yet. I thought we could go over the material while we figure out what to do."

I drank half of the coffee in two quick gulps and burned the roof of my mouth. The whiskey burned my throat. I set down the cup on the coffee table, leaned over and picked up the file.

The top sheet contained basic info such as Abarca's name, contact numbers for Batista, a reference to the María Contreras file and so on. The second sheet was the printout of the photograph Batista had promised. Rosa had made it a full page, which she must've thought would help. Under the photo were a dozen or so more pages from Batista that included copies of police reports in Spanish that I assumed described Paco's arrest, documents that bore official logos and seals that appeared to come from the prison and notes from Batista written in English with a few Spanish phrases. The final two pages were Móntez's notes.

I moved away from the fire. My butt had warmed up enough.

"It's kind of grainy but this should help us." I pulled back the top sheet and showed Luis the photograph.

He jumped to his feet. "Let me see that." He grabbed the file and stared at the picture.

"Goddamn. Goddamn."

I didn't want to ask but Luis simply stood on his fancy rug without saying a word.

"What is it now?"

"This guy," he finally said, pointing at the photo. "Look at those eyes. The face is changed a bit, somehow, and the beard and mustache get in the way, but those eyes are the clincher."

I looked where Luis pointed. The poor quality made it almost impossible for me to really see his eyes, but even with the limitations there was no doubt that they were intense, strong. I remembered that Luis once talked about Sam Contreras' eyes and how he could make drunks leave his bar merely by looking at them.

"You think that's Sam Contreras?" I asked. I grabbed the file from him.

"That's exactly what I think. Paco Abarca and Sam Contreras are the same guy. And I'll bet everything in my meager savings account that Paco or Sam is on his way back to Denver."

"Batista didn't know that? Wasn't he investigating Contreras' killing? He must have had a photo of the victim."

"Maybe he only had a photo of the dead guy—who wasn't Contreras. And remember that María said she buried Sam in Mexico. If she said the dead guy was Sam, then that would've been all they needed down there to conclude that it was Sam."

"You're right," I said.

"Even if Batista knew what Sam looked like," Luis continued, "he might not recognize him today. He has changed. Probably some plastic surgery. I spent many nights in his bar, sitting across from him as he served drinks. I saw him up close. Batista doesn't have that history."

Luis sat on the couch, leaned his head into the soft leather and closed his eyes. He appeared to smile. His hands rested on his lap. Had he finally found peace?

I studied the photograph. I resisted the idea that grew from a nagging pinprick to the slash of a cold blade. I turned the photograph on its side, then upside down. I held the photo up to the light.

"What are you doing?" he asked, his eyes still closed.

"Trying to shake this thing that . . . that's a little hard for me to understand."

"What could be harder to understand than the fact that a guy everyone thought was dead is not only alive but apparently living the life of a Mexican smuggler? It makes easy sense. Or that this same guy is probably responsible for the death of his wife, some-way, somehow?"

"Yeah, I get that's a lot to take in. I'm not trying to complicate shit, but I think there's something else that you might find interesting."

He opened his eyes. "What are you talking about?" He sat up. His left foot tapped a steady rhythm on the rug.

"The night I staked out the house in Westwood? The female Contreras was there, as well as another guy in a hoody sweatshirt, and someone who looked dead."

"Yeah? I remember."

"Give the guy in this photo a shave, rearrange his nose a bit, make it bigger, and he's the dead ringer for the man in the hoody. Maybe dead ain't the right word. But you get what I mean."

Luis shook his head in frustration. Without saying anything he yanked the cup of coffee and whiskey from the end table and finished it.

20 [Luis]

people get ready, there's a train a comin'

It all looked obvious after the fact. Maybe I should have put it together before Gus identified Paco as Sam. I think I was hit hardest not by the actual revelation but, rather, by what my slowness in figuring it out said about me. I not only wanted to retire; it was in everyone's interest if I did.

The little things that creep up on an aging man suddenly were bigger things that worried an old man. Sometimes in conversations I would have a relevant thought about whatever was the topic, but before I could inject my idea into the discourse, I'd forgotten it. Other times I couldn't think of the right word and I stammered as my mouth waited for my brain to catch up. I hadn't had an uninterrupted night of sleep in years, and lately I'd found myself clumping to the bathroom four or five times a night because I couldn't resist the urge (if not the actual need) to urinate. If I didn't put something in its usual place, like keys, wallet or reading glasses, I paid for my indiscretion by forgetting where I laid the damn thing and then having to look all over the house or office for several minutes—the frustration growing into an ugly boiling mass in my gut. With every so-called senior moment, my confidence shriveled, along with other critical parts of my being. Old age, decrepitude and dementia bore down on me like an out-of-control freight train.

When I told Rosa about the latest developments in the Contreras matter, I made the mistake of complaining about my advancing senility.

"Shut up," she said. No emotion. Only a direct command. "Shut up about your age. I hate it when people start whining about

141

getting older. It happens to everyone. No big deal. Be grateful you're not dying, or dead."

"Words of wisdom, but then you're not even forty-five."

"And you're not old, not really. I don't think you've earned the right to call yourself an old man, not yet. You got all your smarts, you can walk and talk okay most of the time. You have plans, right? I thought you wanted to retire so you could do all those things people want to do, like see Paris and Havana or hike up a volcano in Hawaii? Better get with it, Móntez. You aren't old but you aren't getting any younger."

Apparently she'd given my retirement some thought.

"Thanks for the pep talk. Not sure where that's coming from. You can't deny that I'm slower than when you first started working here, what, more than a dozen years ago? I've lost a step in the courtroom. I've . . . "

She waved her hands in the air and shook her head. "I don't want to hear it. I can't dance all night anymore, like I did when I was eighteen. I can't eat two of the giant burritos at Tacos de México, like I could when I was twenty-five. I can't drink more than four beers before I start slurring my words. It's all part of the circle, Luis. Enjoy it, because there's no jumping off at this point."

"You've gotten quite philosophical in your old age."

She grabbed for me but I managed to jump away. She held only air.

"Hey, still have decent reflexes, don't I?"

"I don't have time for this," she said as she walked away. "When you figure out what you're going to do about this guy who's coming to Denver and who might want to shoot you, let me know. I'll want to make sure I have a safe place to hide."

Gus and I'd decided on a plan, of sorts. He wanted me to go over the situation with his old running buddy, Jerome Rodríguez. I knew Jerome's reputation, and from what I understood about the shoot-out that ended with Gus in prison, I believed that if anybody could help us prepare for the return of Sam Contreras, Jerome was that guy. What else he brought to the table remained to be seen.

They walked into my office late in the day. Jerome looked exactly as I expected. The man had done a little bit of everything during his life, as verified by dings and scratches that couldn't be smoothed out by age or an expensive haircut. Scars marked the backs of his hands, his neck and his hairline. He walked like a professional fighter, maybe a boxer or a lucha libre masked hero. His eyes didn't rest on one thing or person for too long; he constantly surveyed his surroundings, even when they were only the boxed-up furnishings of my law office.

"Not sure I can be much help," he said when we settled around my conference table. "Gus tells me the cops are watching for this guy Sam. You and your staff are being careful, I assume. You carrying a gun?"

"Me? No. I won't do that. And Gus can't."

He glanced at Gus. "Gus knows what he has to do." His attention refocused on me. "If you're not armed, how do you expect to deal with this guy if he comes after you?"

"I don't. I'm counting on the police to handle him. My days of trying to be a tough guy are over. I just want to do all I can to keep Gus, Rosa my secretary and whoever else might be at risk, out of harm's way. If necessary, I'll close up the office."

"Again?" Gus asked. "You just opened up."

"So it won't be much of a drop in business. I'm closing shop, Jerome."

He nodded.

"Maybe it makes sense to just shut it all down now, instead of in another month or two. That way, we're not sitting ducks in one place. Gus and Rosa can get on with their lives."

Jerome shrugged and twisted his mouth. "Uh, yeah, maybe."

"Jerome's not exactly a wait-and-see kind of man," Gus said. "He'd rather take the offensive. Right?"

"If it was me," Jerome said, "I wouldn't wait to be surprised by this guy. But maybe that's just me. He's a killer, a thug. I'd want to meet him on my turf, with the odds in my favor. Wishful thinking maybe, but at least I'd try to prepare for that."

"It may be more than we can do," I said.

"You don't need a tank. Any preparation is better than nothing. Everyone who works for you should be on the alert. You all should know what to do if there is trouble, what number to call, where the exits are, how to hunker down in your offices here if necessary, what the signal is if something is coming down. Things like that."

I made quick notes on my legal pad. "Thanks, Jerome. I'll do all that with Rosa and Gus."

"You should do it quick. The prison break was days ago. Paco or Sam or whoever could already be in Denver."

I nodded.

"Thanks, Jerome. We should go," Gus said.

"Yeah," Jerome said as he put on his overcoat. "I'll think some more on this. If I come up with anything specific, I'll pass it on to Gus."

"You want me to stick around until you're ready to leave?" Gus asked.

"Go home. Nothing for you to do here. I'll be leaving in a few."

When I was alone with only the ticking of the office clock, I struggled again with the depression that the idea of retirement stirred up. That idea now mixed with the possible danger from Sam Contreras. The short days, freezing nights and gray scenery of winter surrounded me with melancholy. I paced from one end of the office suite to the other, mumbling broken sentences. I'd argued with myself for months about whether I should retire. No one forced me to quit. I could continue, turn down my practice and take on only the basic, simple tasks a lawyer can do without ever having to see the inside of a courtroom or hear the hostile voice of an opposing counsel. I could counsel wealthy widows on selling their too-big homes, or review business contracts for bearded hipsters looking for unique ways to spend their fathers' money.

Then I bounced back when I remembered the uncertain threat from Sam Contreras. That problem began as a simple run-of-the-mill legal matter that I thought I could handle with a few phone calls. Did I really need to go over all the good reasons for stepping down? Did I really need to re-examine my life again, just so I could end up back where I started? Listen to Rosa, I told myself. The woman knows what she's talking about.

I walked into the cold Denver night. Downtown noises mixed with a brisk wind. The skyline glittered against the black winter sky. I'd stared at some of these buildings all my life; others were new and unknown to me. The buildings changed faster than I could track. Old structures collapsed into dust and rubble, replaced with new towers of steel, glass and greed. I quickly forgot what had been before.

I imagined that somewhere in the noise and traffic, a desperate man on the run searched for money he thought was his. I felt him watching, waiting. I could see him recreating the last days of the woman who had the money. She'd escaped from him, somehow, some way. She'd always been smart. He traced her steps on the final day of her life, the day she visited the office of a lawyer she'd initially hired to help her double-cross the desperate man's partner. He calculated what the woman must have told the lawyer. He was confident that the lawyer held the information he needed.

Cut the crap, Móntez. I hurried to my car in the parking lot across the street from the office. My shoes slid on the pavement and I had to catch my balance more than once. I opened my car, glanced over my shoulder and quickly jumped in. The inside of the car was as cold as the outside air. I felt like I sat on a block of ice. I locked the doors, pressed the ignition button, let the car engine warm up some and slowly drove away.

I'd fooled myself into thinking that someone waited for me in the night. I had to believe that the black SUV that entered the street the same time as me was only a coincidence, and that the coincidence stayed in my rearview mirror for several blocks only because we were going in the same direction. I lost the SUV in the traffic on Speer. I kept looking in the mirror but it was impossible to see if the SUV was behind me. When I parked in front of my house I waited for several minutes before I climbed out. No other cars drove along the street. No one followed me. No dark SUV waited with its lights out.

I sat in the dark in my warm house on my leather couch, holding a glass of scotch. I finished the liquor and poured a second one, then a third. To fight back the negativity I thought about all the good things that happened to me since I'd become a lawyer, and how I enjoyed the comfortable life I'd naïvely mocked in my youth as bourgeois and self-indulgent. I'd done all right, considering.

I stretched out on the couch, dropped the dregs of my fourth glass of scotch on the rug and strained to keep my eyes open. I stared outside through the front window of my house and, before I passed out, I saw a black SUV parked in the street.

Part Three

The Mexican Cop

21 [Gus]

en tu casa no me quieren por borracho

When Jerome and I left Luis in his office, I wasn't sure it was a good idea for him to be alone. The guy who was careful about his work and who took his time to carefully analyze every situation had moved past me in the nervous department. I could tell that he was concerned about Rosa and me, and I respected that, but I wasn't sure what I could do to help.

"He'll be all right," Jerome said. "He's shook up but he looked to have a grip on what's happening. You can't be with him all the time, anyway, and he wouldn't want that."

I drove the Kia. We were headed towards Berkeley Park and Jerome's house. Patches of snow and ice dotted the street but it was nothing like we'd faced the past few days.

We agreed to stop for a drink in one of the new bars along Thirty-Eighth Avenue. The cold temperatures hadn't kept customers from the place, and like so many other joints in my gentrified part of town, we had to deal with standing room only. The name of the place was Calhoun's. That's about all I remember of the club. Nothing stood out about it that was any different from the dozen or so other bars that burst onto the Northside scene. It was a watering hole with noisy drunks, meaningless music in the background and overpriced craft beers. We had two beers each with very little conversation, and then Jerome nodded at me and we left.

As we walked out the bar Ana's youngest brother, Chris, entered. He saw me coming and made a move like he was going to bump me with his elbow. I stepped aside and he glided by me and into one of the waitresses. She fell backwards and dropped the tray of drinks she carried.

"Goddamn!" the waitress shouted.

Chris Domingo stayed on his feet, but the way he wobbled told me he'd reached his limit that night.

"Hey, Chris," I said. "You okay?" He flipped me the bird.

"What's going on?" Jerome asked.

One of the men who walked in with Chris grabbed him by the elbow. "Take it easy, Chris. Come on, let's get that drink." The crowd that surrounded Chris and the waitress moved as one and they disappeared into the bar.

"That's Ana's brother," I said.

"Apparently not a fan."

"Her brothers hate me, all of them. They can't believe their sister is mixed up with a lowlife like me."

"And I can't believe that you're mixed up with a cop."

"It is kinda strange, no?"

"Strange is craving a Quesarito from Taco Bell. What you're into qualifies for Ripley's. I hope you know what you're doing."

I laughed.

"That guy gonna bother you?" Jerome said. "Do we need to do something about him?"

"No, man. He's my girlfriend's brother. I'm not going to do anything. He has to learn to live with me. It's an adjustment. Change ain't easy. If you can stand me, he should be able to deal with it."

I focused on driving and getting Jerome home. We listened to a news radio station but we didn't pay it much attention. We were lost in our own dark thoughts. I pulled up under a snow covered tree in front of his house. He climbed out and I waited while he made his way to his front door.

Lights exploded in front of me and I hunkered down below the dash, out of instinct, only for a second. When I looked back up, a pickup truck's lights blinded me for a few heartbeats. The truck had screeched to a stop only inches from the Kia's front end. Chris Domingo jumped out of the passenger side. The guy who'd pulled him away in the bar jumped out of the driver's side. He ran after

Jerome, and I flashed on the thought that the driver had made a serious mistake. Chris ran towards me, hollering obscenities.

I timed my reaction based on Chris's staggering dash. At the right instant I whipped open the Kia's door and smashed Chris. A hollow thump echoed in the cold air. He clutched his chest and opened his mouth like a fish. He fell in the snow with a dull thud. I climbed out of the Kia and stood over Chris. He was having trouble breathing. In the background I could hear Jerome beating up Chris' friend. I cringed with each crunch and groan.

Chris continued to grab at his chest. His eyes popped like they were going to fall out of his face.

"You got the wind knocked out of your lungs. It's gonna hurt like hell for a few minutes. You think you'll never breathe again, but you will. It's happened to me. You think you're dying, but you're not."

He kicked futilely at me but he wasn't trying to stand up.

"You and Ana should have a talk, Chris. In fact, all of you Domingo brother assholes should sit down and let Ana straighten you out. You, Junior, Paul and Baby Gaby, that's what you call him, right?"

He managed to get to his knees.

"You . . . son . . . of . . . a . . . bitch."

"Yeah, yeah. Get out of the way. Go pick up your buddy and get the hell out of here before the cops arrest you for littering the landscape."

I walked over to Jerome, who sat on his front porch. Chris' friend sprawled in the snow, unconscious.

"You okay?" I asked.

"What I tell you, Gus? Every damn time you get into some mess, I get caught up in it too. What is it with you, man?"

"I love you too, pal. Let's throw this guy back in his truck and see if we can get that piece of shit crawling in the street behind the wheel so he can get out of here. Okay?"

When we finished and Chris drove away, I turned on the Kia. I looked for Jerome so I could tell him thanks, but he'd entered his house and turned out the lights.

I played around with the idea of calling Ana. I didn't follow through. I figured her brothers would fill her in on what happened soon enough, and then it would be up to me to convince her that I told the truth.

22 [Luis]

I'm here to tell ya honey
that I'm bad to the bone

When I woke up I was still on the couch. Sunlight filled the front window. My eyes adjusted slowly. The black SUV no longer sat in the street. I wasn't sure if I'd dreamed it.

I found my cell phone and Gus' message. He wanted to verify that I'd made it home okay. "Call me as soon as you get this."

I had two glasses of water, threw more water on my face, and then I called him.

"You at your house?" he asked.

"Yeah. I gotta ask you something." I sounded like my throat had been ripped open and then sewn shut with wire. "You see anything funny last night?"

"Funny?"

"Different. Like you were being followed?"

"Oh, I was followed. Talk about funny. But it's not what you think."

"If it was a black SUV, then it's exactly what I think."

"Someone followed you home?"

"I think so. Actually, I'm not sure. That's why I'm asking you."

He told me about his fight with one of Ana's brothers. "That can't be what you're talking about," he said at the end of his story. "I don't know anything about a black SUV."

"It might not have been black. A dark color. It was behind me when I left the office, then I thought I saw it again here at the house, but . . . I can't be sure."

"Didn't you check it out?"

"No, not really."

"What make? Or year?"

"Hell, they all look alike to me. My father liked to say SUVs looked like pregnant roller skates. Maybe SUV is the wrong word. They used to be called station wagons. But I don't know for sure."

"I don't get it. Was there someone following you or not?"

"The truth is, I was knocked out on my couch. I got so worked up I chugged too much scotch. Booze just seems to put me to sleep now. There could've been someone here, or not."

"You think it was our pal, Paco? No one's outside now?"

"No. The street is clear. If there was someone, he left me alone last night, although if he busted in with a wrecking ball I wouldn't have known it. And he's not around now. Probably just my imagination."

"Be careful, Luis. We don't know what's going on. Maybe Ana's heard something. Or that cop, Batista? You talk with him yet?"

"Not yet. That's next."

"Okay. I'll get back to you after I talk with Ana. Meanwhile, you going to the office?"

"Yeah. Rosa's there and I don't want her to be alone."

"Good point. I'll come on in myself. We should go over with her what we're thinking. Maybe she ought to just stay home?"

"I suggested that already. Not going to happen, according to her."

"No surprise. All right, I'll check you later."

I tried Batista's cell phone but all I heard was a message that the line was out of service.

The weather had finally broken. Not only was the sun out in full force, but the temperature was rising every quarter hour. The weatherman predicted we would overtake the freezing mark. The day promised to be clear, no snow, with a good deal of melting on the agenda. Except for my headache and the nagging feeling that someone watched me, I felt good.

I cleaned up, had a bowl of cereal and called Rosa to tell her I was coming in. I asked if she was okay, and she acted like I had no reason to ask that question.

I drove as quickly as I could to the office and parked the car. At the corner, I shivered in the bright cold sunshine as I waited for the pedestrian light so I could cross the street.

"Señor Móntez?" I turned abruptly to face the person who asked the question. A man leaned against the corner of the building to my left. I hadn't seen him standing in the shade.

I couldn't see his face clearly. My first thought was that it was Paco. I tensed up.

He repeated, "Señor Móntez?" He stepped out of the shadow. I recognized the Mexican cop.

"Batista? What are you . . . ?"

"I waited out here, rather than your office. I didn't want to interfere with your staff. We should talk."

"Sure. But let's get inside."

We crossed the street and walked in the building. I took him to my back office under Rosa's watchful eye.

His scar was much more noticeable in person, under the bright lights.

"This is a surprise," I said. "Uh, you want something? Coffee, water?"

"Café. Sí. Denver is cold. Gracias."

"Black or . . . ?"

"Just the coffee, por favor."

I found the freshly brewed pot Rosa had made and poured two cups.

I waited while he had a sip or two and settled back in his chair.

"This is unexpected, I know," he said.

"You didn't say you were coming to Denver when we talked. Why the surprise?"

"I didn't know I was headed up north. I learned after our call that Abarca was on his way here. I left as soon as I knew. I didn't take time to call you."

"How do you know he's here?"

"Informants."

"Really?"

"Men who decided they had better things to do than endure our questioning. A few cooperated after we explained their options. That happened after we talked."

"You tortured them?"

He looked at the books in the nearest bookcase. "The criminals I hunt are animals. They don't respond to usual techniques. We learned that from your anti-terrorist officials. We work closely with them. In the right case."

The guy intimidated me on Skype but in person he was a hundred times scarier. I didn't want to know any more about how he knew his fugitive was in Denver.

"So Sam Contreras is back?"

"Sam Contreras?" He shook his head.

"The actual name of the man you know as Paco Abarca. We recognized him from the photo you sent."

"Contreras? I don't understand."

I began with Sam in Denver, running the bar, but also involved with Richard Valdez in drug smuggling. I reminded him of María Contreras and her story about Valdez and the missing money. I explained my belief that Valdez had been killed by Sam or María, or both, and that Sam had operated in Mexico as Paco Abarca.

"But Abarca is not a recent creation," Batista said. "He's been known to us since the alleged attack on the fishing boat and what we thought was the death of Contreras and the guide."

"The guide, Abarca, or whatever name he had, may have been real. He probably died on the boat. Sam assumed his identity. Actually, I think he created the Paco Abarca person. The real guide was probably too well-known for Contreras' purposes."

"Contreras killed the guide?"

"I don't know. There are many possibilities. Somehow Contreras made it look as though he died in the boat, too. Since then, I believe he's been going back and forth between Mexico and the U.S., as Abarca, running drugs, other contraband. You caught him smuggling again, but I think he was also involved in the killing of Valdez up here."

He finished the coffee and put the cup on my desk.

"You want more?" I asked.

"No. Gracias. I was thinking, though, that if what you say is true, it explains a lot."

"Such as?"

"The man I knew as Paco Abarca was apparently a man of influence. I think I told you that. The way he lived in prison, the escape he pulled off during the riot. I have since learned that he was connected to several major criminals on both sides of the border. He was a drug smuggler, but that was not his main business."

"It's not? I find that hard to believe."

"I've interrogated the others that were captured at the same time we captured him. These other men confirm that Abarca was not just one of the hired hands. He was jefe, chief of human smuggling operations, a business that paid off in huge profits for him and his associates."

"Human trafficking?"

"Yes. He transported women and children to the U.S. for the sex trade. He smuggled workers, with promises of jobs, only to have them end up as slaves, isolated and unpaid, in various jobs in your Midwest states. Construction in the cities, sheepherding in the mountains, maids and other domestic workers everywhere. It was a very profitable business. He was on the move constantly, back and forth across the border. Overseeing the operation, we assume."

I whistled through my teeth. "Drugs, trafficking. A real sweetheart, this guy. Anything else?"

Batista nodded. "These criminals are always expanding their business. Apparently, Abarca, or Contreras, had something to do with the marijuana trade here in your state. The legalization of that drug opened new opportunities that he wanted to get involved with. He may have already dipped into that venture. We aren't sure at this point."

"I don't understand. The legalization of marijuana was supposed to get rid of the illegal element. What's in it for a guy like Contreras?"

"There's too much money on the table for these people to ignore. They will find a way to get their share. As they always do. In any case, his partners protected him after he was arrested and helped him escape. We know he's here in your city. I didn't know precisely why he would come here, other than the thin connection to your dead client. But if, in fact, he is your dead client's husband, and she had some of his money, then it fits together."

"You think he intends to operate out of Denver?"

"It's a possibility. But sooner or later there will be a change in his popularity, so to speak. He has to be running out of money. Even his powerful friends can't help him when he's on the run, hiding from everyone. I assume whatever he had when he escaped has been used to get this far. He requires fresh resources. Your client's missing money is exactly what he needs now."

"What do you mean a change in his popularity?"

"At some point, Contreras will be more of a liability than an asset to his friends. He was more useful to them in prison than on the run, if you can believe that. They will cut him off, maybe try to limit their exposure."

"So they'll hunt him, too?"

"It's the way these people live. And die."

And if it happened the way Batista outlined, Sam Contreras would become a more desperate, and dangerous, man.

"What do the Denver police say about this?" I asked. "You working with them?"

He hesitated. "I haven't talked with the police here, yet. Not since I arrived. I came to see you first. I wanted to talk with you last night, but I lost you in the traffic, and when I finally found your house, it was late and you didn't answer when I knocked. So I waited until today."

"That was you following me?"

"I was trying to make contact. I did a sloppy job."

"You have no idea."

"I apologize."

"No matter. Why not work with the Denver police?"

"I don't have any authority here. I would have to be asked by Denver police to even observe a matter here in la gabacha, or at least they would have to approve a formal request from the Mexican government. And when a Mexican fugitive escapes into the United States, several diplomatic and political protocols have to be followed. Certain officials from my country have to talk with officials from yours. There are papers, forms, legal documents that have to be processed. I've been through all that in the past."

"You didn't want to go through it again?"

He nodded. "I would, in the routine case. But . . . this man escaped after I locked him in prison. That's never happened to me. I have a responsibility to take him back. He's accountable for the suffering of hundreds, if not thousands, of Mexican citizens. He's a killer. I couldn't wait for the politicians to make a decision."

His rigid face and clenched fists emphasized his words. I had no doubt about the man's commitment to capturing his escaped prisoner and making him pay. I took it to be more than professional pride. There was something personal about the way Batista spoke about the fugitive. Alone, in a foreign country, without any legal authority, he was on a dangerous road.

"And you couldn't risk that one of his friends would find out about your formal request?"

He intertwined the fingers of his two hands and held them in front of his chest. Several small scars dotted his hands. They could have been burns.

"The connection between some of the politicians and the men who worked with Abarca, uh, Contreras, is close. I'm sure the fact that I left the country and am here in Denver is known to several of my superiors. Let's hope none of them are involved with Contreras. I won't be surprised if I'm summoned back."

"So, you're here unofficially? You're on your own?"

"Sí. Así es."

He reminded me of Mexican relatives I hadn't visited in years. Dark skin from indigenous ancestors, height and bone mass from an African or two, pale brown Spanish eyes.

"Do you have an idea how you're going to find Contreras?"

He smiled and the scar on his cheek wiggled like a snake.

"I was hoping you would lead me to him."

"You want to use me as bait?"

"I hadn't thought of it that way, señor. The money is the key, I believe. If Contreras thinks you know where the missing money is, he will show himself to get it."

I could see where he was headed with his plan, and I didn't particularly like it.

"Before you get too carried away, you should meet my assistant, Gus. We should go over everything with him. If there is anything we can do to help, I need to hear what he thinks."

"This Gus who works for you? You want him involved?"

"He's been involved since the beginning. I need his help. He can help you, too."

I tried to imagine Gus' reaction to Batista's story. The best I could do was think of his smile that wasn't really a smile, his frown that wasn't really a frown. But he certainly would find Batista's words interesting.

"I can use whatever help you offer. But you know the danger."

"I understand, and so does Gus. How should we work this?"

"Señor, I believe I will have another cup of coffee."

23 [Gus]

get along little doggies it's your misfortune and none of my own

The conversation with Ana went easier than I expected. She summoned me to her office, where she was trying to finish up a few projects left over from the previous year. No hugs or kisses, no "how have you been?" Her cool reception and business tone were her way of telling me that I had messed up.

"Chris is a hothead," she said, after I explained my side of the confrontation with her brother.

I thought I presented a pretty good defense. "He wanted to kill me. He's lucky I didn't call the cops." I would never do that.

"But you shouldn't have hurt him. He had to go to a doctor to check out his ribs. His sternum, really. Nothing's broken but he has a bruise that covers his entire chest."

"I protected myself. He was determined to beat me up. I ended it as quickly as I could."

"He won't forget. I've had to get all up in his face—and my other brothers'—about leaving you alone. Chris is the worst, the most stubborn, just like our father. He's always treated me like I'm made out of glass. He gave hell to every boyfriend I've ever had."

"I think my arrest record has more to do with the way he acted than his thinking he needed to protect you."

"Whatever. If you see any of my brothers, avoid them. Walk away."

"How can I avoid your brothers if I'm going to keep on seeing you? We're bound to run into each other."

"Just stay away from them."

"Nothing would make me happier. But it's not entirely under my control."

She shrugged. "Guess that's the best I'll get from you."

"I'm not looking for trouble with your brothers, but I won't run away from them either."

She nodded. "Goddamn men."

We talked for a few more minutes until she ran out of cusswords and orders about how I was to act around her family.

Then she asked for a favor.

"Let's go to the parade. I've never seen it."

"Parade?"

The newspaper and TV news shows were filled with stories about the annual mid-January National Western Stock Show that brought thousands of visitors to Denver and poured hundreds of thousands of dollars into the city's economy. The city dressed up like one giant cowboy and showcased its history as a cow town.

"I've lived in Denver all my life and I've never even been to the stock show."

"You can't be serious."

"Of course I am. The parade starts in about a half hour, over by Union Station, then it goes down Seventeenth. The cowboys herd a bunch of cattle through the streets. They're all dressed up for the rodeo. I want to see it, and if we leave now, we'll make it just in time. We can walk."

The cowboy parade was a better alternative than continuing to talk with her about her nut job brothers.

The long shadows of winter crisscrossed the streets and sidewalks of downtown Denver. We walked to the mall, between the skyscrapers, through the shadows and against a stiff breeze that whipped the crowd assembled for the parade.

My cell buzzed.

"Where are you?" Luis said. "Batista's in town and the three of us should meet."

"Batista? What? You won't believe where I am. I'm walking to the stock show parade with Ana."

"You're serious?"

"That's what I said. But here I am."

"Can you come back to the office? We really do need to talk . . . uh, wait a minute."

Someone in the background said something about seeing the city, getting some fresh air.

"Hang on, Gus."

Ana and I continued on our trek to the beginning of the parade. People were lined up along the street.

"I'll never see anything," Ana said. "I'm too short."

We moved in as close as we could to the sidewalk but we were still several rows back. I held my phone to my ear and waited for Luis to finish the call.

"Batista and I will walk downtown, meet you," Luis said over the phone. "He could use some breakfast. Brunch now, I guess. Where are you?"

"We'll be at Blake and Seventeenth, a couple blocks from Union Station."

Ana and I huddled close in the crowd. "That wind is cold," she said. I hugged her closer and felt her warmth. We waited among the watchers—kids dressed up like cowboys with their parents or grandparents, office workers taking an early lunch, tourists in town for the show, ranchers and farmers on their annual journey to the big city. Union Station sat like an ancient monument at the end of the street.

"The parade will come from around that corner." I pointed in the direction of the station. "Here come some cowboys now." A group of men mounted on horses rode up the street, followed by a 1940s Ford pickup decorated with bunting and flags. The shiny midnight blue truck crawled along the street with a smooth purr. A tall black man wearing a stylish Stetson waved from the back of the pickup.

"That's the parade's Grand Marshal," Ana said.

"Is that . . . ?"

"Yeah, the ball player. Denver native."

The pickup passed on and, for a few seconds, no one followed. Then more cowboys filled the street. They wore chaps, boots and ten-gallon hats. They twirled ropes and a few threw candy to the children in the crowd. They appeared authentic to me, but what did I really know about cowboys? When that group passed, the crowd stirred with a buzz.

"Here they come," I announced.

Ana stretched on her toes to get a better view of the cattle that rushed around the corner. She leaned on me for balance. Through our coats I felt her tight body, hard from exercise and police training.

The longhorns seemed too big for the street. The brown or gray animals lumbered straight ahead, one following the other. I expected them to smash their enormous horns together but they marched as one huge beast under the guidance and prompting of the cowboys. The herders kept the cows moving with twisting ropes and the sleek muscle of their horses. A few of the drovers hollered "yip" or "ay-ay."

"I can't see," Ana said. "I need to get up front for a better look." Before I could say or do anything to stop her, she pushed her way to the curb only a few inches from the cattle.

"Ana, wait." She eased through the crowd by slipping by a woman who struggled to keep her young son secure in her arms. "Ana!" I shouted.

The woman looked up at me. Ana stopped. The boy screamed and squirmed lose from his mother. He stumbled to the street. Ana reached to grab him but she tripped on the curb and fell face first. A ribbon of blood appeared on her forehead. The boy regained his balance, then ran back to his mother. Ana tried to stand up but she bumped into one of the steers, who jerked back and hit another one of the longhorns. The sudden movement caused the animals to speed up. Ana fell back on the street.

The parade watchers retreated from the street. I was caught up in the rush away from Ana. I heard someone say "stampede." I peered through the crowd and saw Ana try to stand up again, but one of the longhorns pushed against her and she fell for a third time. The boy screamed again when his mother tried to retreat to the back of the crowd. The herd picked up more speed. They grunted and tossed their horns in every direction. Some were so close to Ana that I lost sight of her as I pushed and shoved kids and tourists. A man smashed against my shoulder as he ran from the street. I couldn't see Ana.

I kept fighting against the crowd until I made it to the sidewalk. The cattle were gone. I looked up the street. The cowboys regained control and the rush of frightened cattle ended with a few seconds of excitement for the drovers and watchers.

Ana sat on the curb. She held her hand on the cut on her head. Luis Móntez stood next to Ana, and next to him was a tall dark Mexican who looked like a cop.

I sat down with Ana and hugged her around the shoulders.

"He saved me," she said. She pointed at the cop.

I stood up and looked at Luis. "We saw Ana on the street, getting shoved around by those cows," he said. "This guy jumped in and pulled her to safety." Luis pointed at Fulgencio Batista. "He turned one of the animals away by swatting him on the nose," Luis continued. "I never saw anything quite like that. It was over before I knew what was happening."

Batista extended his hand. I shook it, introduced myself. "You've already met Ana." I said.

He stared at the sitting Ana. "In a manner of speaking. El placer es mío."

Luis, Batista and I made small talk while Ana sat and watched the rest of the parade. Batista ate a hot dog he bought from a corner vendor. I didn't pay much attention to the rest of the parade.

The parade ended and the crowd broke up. Street cleaning machines followed the cowboys, cowgirls, horses and cows.

Ana stood up. She hugged Batista, kissed him on his scar. "Muchísimas gracias," she said. That's the first time I heard her speak Spanish.

24 [Luis]

es que la vecina me puso el dedo

Batista's quick thinking impressed me. He saved Ana from injury, at the least, and he did it without real violence to the steer. He was chivalrous, bold and kind to spooked animals. The guy was a saint—a saint with a scarred face.

We made sure Ana was okay, then we walked back to my office, none of us saying much.

We sat at the round conference table. The Mexican cop, the Chicana cop, the ex-con and me, the lawyer. Rosa worked at her desk, typing more goodbye letters for clients. We held cups of coffee.

"I don't get it," Gus said. "This guy, Sam or Paco, or whatever. Why Denver? Compared to the money from working with cartels and human traffickers, drug smuggling, all of it—the quarter of a million is peanuts. You think he'd come all this way for that?"

"The money he's chasing is more than that," Batista answered. "From what Luis told me, the two hundred and fifty thousand dollars is what a man named Valdez was after. But the information is that was only part of the money. There is more, much more."

"How much are we talking about?" Ana said. She had recovered nicely, with only a small Band-Aid on her forehead. No one would know from looking at her that an hour before, she'd almost been run over by a mad cow.

Batista cleared his throat. "It has to be in the millions. The amounts of money that these criminals operate with, and hide away, are amazing, unbelievable."

Gus smiled at me. I looked away. I didn't like that smile.

"These men and women operate like independent countries with their own armies, laws and legal system. They have the money to do as they please. Men like Contreras may not be completely inside a cartel, but they work very close, and they, too, make millions."

"And Valdez knew only about the quarter million? Maybe that money was legit, from the import business?" I asked.

Batista slowly shook his head. "I doubt that this man and anyone working with him ever made any honest money."

"He ran a bar, here in Denver," Gus said.

"A cover for laundering some of the money," Batista said. "There's so much, they have to invent ways to use it."

"This money's not in a bank somewhere offshore?" Gus asked. "Or Switzerland?"

Batista grinned. "Like on American TV? If Contreras does what so many of the others do, the money's stacked in a warehouse or buried in the desert, or a cave. Around here, down a mineshaft. They can't use all that they get but they continue to accumulate it."

Ana grabbed Gus' hand. "Then he must know where it is. Why would he bother with Luis or any of us?"

"That may be the reality," Batista said. "Which means he's already retrieved the money and may be gone. Or . . . "

"What?" Ana said.

"Or María or Valdez moved it," Gus said. "And Contreras might think that María, or Valdez, told Luis about it."

"Well, he'd be wrong," I said. "No one told me anything about a cache of millions hidden somewhere in Colorado. María denied knowing anything about the money. And Valdez insisted she had it. Neither of them seemed to know where the money was."

Gus and Ana drank coffee. Batista stood up. "I have to move around. Do something," he said.

"María could have lied to you, Luis," Gus said. "We've talked about that. She played out her role of ex-wife in the dark to throw off Valdez. She hired a lawyer to help her, to make her play more on the level. Valdez might have fallen for it, but he was planning to talk with you. Then he was killed."

"Yeah, and she was around when he was killed," I said. "But that involved Sam, too."

"She tried to fool Sam. Probably fingered Valdez. Laid it all on him. Said he had the money. Set him up for Sam, but Valdez didn't talk. Sam lost his patience. They tried to clean it up with the fire, then he got rid of the body."

"That makes sense," Ana said.

"And after Valdez died, and Sam had time to think about it, he turned his attention to his ex-wife," Gus added. "That's why she was half-dead when she reappeared."

"He put her through hell to get to his money," I said. "Whatever he did to her, it must have contributed to her heart attack, to her dying in my office."

"But she didn't talk either?" Ana asked. "Was she that tough?"

"We don't really know," I said. "It's all guesswork. Only Sam knows what happened."

The inference that María might have resisted Contreras' torture agitated Batista.

"Contreras would know how to make anyone talk. That's a certainty. Valdez died because he didn't know anything about the missing money. He couldn't satisfy Contreras. He died because he chose the wrong partner for his business."

"And María?" I asked.

"An interesting woman, obviously. Somehow she escaped Sam. By returning here, to this lawyer's office, I believe she escaped before she gave in and before she was forced to reveal whatever she knew about the money. She still needed Luis. If she talked, he would have killed her since he didn't need her anymore. But from what you say, she wasn't above sacrificing this Valdez person."

His deductions were logical.

"It's a puzzle why she would have come back to you, Señor Móntez. It certainly looks like she trusted you, maybe told you something that Contreras wants to know."

So long, logic. I tried to laugh. Didn't happen.

"I repeat. She didn't tell me anything about the money. She was very convincing that she didn't know anything about it."

An uncomfortable moment slipped by.

"Por favor, I apologize," Batista said. "I meant nothing. I believe you. I'm only saying it looks like she confided in you."

"You mean to Contreras, right?" Ana said. There was something in the way she asked the question.

Batista sat down at the table again. "Yes. Of course. To the criminal, Contreras."

It was only my imagination, but it felt like everyone in the room breathed deeply at the same time. I looked at each of their faces for any sign about what they were thinking. I had to believe that Gus didn't doubt what I said. I wasn't sure about Batista or Ana. My imagination had taken off and I read too much in the way that Ana and Batista looked at each other across the table. At that moment, in the slightly heavy, uncomfortable air of my messy office overrun with boxes, file folders and loose papers, I would've sworn on my soon-to-be retired lawyer's license that the two cops weren't all that sure about me.

25 [Gus]

chaparra de mis penares

The meeting at Luis' office ended without any resolution of the next step. We swam in uncharted waters, on the lookout for a shark, but that was about all we really knew. Luis simply nodded when we told him to be careful. Batista volunteered for bodyguard duty, but Luis turned him down. At the end, we went our separate ways. I assumed I was responsible for Luis and I told him I would check up on him later. He shrugged.

Ana offered to help Batista find a place to stay—he had a room at the Brown Palace in downtown Denver, but she argued that the hotel was too expensive and too touristy for a policeman's budget.

"Something closer to Luis' house makes most sense," she said.

"I like the name of the hotel," Batista said. "Feel at home in a palace that's brown." He faked a laugh. "Get it? ¿El palacio castaño?"

"Your joke didn't work," Ana said. "Nice try. Maybe it's funnier in Spanish?"

His face folded into a puzzled frown.

"You need a ride to Corrine's?" Ana asked.

"I'm good," I said.

She nodded and walked out with Batista.

I called my sister about her plans. Corrine insisted that Max and I meet her for a drink. When I tried to beg off, she said she wanted to catch up.

"I've got a lot going on," I said. "Ana, Luis and Batista. It's complicated."

"You got no time for your sisters? That you ain't spent any quality time with for weeks?" Corrine said. "Just the police, your new friends and that girlfriend with the idiot brothers. Can't compete with that. Even though you're living in my house, I never see you." She made a strange sound with her throat. "Sure, I get it." She knew that playing the family guilt trip card would work. "I'll meet you at the Dark Knight, okay?" I said. "Give me about a half hour."

≫ ≫ ≫

My sisters waited at a booth along one side of the bar. Móntez told me about the place, said it used to be his hangout back when he needed to hang out. He found isolation there, he said. According to Luis, it hadn't changed in twenty years. When I walked in, I believed him.

Retro dark paneling, red vinyl bar stools and booth benches; neon or what looked like neon signs glowed over the bar and along the walls. Photographs of hot rods and customized convertibles lined the hall to the restrooms. The bartender looked as though she had come to work straight from her role as one of the Pink Ladies in *Grease*. We watched that flick in the joint, about a hundred times.

"Why they call this place the Dark Knight?" I asked when I sat down with Corrine and Max.

"Name doesn't fit the décor," Maxine said.

"Used to have a different ambience," Corrine said. "Back in the day, swords hung on the walls and a knight's armor stood in the corner by the jukebox, right over there." She pointed to a trash can. "The armor was black, of course. Shiny. Place had attitude."

"And Móntez drank here?" I asked.

Corrine nodded.

"He said it hadn't changed since he was a regular."

Corrine shook her head. "Nah. It's changed. Some of the customers haven't. Must be what he meant."

There were a few other people in the place. A grizzled older man hunched at the bar, sipping on a beer and a glass of amber liquor. A man and two women huddled around a table near the door. The bearded man wore a black and red flannel shirt, black jeans and boots. The women wore the same outfit. They whispered.

"Sure is quiet for a bar," Max said.

The bartender found us. "Hello. I'm Joyce. What ya drinkin'?"

Max ordered a Moscow Mule. Corrine wanted a shot of Herradura and a Fat Tire. I asked for a lite beer.

"That all?" Corrine asked. Joyce walked away.

"Yeah. My parole, remember? Can't drink too much, especially the heavy stuff."

"I thought that was over, that they weren't hassling you anymore."

"It's lightened up, a lot. But every once in a while I have to go through the motions with someone down at the parole office. I don't drink that much anyway."

"You really changed, you know that?" Corrine said.

"I've learned the value of patience, I'll give you that. I can wait now. Can't be in too much of a hurry in lockup. That could be dangerous."

They squirmed in their seats. Corrine continued. "I mean, you don't drink, you're working a regular honest job and you're dating a cop. I never would have thought that the little Northside gangster, Gus Corral, would end up on the straight and narrow."

"Prison might have had something to do with the changes," I said.

"It's more than that, Gus," Max added. "You've grown up. You're more focused, serious." She looked at Corrine. "Not as much fun, though, eh?" Corrine nodded.

"Guess prison was the best thing that could have happened to me," I said.

They both shook their heads. "No, no. That's not what I mean," Max insisted. "You've always been the smartest one in the family. We've told you that your whole life. Now you're using your smarts. You work for a lawyer. You have heavy responsibilities and get a regular paycheck. It's all good, Gus."

"Believe it or not, Gus, we believe in you. And . . . we love you," Corrine said.

Max nodded. "You know it," she said.

"Whoa, that came out of nowhere," I said. "You guys been drinking before you got here?"

Corrine punched my arm and we all laughed.

Joyce wiggled to our table with the drinks. I helped myself to a healthy slug of beer.

"This why you wanted to get together? Do a hug and kiss? Talk about my changes and new outlook on life? I can tell you, it ain't no big thing." I took another slug. "When you get down to it, I haven't changed all that much."

"I want to know more about Ana," Max said. "You serious about her?"

"This gonna be all about me?" I said.

"Maybe," Corrine said.

Max laughed again.

"No, it's not," Corrine said. "We're just talking. I'm curious about my brother's girlfriend. That's all. It's not like you've ever really been long term with a significant other, you know. Not in high school, not even when you married Sylvia. So I ask. How serious is this?"

I shrugged. "We have a good time. That's where we're at. You don't want details about that, I'm sure. But to answer your follow-up questions, we aren't planning or talking about anything else."

"Do you even like her?" Corrine asked.

"Of course, he does," Max said. "It's obvious to me."

"Jesus. This is too much. Yes. I like her. No, there's nothing serious in the works. Is that enough? Let's move on with the family news, all right? Let's talk about you guys."

We spent the next few minutes going over Max's plans for her wedding. She, Sandra and Jackie O had worked through the details of the ceremony, the vows and the location. Next on her agenda was finding a band and a hall for the reception dance. Then a caterer.

"I told her to ask one of the Chicano bands. Mood Express. Next In Line. Los Latineeerz. Chicano Heat. Rick Garcia," Corrine said. "Bands like that."

"All good," I said.

"I'm gonna follow through," Max said. "But . . . "

"That's not your type of music, is that it?" I said.

"I like all those bands. They're tight. I just don't . . . "

"I thought your band, the Rakers, were gonna play?"

"That was the original plan. But Sandra and I didn't want to be stuck performing at our own wedding. We want to dance!"

"Then I think that settles it," I said. "Hire a band and get the party started."

Corrine caught Joyce's attention and signaled for another round.

"What I actually wanted to talk to you about is all this business going on with Móntez's case," Corrine said. "The woman who died in his office, and now this federal cop from Mexico. How risky is this? You don't need another shoot-out with Mexican gangsters. I think one per lifetime should be enough."

"I'm worried, too, Gus," Max said. "What's it all about? Why are you involved?"

I'd said it before. I loved my sisters. But they could be a pain.

I calculated that I wasn't getting out of the bar until I satisfied their curiosity and their concern. So I walked them through the history of the Contreras case, beginning with the woman who said she wanted help keeping her dead husband's business partner at bay and who denied knowing anything about any missing money. I went through the late night get-together at the house that burned down, the woman's disappearance, strange reappearance and stranger death. I described the nationwide hunt for a man we thought died years ago and who turned out to be somebody completely different. I described Batista and his heroics at the rodeo parade. I told them about the drug smuggling and human trafficking. I ended with the idea that Móntez was at risk and that we all had to be careful and watch for Sam Contreras.

Corrine and Max went through another drink as I worked my way through the story. They didn't say much.

At one point, Corrine said, "Damn, Gus. You know better."

At another, Max said, "This is unreal."

"It's too real for me," I said. "Luis knew Contreras when he ran the bar. Contreras apparently thinks Luis may know something about the money. I think that means that anyone close to Luis may be in danger."

"Móntez doesn't know anything about the cash?" Corrine asked. She looked over the rim of her drink as though she were talking out of turn in church.

I thought about how I should answer. I thought hard and I took my time.

"You know if he did, he'd have told us, or the cops, at least. The woman died before she could tell him anything. I'm sure of that. No doubt in my mind. Luis is not the type to play fast and loose with information that could put a target on others. Right?"

Corrine and Max both nodded. "Yeah, yeah, no doubt," Corrine said. "I had to ask, that's all."

"What's the next step?" Max could absorb just about anything and not let it ruffle her. She was into planning, anticipating and avoiding surprises. It was only natural for her to think that Luis and I had thought about all the options and consequences, and that we were ready for whatever came at us.

Corrine and Max were as different as night and day, but they had one thing in common. They were more together and had more on the ball than their wayward brother would ever manage.

"We wait, for the most part. I want to get together with Batista again and review what we know and maybe go on the offensive, if we can figure it out. But first Luis and me will clear up about how we should deal with this, and what our actions should be if Contreras does show up."

"That's a certainty, isn't it?" Max said. "It's too much money for him to walk away from. It's too much money for this to just go away."

I couldn't disagree. "Well, that's probably true, but there might be a few other possibilities. None good. We don't know who Sam was hooked up with, other than Valdez. Anyone out there could be after the money, could be after Luis. We just don't know at this point."

Corrine and Max frowned.

"I don't like it, Gus," Corrine said. "You're getting in deep again. Remember the last time. This could go all wrong for you."

I tried to smile at her. "I guess. But this time, I'm working with the cops, if you can believe that. I'm doing the right thing."

The lumberjack-looking man and his companions had left. Joyce helped the older man who sat at the bar find his jacket, which had fallen to the floor. It looked like he was getting ready to leave.

The front door opened and a man in a long overcoat walked in, looked around, stopped when he saw us sitting in our booth and then he backed out of the door. That spooked the shit out of me.

We hugged goodnight all around. Corrine had come with Max, and I continued to borrow Corrine's car. My sisters drove away laughing about something. For some reason they often laughed when they told me goodbye.

I sat in the Kia and tried to connect with Ana. I called her but only got her voicemail. I left a message, which she usually answered within minutes. After fifteen, I called again and left another message.

I thought I should pay her a visit. On the way, I called Luis.

"You okay?"

"Sure, why wouldn't I be?" he said.

"Where are you?"

"I'm on my way to Rosa's. She invited me for a late dinner."

"Good. Don't be alone if possible. Okay?"

"I think I'll be all right."

"Don't go all macho, okay? This is what we agreed on when we talked. We have to watch out for each other until we know what this guy Sam is going to do."

"Got it. I'll be with Rosa, then at my house. And you?"

"Ana's. Don't know how long. If it's early, I'll swing by."

I drove in silence. The quiet helped my mood.

I parked and was about to climb out when I saw a cab idling in the street in front of Ana's apartment complex. At the same time that I put my hand on the car door handle, the apartment building door opened. Ana walked out, followed by Fulgencio Batista. I didn't call to them. I watched as they strolled to the taxi. He leaned down and kissed her, fast but hard. She stood on the curb while the cab pulled away. I thought about opening the door and confronting her, but again I waited. I sped away when she entered the building.

I drove aimlessly for several minutes. I crossed streets and intersections I'd known all my life but none of it registered. Eventually I found myself on Seventeenth Avenue, near the corner where Batista rescued Ana from the angry cattle. With practically no traffic, the city looked vacant, almost deserted to my jaded eyes.

I shrugged mentally. It's not like we were committed. That's what I'd said to my sisters. There was always something lacking. She was too serious for me. Never made me laugh. I pushed thoughts of Ana out of my head and decided to go home.

Luis would still be at Rosa's dinner. I planned to get to him early in the morning. I believed we could put an end to the situation we found ourselves in. At least, I concluded, we could learn what was really going on.

26 [Luis]

nobody loves me but my mother and she could be jivin' too

Rosa invited me to dinner at her place. I passed. She made dynamite pozole, perfect comfort food for the winter cold, but I didn't have much of an appetite. I asked her to bring me a bowl in the morning. When she hesitated, I told her not to worry. I was okay, I said. Or as okay as I could get, given the circumstances. Everything I told her was the truth.

I was alone in my office. The only light came from the hall. Everyone had cleared out an hour earlier, but I hadn't moved. I stared at file folders, notepads and a constantly changing computer screen saver.

Maybe it was the unknown threat from Contreras, or the banal toughness of the scarred Batista, or Gus' bad boy act, or the wild scene at the parade. Maybe it was the weather. I could come up with a thousand different reasons for feeling the way I did and each reason would have a logical base and it would be untrue. I'd never really understood my motivation for many of the things I'd done in my life. If I was honest, I had no excuse for making the mistakes I'd made most of my life. But I was too old to begin any deep self-analysis.

I sat at my desk in the semi-darkness, going over insignificant episodes in my personal and professional realities, tossing each one aside as something else popped into my worried brain. Finally, I confessed to the plastic glow-in-the-dark skull sitting on the corner of my desk that Batista spooked me with his story about the fake Sam Contreras and the piles of money driving men and women to violence. The calavera ignored me.

The ghost of María Contreras hovered in the corners of my office. The material woman who started this was not around to see how it played out. Ghosts don't have to deal with consequences. "Not really fair, is it?" I heard myself say.

My cell phone vibrated on my desk, then lit up.

Rosa's number flashed on the screen.

"You're still at the office, aren't you?"

"No, no. I'm on my way home."

"You're lying, Luis. You're not a good liar. Why haven't you left? It's been almost two hours."

"Really, I'm on my way out. Locking the door now. What's the problem?"

"I'm worried about you. If that isn't enough, I'm worried for myself."

I hesitated. "What do you want me to do?"

"Go home. Or come over here. Don't stay at the office. That's the first place this killer will look. I knew I should have forced you to leave."

She did sound worried. Rosa was strong. I relied on her to be a rock when cases and clients whirled around the office like dead leaves caught in a windy tunnel. This was different.

"I'll swing by your house. We can have dinner somewhere, maybe a drink. Okay?"

Slight pause. "Okay. I got food here. But leave now."

Gus called almost as soon as Rosa hung up. I told him I was on my way to Rosa's. He assumed he would stop by Ana's.

I thought about calling Batista. When I realized I wasn't sure what I would talk to him about, or what questions I wanted him to answer, I stuck my phone in my coat pocket. He knew everything I knew about the Contreras family. I trusted that he also knew what he was doing. If anyone could find Sam Contreras it would be Fulgencio Batista, a hard-nosed Mexican cop on the trail of the man that got away. My trust didn't put me at ease, but it was all I had.

I drove to Rosa's rolling through about a hundred different scenarios. My brain wouldn't turn off. I knew it was irrational. No one had actually threatened me. No one had taken a shot at me or tried to force out of me the hiding place for the missing money. I'd done nothing wrong and yet I was compelled to wear guilt, or something very close to guilt.

Batista probably had it all covered, I reminded myself again.

Then I'd jump to thinking about all the bad that could happen even with Batista's help.

That downer was followed with my insecurity about retirement and leaving the only life I'd known for forty years. What would I do in the morning when I had no place to be, no appointments to keep, no problems to solve or clients to help?

I realized I was alone, as alone as one man can be. No wife or lover. Children spread across the country, hundreds of miles away. No real plans, no real money. What was I doing, and who was I supposed to do it with? I hunched over the steering wheel, almost as if I expected a bullet to crash through the windshield, or a semi to T-bone my car at the next intersection.

Rosa's little house sat near City Park on the east side of Denver. She lived with a cat, a fish tank and a stuffed parrot—her dead pal, she said. When I knocked on her door, she answered quickly with a worried look on her face. She pulled me inside.

Rosa kept a clean and neat home. Tidy. In her youth, she wore bright colors, drove tricked-out cars and decorated various apartments with native pottery and Chicana flash. Her style had mellowed. The walls were subdued shades of brown and yellow. She displayed a few black and white photographs. That was it for decoration. Her home didn't have a pillow out of place, or a dirty cup on a counter.

"What's wrong?" I asked.

"I got the strangest call. Just now. Freaked me out a little."

"Who called?"

"Gus' girlfriend, Ana what's-her-name."

"Ana Domingo called you?"

"Yeah. Not like we've ever talked."

"What'd she want?"

"She asked for María's file, said she wanted to look over a few things; mentioned something about a timeline. Our office file.

She's checking on dates, whatever. Tell you the truth, she didn't make a lot of sense."

"She asked you? Why not call me? Or go to Gus? What could she be up to?"

"You tell me. It didn't sound right. I put her off. Said I wasn't feeling too good and that I would get back to her tomorrow. She didn't call you?"

"Hell no. She's up to something. You know she can't see the file?"

"Of course. She has to know that, too. What the . . . ? She left with Batista, remember? Maybe he put her up to it?"

"Christ, what could that mean?"

"That they're working together. They're both police, so it makes sense. He's unofficially here, you said, right? She's helping him, probably all he's got for backup."

"They just met today and she's already working on his investigation?"

"Maybe they just met today. We don't really know, do we? I thought there was something between them. He could've talked with her before he even came out here."

"Unlikely. How would he know about her?"

She shrugged. "Or else he swept her off her feet when he saved her ass from getting run over at the parade. Some girls might be impressed with that."

"More likely."

"But she's supposed to be hot after Gus," Rosa said. "The poor guy almost got beat up because of her."

I held up my hands. Rosa had gone where I regretted leading her. "Whoa. We don't know what kind of relationship there is between Ana and Batista, if there even is one. Could be totally legit. All on the up-and-up." She wrinkled her eyebrows at me. "Or she could just be doing her own thing, maybe trying to help Gus. That's possible, don't you think?"

"Sure, Luis. Whatever you say."

She walked me to her dining table where a steaming bowl of pozole waited. She had prepared small plates of chopped onions, radishes and cabbage, sliced limes and oregano. The pungent smell of New Mexico red chile powder floated from the kitchen to the table.

My appetite returned. We ate two big bowls of the spicy stew. The warm tortillas and cold beer made the meal one of the best I'd had in days. The comfortable feeling that overtook me at her table translated into conversation that extended into her living room and late into the night.

We talked about María Contreras, Fulgencio Batista, Ana Domingo and Gus Corral. These were new people in our lives, but they'd assumed an importance that we agreed was unexpected. Rosa confirmed that she didn't trust any of the four, although she grudgingly gave Gus one of her "Oh, he's all right, I guess."

We joked about judges and other lawyers, even a few cops. We had years of legal battles to pick from.

We laughed at some of my crazier antics, most of which had to do with my drinking.

We talked about what to expect after I closed my practice. Neither one of us was on strong ground regarding our respective futures.

We were most engaged when we talked about various clients and cases over the years. She surprised me with what she remembered. She had retained important details—dates, names and places—that I could never recall because they had been buried by hundreds of other dates, names and places that bumped up against each other like marbles in a hyper pinball game. She helped me see that every once in a while we had done some good, often in spite of my careless work ethic and self-destructive tendencies.

About midnight, after we drank one beer too many and laughed at one story too much, a strange thought crossed my mind that losing Rosa was going to be the most difficult part of retiring. I quickly said goodnight. I left her house feeling something I didn't quite understand.

27 [Gus]

my mother used to tell me, she said,
son, there's gonna be days like this

I'd intended to sleep. That turned out to be impossible. My brain was hot with thoughts and images of Ana and Batista and Sam Contreras and stacks of dirty money. It was late, too late, but I threw on my running shoes. I sprinted out of Corrine's house into the darkness. Her motion light caught me before I left the yard. Then, more darkness until the trees parted and the street lights marked the sidewalk. I ran in the general direction of downtown Denver, south and east. I left the sidewalk and ran down the middle of the streets. I moved my legs as fast as I could, daring my body to break down, hoping that it didn't.

The new condos on Tejon Street loomed above me. I worried that a rich hipster would panic when he saw the Chicano cholo running down the street way past midnight. I calculated the odds that I'd be shot by a bearded marksman from a condo balcony. They weren't in my favor. And still I thought of Ana and Batista and Sam Contreras.

I'd never met Sam Contreras. Luis had been one of Sam's customers, and what I did know about the man I learned from my lawyer. He'd described Sam as a "throwback," someone who could make a person run out of his bar simply with a look. Tough. He caused his wife's death, most likely from torture, and probably killed his business partner. He was a drug and human smuggler and he laundered money for marijuana tycoons. He escaped from a Mexican prison during a bloody, deadly riot. He did business with crime cartels. I didn't like the Sam Contreras that Luis described.

I added one more point to the mental picture of Sam Contreras. He wanted his money and he would do anything to get it. I wanted to holler when I remembered the kiss Batista gave to Ana. I stayed silent except for the urgent rush of my breath in and out of my lungs. No screaming homeboy in the streets to wake up the gentry. No wild loco to arouse the remaining raza in the small houses and weary-looking duplexes. Only a dark flash in the night, sprinting through the Northside, oblivious to anyone and anything.

Dogs barked at me as I passed their yards. I barely glanced at the former mortuary, now-hip restaurant and the giant milk can ice cream joint as I sped down the hill that looped towards the freeway. I made it to the Highland Bridge across I-25. I trudged on. I circled Commons Park, stopped at the Millennium Bridge and turned around. People slept in the weeds and brush along the South Platte River. A man with a stringy beard, wearing a patched parka and holding a dirty American flag, watched me glide by. He looked like he hated me. I crossed I-25 again and headed home.

I sat on my lumpy bed in Corrine's basement, sweating and thinking about how we could draw out Sam Contreras. It was not an enjoyable exercise. Truth be told, I didn't want to ever meet Sam Contreras, but it didn't look like I had a choice.

The same solution circled around repeatedly. Sam had to think that Luis knew where to find his money. Maybe even that Luis had the money. María Contreras could have given him the loot the night she died in his office. As her lawyer, he had a duty to protect her property. Why else was she there?

It was an easy enough idea to believe. Even Batista and Ana acted as though Luis knew more than he was letting on—when they had the spare time to think about the fugitive that brought the Mexican cop to gringolandia.

When I finally crawled under the blankets, I had the beginning of an idea. I wasn't sure that Luis Móntez would go along. I planned to cross that bridge in the morning.

≫ ≫ ≫

I found Luis standing in the middle of the remains of what had been my place of work. A lawyer's office is built on paper, no matter what the computer geeks say, and it looked like a ton of that foundation had been dumped on the floor. Filing cabinet drawers were strewn around the place, folders were ripped and page after page of legal documents scattered across the floor as though they'd been tossed in the air and left to drift in the wind.

Luis held a manila folder in one hand and a cardboard box in the other. He looked lost.

"What happened?" I asked. I already knew the answer.

"Someone broke in, trashed the place. Not sure if they found what they were looking for. I called the police. They should be here any minute."

"No one else around? The place clear?"

Luis nodded. "I just got here, but there's no one else. Rosa's probably on her way."

"How'd they get in?"

"I think they just jimmied the front door lock. It wouldn't be that hard. Rosa was always on me to add more security. I told the building manager he needed to be more proactive, but it's never happened."

"No alarms or cameras?"

He looked at me like I had a snake crawling out of my mouth.

"We're not exactly on Seventeenth Street here, Gus. There's a camera at the building front entrance. It's not always on, the janitor says. That's all I know about."

The place was wrecked, but it didn't look like anything had been broken. The burglars weren't into mischief. They wanted something specific.

"My computer was taken," Luis said. "The only good thing is that most of this stuff is closed, over with. Not too many active cases left. I was gonna ditch that computer anyway. But we'll have to let the clients know."

"The Contreras file?"

He nodded. "Plus, I don't see the paper file."

"Really? You have a copy?"

He nodded again. "Most of it, yeah. When we started closing out files and returning documents to clients, I asked Rosa to keep copies. Standard procedure. We kept a paper file from the first day María Contreras showed her face here. Lately, Rosa added whatever else we had on the computer. That was a no-brainer."

"Where could it be?"

"We have a storage room in the building basement. She might have put it there already. I haven't checked it yet. I'll go down there now."

He rushed to his desk and plucked a set of keys out of the top drawer.

"Maybe I should go with you?"

He paused. "No, no. Wait for Rosa and the cops. I'll be right back. Just a few minutes. I'll know right away if they got to the storage room."

He sprinted to the elevator, then changed his mind and walked through the door to the stairwell.

The office turned into a surreal circus when the police arrived a few minutes later. The first thing that happened was that I was immediately surrounded by a pair of Denver's finest. I'm sure I looked the part, so I didn't really blame the two for doing their jobs. It took a few minutes but I patiently corrected any misconception.

The office was yet another crime scene.

The cops wanted to speak to Luis. I said he would be right back from the basement. Immediately one of the uniforms ran to the stairway door and headed for the lower level. She jerked open the door and disappeared.

I watched from my desk and answered all the questions. Uniforms and plainclothes walked through the office quickly or huddled together and whispered. Some type of police technician looked over the door and confirmed that the lock had been broken. Men in suits and sweaters took photographs, rolled out measuring tape and squinted at file drawers and paper scraps. Suddenly four policemen sprinted to the stairway door. "What's going on?" I shouted at one of the cops. "There's a woman, hurt. They found her in the stairwell." He joined the group running down the stairs. Someone barked an order to send more men to the back door of the building.

≫ ≫ ≫

We paced around St. Joseph's emergency waiting room. That's when I told Luis how I thought we might smoke out Sam Contreras.

He wouldn't even listen at first. "I can't think about that now," he said. "We're here for Rosa."

After about an hour he finally talked with me about what we could do. We stood in front of a coffee vending machine.

"It looks like he's already found us—found me. And Rosa paid the price."

"It looks like that, but until Rosa tells us, we don't know for sure what happened in the basement."

"It's got to be him. What else could it be? He was looking for whatever María Contreras might have given me. He ransacked the office, then figured out we had storage, wanted to make sure he had everything and then was surprised by Rosa." He pounded his fist against the coffee machine. "Damn. She shouldn't have been alone."

"Don't blame yourself. Nothing we could have done."

He shook his head. He reached into the machine and pulled out a cup of gray coffee.

Luis had found Rosa bleeding in the stairwell, unconscious. She had a nasty cut on the back of her head. He called for an ambulance and was trying to stop the blood when a cop found him. Luis looked up into the drawn revolver of the police woman. He stepped away from Rosa and explained what he was doing. The cop called for backup. Eventually the situation was sorted out. We guessed that Rosa had arrived before Luis and then had the same idea to check on the storage room. She must have surprised the burglar, who knocked her out.

"We'll get the son-of-a-bitch. Whatever it takes."

I nodded. "Yeah. I know."

Part Four

My Bad

28 [Luis]

and I'm so afraid I'm gonna find you with a so-called smoking gun

Rosa had a concussion and required a few stiches, but she was released from the hospital after one long night. She didn't see the person who knocked her on the head. She was in the stairwell, looking through a small window in the stairwell door to the storage room door trying to see whether that door had been breached, when she heard something behind her, then . . . nothing. She woke up in the ambulance.

My office was closed by the police, again, while they tried to gather evidence. I explained to them what I thought was going on, but no one I talked to seemed interested in a possible Mexican prison escapee who was supposed to be dead. After that, I didn't have the heart to go back and try to straighten out the mess in the office, especially with Rosa laid up at her house.

Gus and I agreed everyone should meet at Corrine's house to talk about what to do. Corrine wandered in and out with offers of drinks and food. I sat on the couch and faced Ana, Batista and Gus, all sitting in chairs that formed a semicircle in front of the couch.

"Nothing's happened since the break-in and attack on Rosa?" Ana asked.

Gus had let me know that he and Ana were no longer an item, but he didn't offer an explanation. I figured he'd tell me it and when he felt I should know. There was a certain tension between them that everyone noticed. No one said anything about it.

"I haven't left my house," I answered. "The office is a mess, Rosa's still laid up, and Sam or Paco or whoever was after me hasn't made a move."

"That's right," Gus said. "That's why I think it's time we did something."

Batista stared at Gus. "Like what?" he said. "What do you have in mind?"

I jumped in before Gus responded. "It's not that we have anything definite to do, it's just that Gus and I have looked again through all the stuff that María Contreras gave us. We think we might have found something."

"You found something? What the hell does that mean?" Ana's question carried an obvious note of irritation.

"The way it looks, to us at least," Gus said, "is that María knew a hell of a lot more than she let on. She was in it all along, from the beginning, and deep. She used us—Luis and me—to get at the poor sucker Valdez. She drew him out when he sniffed around for the missing money that he thought was owed him. She didn't want him messing up her good thing."

"What good thing is that?" Ana said.

"The way we think it played out, is that she guarded Sam's money, or at least she knew where it was," I said. "It built up for years, since Sam pulled his disappearing act down in Mexico. He was into a lot of stuff and he added to his stash all the time. Then, out of the blue, this guy Valdez is released from prison and wants his cut. He's a loose end. Knew too much about Sam's and María's real business. But he played it coy, kept pressure on her, made her nervous, and she didn't think she had an opportunity to move the money. She needed a ruse to draw him out, or to find out where he was, so she brought in a lawyer, me, and acted like she didn't know the real dope."

"There's one thing that's bothered me about that scenario," Ana said.

"What's that?" I asked.

"María used you guys to find out where Valdez was. The house in Westwood. But that was Sam's place. Why would he stay there? And why didn't María know it?"

"Yeah, that bothered me, too. Then I reviewed the timeline. Valdez first contacted María at a time when Sam was out of the country. He must have known about the house and hid there. Sam wasn't using it anymore. In fact, Valdez thought Sam was dead, like the rest of us. María got the address from me, but by that time, Sam was back in Denver. They probably surprised Valdez at the house and eventually killed him. Then Sam turned on María."

"Both Valdez and María played roles for Luis. It cost Valdez his life," Gus said.

"So she took care of him?" Ana said.

Gus and I nodded.

"She and Sam," Gus said. "They killed him, burned the evidence, got rid of the body."

"That starts a chain reaction involving Sam and María," I said.

Batista sat back quietly while Gus and I talked. "How are you so certain about all this?" he asked. He looked squarely at Gus.

Gus looked at Ana.

"Most of this is what we know from María herself, if we fill in the holes of her story."

"And we used what we've learned about Sam," Gus added. He continued to stare at Ana.

"It's guesswork, what you lawyers call 'speculation,'" Batista said. He stood and paced, his usual mode of conversation. "You don't have any hard proof."

Gus had seen enough at the Westwood house to confirm much of what we presented, but Batista didn't need to know all the details about that.

"Actually, we have a bit more than guesswork," I said.

"Really? Like what?" Ana asked.

"We found notes and other things in the file that María must have overlooked when she dumped the pile of papers on my desk. We didn't pay attention to those kinds of things when she disappeared. You remember, it all came down quick. One day we had a client, the next, we didn't. We didn't even think about her for months, not to mention the husband we thought was dead. Only now, after we've gone through everything again, are we seeing a pattern that tells us the story."

"It's nothing like a smoking gun," Gus said. "But there's a map in the papers that we didn't think meant anything until we read a sticky note that was stuck on the map."

Ana and Batista waited for the rest from Gus. Corrine was in the room and she, too, waited.

"The note says, 'Paco's safe.'"

"Paco's safe?" Ana said. "Like, he's okay, all right?"

"Maybe," I said. "Or, that there's a safe place used by Paco."

"A place where money could be kept," Batista said.

"That's what we're thinking," Gus said.

29 [Gus]

good and bad, I define these terms quite clear, no doubt, somehow

The map told an interesting story; at least, I found it interesting. That night in Corrine's house with all the players present, except for Sam, it was easy to see that Batista had a hard time believing what Luis and I told them. Ana, on the other hand, looked to be inclined to buy into what we said. Or maybe it was that she hoped we were correct. One thing about that woman, she knew what she wanted. Right then, in my sister's home, I had no difficulty with the concept that my ex-girlfriend, the human resources cop, wanted nothing as bad as getting the chance to see a pile of money snatched from gangsters who didn't know what to do with all that cash, and not because she was civic-minded. Ana liked the idea of piles of money. That was me giving her the benefit of the doubt.

I'd ended whatever our thing was with a quick visit to tell her that I thought it was time to move on. I didn't explain that I'd seen her with Batista, and she didn't admit that she'd already moved on and that I was way behind the curve. She took it with grace, which I admired, and a sense of relief, which I didn't. And just like that, I was her ex and she was another name on a list that had no use.

So, when we met at Corrine's, we both understood the situation. I couldn't help looking at her with some regret. She was, after all, an attractive, sexy woman. But then, aren't they all?

What bothered me the most was how I was supposed to deal with Fulgencio Batista. Apparently, they didn't want to share the news about their new-found relationship, and I wasn't going to bring it up. I'd let Luis know that Ana and I were no longer a duet, but that was all. I figured, if the Mexican cop and Ana wanted to share their happiness with the rest of us, they could do it much better than I. I let it all go and concentrated on what we had to do to bring down Sam Contreras.

The wrinkled map lay unfolded on Corrine's kitchen table. One crease had a tear and coffee stains spotted one edge. We stood around the table, studying the map. It was a basic highway guide, given out at tourist information centers and sold at gas stations for five bucks.

"What place is this, in the map?" Batista said. "What are we looking at?"

"That's the I-70 highway," I said, pointing to a long blue line that twisted out of Denver into the mountains. "It's hard to see at first, but there's a small triangle drawn in pencil near the exit to Frisco."

"What's a Frisco?" Batista asked.

"Small town about an hour and half from Denver," Luis said. "In the mountains, near the ski resorts. Copper Mountain, Breckenridge, Keystone, Arapahoe Basin." He pointed to each resort on the map. "Very popular, very turista."

"What does Frisco have to do with Sam Contreras?" Ana asked.

"We didn't think anything until we looked closer at the receipts María gave us to show that the import business didn't have any money left after Sam supposedly died and Valdez went to prison." Luis pulled out a few sheets of paper from his briefcase and spread them next to the map. "There was a monthly charge for a storage unit in a place called Alpine Storage and Security, in Frisco. The monthly bill was seventy-five dollars. Paid every month for three years."

"A small debit each month, hardly noticeable," I said. "And we didn't notice it at first. It must be a walk-in closet unit. Only big enough to hold a few boxes or crates of money, but that's all."

"This doesn't help," Ana said. "If Sam was using a storage unit for the money, then he's gone up there and taken out the money, and probably is back in Mexico already. Christ, this is useless."

"It's easy to jump to that conclusion," I said. "But look closer at the receipts Luis pulled. Look who paid them. It wasn't Sam."

Ana and Batista pored over the papers. "The receipts don't always say, but some of them show that María paid the fee. So, it was her storage unit?"

"Looks like it," I said. "I think she used the map when she went up to Frisco to find a storage place. She wanted it far enough from Denver to not attract attention, but not too far away in case she needed to get to it fast."

"You think the money is still there?"

"We can't say for sure," Luis said. "We don't know how much María told Sam, or how much he figured out on his own. We had all these papers from the first time she came to our office. Maybe he never put it together. Maybe he's waiting for me or one of you to make a move to the money. We just don't really know."

"Wait a minute," Ana said. "María's been dead for months. The bill hasn't been paid. These places give you thirty days and then they open the units and sell the junk. Except in this case, the storage owner would find the money. He'd have it now."

Luis drew out one more receipt. "Look at this. She paid up for a year in advance. It was right around the time she came to me. She covered her bases. She knew Valdez was closing in, so she wanted to guarantee there weren't any glitches with the unit. But you're right to be concerned. We can't risk that the storage company will open the unit."

"I don't understand," Batista said. His words surprised me. I thought the guy would understand all of this better than anyone at the table. "Was this woman working with Paco or Sam, as you call him? Or didn't she know he was alive?"

"We'll never know the answer to that, but I think she wasn't sure," Luis said. "He had her hide the money while he took care of business in Mexico and the Southwest. He was reported dead but that was to throw off all the cop heat. She moved the money to the storage unit and waited, bided her time. She had to know how he operated. She must have had doubts that he was really dead. Or she and Sam were still actively working together. It doesn't really matter, does it? And then when Valdez made demands, it set off her alarms and she tried to go on the offensive. That got her killed."

Batista shrugged his shoulders.

"What's the plan?" Ana asked. "What does this mean as far as dealing with Contreras?"

"We have to believe that he's watching us," I said. "He tore through Luis' office looking for the same thing we were—a sign or clue about where María hid the money. He has her electronic file, he may figure out what she did. But the good thing is that the storage unit receipts weren't in the computer file, so he couldn't get them. We think he's still in the dark and waiting to see what we do."

"What about the paper file? Didn't he get that?" Ana kept coming up with questions.

"No," Luis said. "He never made it into the office storage room. Rosa interrupted him and he must have run after he knocked her out. But he wouldn't have found them anyway. Rosa had them, at her house. They were part of a box of documents she intended to scan and then destroy."

Everyone settled back for a moment.

"I think we can set this guy up," I said. "If he sees that we're going to the mountains, he might look again at the map. It was scanned into the computer file. It might be enough to lead him into a trap."

Luis rubbed the back of his neck. "I'm not as optimistic as Gus. Personally, I think Sam has found the money and left the state. But this storage unit is all we have. Maybe it can be the bait we need. Especially if it looks like I'm heading to the mountains without all of you, like I'm after the money only for myself."

My gaze swept from Luis to Batista to Ana. Each one looked worried, doubtful, angry. My eyes landed on Corrine, who stood in the corner of her kitchen. She shook her head, then smiled. She shook her head again and left the room. She'd done the same whenever she thought I was about to get into trouble. It was her older sister way of telling me to cool it, to slow down, to step back. It rarely worked in the past. But I was older than that now.

≫ ≫ ≫

Two nights before Luis was to drive up to Frisco, a few visitors dropped by the house. Corrine never really liked my friends but she tolerated them. She welcomed Shoe, Ice and Jerome with a six-pack of beer and told them to make themselves at home. Then she pretended to read a book in the kitchen while she listened to us talk.

I spent almost fifteen minutes giving them a summary of the past several months. I wrapped up with an update on what we thought would happen once Luis made his move.

"You want us to wait for your lawyer friend up in the mountains, then save his ass when this bad guy decides to blow his head off?" Jerome cut through my monologue with his typical attitude.

"We're gonna watch out for him, yes. We think this guy, Contreras, will follow him for the money. It's our job to make sure he doesn't do anything more than follow Luis. We grab him when we see him."

"Why so many of us?" Shoe asked.

"There might be others. We think Contreras is running, not only from the Mexican cops, but also from another cartel. There could be a lot of guns."

"Shouldn't you just take this to the cops?" Ice said. He was always the most cautious.

"A Mexican federal agent is involved—Fulgencio Batista. He'll be with us. I wanted us to talk this over without him around. And we don't have enough for the police to do anything, really. Ana ran this by some of her pals on the force. Unofficially. They told her we were all cracked. The way it breaks down is this. Luis is taking a drive to the mountains. We think bad shit could happen, but we got no hard proof. We haven't ever seen Contreras; had no direct contact with him. There was a break-in at Luis' office, but the police have already concluded it was a run-of-the-mill B and E. The police aren't going to waste their time with our theories. So, it's up to me, to us. Are you in?"

"This is wild, even for you, Gus," Jerome said. "Shoe and Ice aren't gunmen—no offense, guys."

I nodded at the way Jerome indirectly pimped his own reputation. Shoe and Ice both smiled at Jerome. They were enjoying this.

"It sounds like you're asking us to take on professionals, men who know what they're doing," added Jerome. "You sure this is a good idea?"

"If we're up there ahead of Luis, waiting at the storage place, I don't see how this is too risky. We wait for Contreras, take him as soon as we see him. He may know what Luis looks like, but he won't know us. We outnumber him; he won't have a choice. The unknown factor is whether there are others watching Contreras. We might have to just get Luis and take off. I don't want a shooting match any more than you."

The three men drank their beer.

"You gonna risk violating your parole?" Jerome said.

"I'm counting on Batista to cover for me. If we nab Contreras, he's got a nice catch to take back to Mexico. I'm hoping he stands up for me when I need it."

"Ain't gonna happen, Gus," Shoe said. "You could end up back in prison, just for having a gun, and worse if there's any kind of shooting. What if someone gets hit? You should rethink this, Gus."

Ice nodded. "You sure it's worth it?" The boys asked the same question in different ways.

I finished off my beer. "Luis Móntez gave me a chance. I'm just helping him out. The way I hope it goes is that we grab Contreras because we surprise him, Batista takes the credit, and the rest of us are just friends of Luis who happened to be around. No guns, no shooting, no pedo. How's that sound?"

"Sounds like a fairy tale and smells like manure, little brother." Corrine hollered from the kitchen. "Sounds like another Gus Corral fiasco. Sounds like you need my help."

My three visitors all laughed. Corrine was serious.

"What do you think you can do to help?" I said. I wouldn't turn her down. She'd shown me long ago that she could handle certain situations much better than I—like the ones where I might be somebody's target.

"These guys will stick out worse than sore thumbs. Look at them—do they look like anybody who hangs out in Frisco, Colorado? No, they look like they came right off the chain gang. These mountain towns may be loaded with immigrants and gente working the kitchens and cleaning the motels, but for the most part those people want to be invisible to the tourists and skiers. Frisco will be covered with snow but that's not what makes it a lily-white town. Your friends need to dress the part. Ski parkas, fancy gloves and boots, maybe some skis in a car rack. And they need a good reason to be in the same area as the storage business. What else is going on there?"

None of us had a ready response.

Shoe squirmed then finally said what was on his mind. "You guys might think this is nuts, but on the lake there's always fishermen. They drill holes in the ice and wait for the fish to snatch their bait. We could be ice fishermen."

"You must be joking," Jerome said. "We don't know the first thing about ice fishing. We don't have the equipment. We'll probably fall through the ice. Think of something else."

"I like it," I said. "It could work, as long as we're not too far away. Just a bunch of city slickers trying to fish in the winter. We can act like we're setting up for a day's worth of fishing. The lake isn't that far from the storage building."

"How do you know that?" Corrine asked.

"When I looked at Frisco on the computer. I did the street level view and saw the storage company, and the lake close by."

Corrine nodded. "Good, good," she said.

I continued with what I thought could be our plan. "We keep our eyes on the place, and when we see Luis pull up, we watch for Contreras. We move to the shore, and jump him when he parks."

"Four city Chicanos on the ice, trying to look like we're after fish?" Jerome said. "Who's that gonna fool?"

"Four Chicanos and one Mexican cop," I said. "Batista will be with us."

"That makes it better?" Jerome said.

"Look. We just have to look the part so that we don't get too much attention. We'll drill a few holes in the ice . . . "

"Wha-a-at?" Ice said. "We have to drill holes in ice that we'll be standing on?"

"What'd you think?" I said. "People do it all the time up there. There'll be others on the lake, fishing. What we'll really be doing is watching for Luis and Contreras. We'll be okay."

Shoe spoke up again. "Jerome made a good point. We don't have any equipment."

I nodded. "I think that means we go up tomorrow, find one of the fishing equipment rental places, and get what we need. We spend the night, then head out to the lake early. Luis can tell us what time he expects to be in Frisco."

Corrine moved towards me. "You should rent motel rooms now. You probably won't get much, but you won't need much, right?"

We all nodded.

"How will you pay for all this?"

They looked at me.

"Hell, I don't know," I said. "Maybe Luis?"

Corrine walked to the desk near the window. She pulled out her wallet and removed a credit card. She handed the card to me. "Here's how I can help. Don't use it for booze."

30 [Luis]

gone is my youth
I look in the mirror every day
and let it tell me the truth

I headed to Frisco early on Saturday morning. The Denver sky was a pure blue canopy lit with sunshine and no clouds to block the view. Spring was working its way to Colorado, which meant the city stretched in warmth while the mountains huddled in a blizzard. And the next day, the reverse could be true.

The kindest thing Rosa said about what I planned to do was that I was an idiot. "An old man idiot," were her exact words. She ordered me out of her house when I explained what was going on. I called her one more time before I hit the road, but she didn't answer and I didn't leave a message. Meanwhile, Gus and a few of his friends were well on their way with their part of the scheme. They worked with Batista. Ana waited at her house for word about how we were doing. We all agreed that a Denver cop didn't need to be more involved than she already was.

I wore lined Carhartt jeans, boots and a sweater. I had a parka, gloves, scarf and a thermos of coffee. GPS—set for the storage outfit address. Cell phone—charged. All the tools were ready. I felt okay, considering that I was an old man idiot. "In the old days . . . ," I started to tell myself. I stopped before I got carried away with too many what-used-to-be's. I just hoped I was as prepared as I tried to show.

I also had my Walther PPK .380 in the glove box. I hadn't fired it in years. It was clean, gleaming and loaded. I gambled it would work if I had to use it.

I made a production out of preparing to leave on the trip and then of loading my car with an obviously empty suitcase. When I was ready, I stood on my front steps, unfolded the map and stared at it for two minutes. I tried to be conspicuous, then I drove out of Denver, speed-limit slow.

I periodically looked in my rearview mirror for any sign that I was being followed, but the highway was so busy that I couldn't say for sure. Several cars trailed me for miles up the steep grade of Floyd Hill. An accident near the exit to the Central City Parkway kept me stalled for a half-hour. My car idled but my heart pumped like a drunken drummer trying to solo. When traffic finally moved again, I'd chugged most of the coffee and realized I needed to find a restroom. Talk about an old man.

Construction work a few miles up the highway stalled me again. I felt pain from my distended bladder. When I accepted that I would have to wet my pants, the flagman released us and the ten-mile line of cars moved forward. Around a bend I saw an exit with a gas station sign and I found relief. So far, the biggest threat had come from my own bodily functions.

By the time I made it through the Eisenhower tunnel, a thin blanket of snow covered the steep hills on the side of the highway. At first, the flakes were big and lazy, sparkling in the white sun against the water sky. I raced past Silverthorne and Dillon until the pretty snow changed into a thin curtain of ugly sleet. I slowed for Exit 203, followed the roundabout, past the Walmart, and eventually I was on Summit Boulevard, on the edge of Lake Dillon and the postcard-perfect town of Frisco.

I needed more coffee. At least, that's how I rationalized my delay. I turned onto Main Street and found a coffee shop. I sat in the car for a few minutes after I parked. I thought about Rosa and whether she was right that I was an old idiot. I sat in the shop for thirty more minutes. I drank straight-up coffee without sugar, cream or anything else. I watched the snow fall and build up on the already icy streets. Thoughts of the dying María Contreras, a bleeding Rosa and a burning house played with my head.

The GPS took me to a business park only a hundred yards or so from the shore of Lake Dillon. I parked on pavement near a shop that offered snowmobile tours and rentals, turned off the motor and checked my surroundings. Gray and black clouds hung low across the mountains. A long squat brown building had a sign that said it was Alpine Storage and Security. There were maybe a half-dozen other cars in the parking lot, and a banged-up, faded pickup at the red doorway to the storage building. I calculated that the door was to the office, and from there a hallway must lead to the various storage units in the building. Maybe they were in the back, behind the building.

I carried the key to the unit that Gus found in María's house when he searched it after she died. We'd finally figured out why the key was important.

I texted Gus: "I'm going in." That's when I saw that I'd missed calls from Gus while I thought about fate and luck in the coffee shop. The phone was buried in one of the deep pockets of my parka, smothered. Too late now, I thought.

I slipped on my gloves, wrapped the scarf around my neck, put the gun in the waistband of my pants, covered it with my sweater and left my car. I didn't think I needed the parka. I felt like an old man idiot.

31 [Gus]

many fish bites if ya got good bait

The first part of our plan went off like clockwork. We made the trip up the mountains on Friday without incident. Five of us huddled in the rented Suburban: Jerome, Shoe, Ice, Batista, me. We'd arranged for rooms and the rental equipment for fishing. Some of the time, it felt like we were just a bunch of regular guys on our way to a weekend of beer and fishing. I expected country music on the radio. Then I'd see the cold stare of Batista in my rearview mirror and the rifles stretched across the laps of Shoe and Ice.

What we hadn't counted on was a surprise late-winter snowstorm.

The guy at the fishing equipment place—Doc's Fishing Supply—let me know that the weather didn't look good for Saturday. His name tag said "Bennett." He had everything we needed piled up on the floor of his shop.

"I understand if you boys want to cancel," Bennett said.

He'd smiled too broadly when we noisily walked into his place of business, and that set off my radar. Maybe it was the accumulated tension of the ride and going over in my head the hundreds of details that could derail our plan, but I didn't like Bennett from the minute I walked in his shop.

I pulled out my wallet. It held the cash we'd taken out of Corrine's ATM card. "We're good. We may not catch too many fish but we want the experience. Know what I mean?"

"Not saying anything about the fishing. More about whether you boys will freeze to death. It gets mighty cold out there on the lake when the wind blows and the snow hits like birdshot. You sure you want to do this?"

Inwardly, I smiled when he repeated the question everyone else had asked me. I didn't like it that he kept calling us boys, but I had to let it pass. We didn't want to attract more attention than we absolutely had to, and I figured a wrestling match between out-of-place city homies and a country ignoramus might bring on just such attention.

"Yeah, we're sure."

"Okay. Your funeral," he said easily. "If a Wildlife Manager asks for your licenses, you have them, right?"

I nodded.

He rang up the bill. "You know how to use the ice auger? The poles? The heater? Any questions?"

Ice and Shoe picked up what they could and then wobbled out the door.

"Nah. Thanks," I said. "If we got questions later, on the ice, I guess we can call you?"

The man laughed. "Sure. Give me a call. My number's on your receipt. If you got any questions at all." He sounded amused, like he was in on a joke where we were the punchlines.

I picked up a pole and fishing tackle. "Looks like a toy, don't it?"

"Oh, it's real. It'll work. You know how to use it?"

I walked away. "I got it."

I threw the stuff in the back of the van. "You hear that guy?" Ice said. "He thinks we're gonna freeze."

"Hope he doesn't turn us in to the wardens or whoever it is that might check us out," Shoe said. "We don't need that hassle."

We had licenses. We'd bought them online and carried proof of payment. But I agreed with Shoe. We wanted no interruptions, not even from a friendly game warden who was only curious about how our fishing luck was holding out.

We checked into the Ski Palace Motel and ate pizza and drank beer at Greco's, a friendly enough mountain bar. Pitchers of beer chased sausage and pepperoni. The food, the motel and the rest of that cold night passed by in a blur of anxious thinking about the next day.

We woke up around six, found a coffee shop, chugged caffeine and then began our play.

The lake was a few minutes away in our van. I liked driving the Suburban. It was big and hefty, powerful. I was glad Corrine suggested it. She said we needed a real mountain car if we wanted to pull off our masquerade.

We didn't expect Luis for another half-hour or so. We set up camp on the shore, put our equipment together, tested that the auger had juice and then began our hike on the ice. Batista carried the auger—basically a hand drill to cut holes in the ice for our lines—while the rest of us hauled the poles, bait, heaters and folding chairs. We picked a spot away from other fishermen and women, but about the same distance from the shore. The ice appeared okay, although when I first stepped on the ice, I heard growling and squeaking. I jumped back on the shore.

"That's just the ice freezing more," Jerome said. "Means the ice is safe."

I didn't know where Jerome picked up his fishing knowledge, but the guy usually knew a little about anything and everything. He led the way and drilled holes while the rest of us jumped at each sound and tried to not think about the frigid water under our feet and the whipping snow blowing in our faces. I called Luis. No answer. I assumed he was busy driving.

When at last we were ready to actually fish, I looked at my watch and realized that we had been on the ice an hour and ten minutes. I looked over at the storage building, sitting against a backdrop of mountains covered in snow and clouds, but didn't see anything that wasn't there when we arrived. But I also knew that I hadn't kept my full attention on the building.

I called Luis. No answer again.

I walked over to Batista, who sat in one of the chairs, facing toward the shore and the building.

"You see anything?" I asked.

"No. But, there was some time when we first got here that I didn't have full eyes on the place. And now, with the snow, it's difficult to see much. I don't think anyone came or went, but if someone entered from the back, we'd never know it. Is there a back door?"

I kneeled down on the ice next to him. "There's a double door that allows access to the storage units from the back—for bigger items like a table or a couch. But you have to go through the front door to get the guy to open the back door."

Batista shrugged. "How do you know this?"

"I checked out Alpine Storage, on the Internet. I looked at everything about this place, this town, on a computer. Even saw pictures of the units. And the guy who's usually working at the units. His name's Lionel Gussler. Looks a little like the mountain man in Doc's place."

"But it's not impossible that someone could come up from behind and be let in through the back doors, and we wouldn't have seen him?"

I nodded. "Not impossible, no. Contreras could have phoned Gussler and had him open the back doors without ever coming through the front."

"Móntez is late. Have you heard from him?"

"No. I'm worried. I called him but no answer. Maybe I should go check on him."

That was the minute when the panic hit. We'd been on the ice longer than we expected. Luis was late and he hadn't called or answered his phone. Sam could be in the storage business waiting for Luis. Batista stood up.

"I'm going over there," he said. "Puede que sea demasiado tarde."

Yeah, we could be too late.

I was about to join him when we saw the State Wildlife Division truck driving along the shore. The truck's headlights were on. It stopped on the shore near us. Batista walked away from me to the shore, but not towards the truck.

"Here comes a warden," I said to the others. "Keep cool."

I turned my attention to the game warden who jogged straight for me.

"Hello there," the warden said. "Kind of snowy for fishing, ain't it?" He waved his hand at the other fishing parties. They were all packing up, calling it a day.

"Yeah, we thought we'd give it a shot. Guess we'll head home."

The warden stood in front of me. He looked over our equipment. "Bennett Smiley over at Doc's told me you guys might be in trouble. Said you didn't look like you were really prepared for the weather. Asked if I'd check. You okay?"

That damn Bennett.

"Yeah, sure. But you're right. We should head in."

He glanced over his shoulder at Batista, who had reached the edge of the lake. "Your friend seems to have already left."

"Yeah. He got cold. He's gonna sit in the truck while we get the gear."

"You guys have any luck?" He nodded at Ice, Shoe and Jerome.

My phone went off. It was a text from Luis. I peered over the warden's shoulder and saw Luis' car parked in the parking lot. I didn't see Batista.

"Uh, nothing really. We just threw in our lines." I made a move like I wanted to get on with packing up.

"I'd like to see your license."

My mouth tightened and I almost told him to go to hell.

"Sure, no problem." I reached for my wallet in the inside pocket of the heavy coat Corrine had bought me for the trip. I wasn't doing anything illegal, but the warden affected me the same as happened whenever I encountered any law enforcement officer. LEOs and I didn't mix. I felt guilty just talking to a cop, any kind of cop, and that included Ana.

"Gus! Gus!" Batista shouted from somewhere on the shore.

A gunshot echoed from the shore, past us and across the lake. We all ducked in reflex, including the warden. Three dark figures struggled in the distance. The warden looked at them, then at me. He unsnapped his holster flap and pulled his weapon. I ran to

Batista. The warden followed behind me. He didn't holler for me to stop, so I kept running.

Batista and two men were rolling on the snow, fists flying. Two large handguns lay on the frozen ground. I grabbed one of the men and yanked him off Batista. He looked surprised, threw a punch, missed. I leaned back on my heels and hit him in the face. He fell back on the ground.

The warden shoved his gun into the back of the man sitting on Batista. The man held up his hands. The man I'd punched also lifted his hands.

Batista lay on the ground, bleeding from a wound on the side of his neck. My boots squished through a mix of red snow and mud.

"We have to get him to a hospital," I shouted at the warden. I rushed my words. "Federal officer. Mexico." I pointed at the storage building. "Fugitive."

We heard another shot, this one from inside the building. I waved my hand at Batista and then at the warden. I ran to the building.

32 [Luis]

send lawyers, guns and money
the shit has hit the fan

The sleet hit when I opened the car door. The wind cut through me as I realized the difference between snowfall in the city and the mountains. I pushed against the wind. I walked the several yards to the red door, regretting that I hadn't taken the time to put on my heavier coat.

I opened the door. I stepped into a small office with a metal desk, a crooked chair and a lumpy divan in front of the desk. No one was in the office.

I looked at the key—#143 was etched in the metal.

I walked past the desk into a well-lit hallway that stretched the length of the building. The hallway was clear. Doors lined up on both sides of the hallway. The limited space between the doors meant that the units had to be small. The first door to my left had metallic numbers attached to it: #100. I walked until I came to #143, about halfway down the hall. The white metal door opened when I used the key. I switched on a light. An empty cardboard box about the size of a fifty-inch TV screen sat in the middle of the narrow room.

I heard something behind me, a door opening. Too late, I turned.

The bartender from the Roundhouse Bar stood in front of me. Contreras' right hand held a handgun, a revolver with a snub nose. His left hand grabbed me and threw me against the wall.

"Where is it?" he shouted.

Behind him I could see the open door to the unit across the hall, and on the floor of the unit the crumpled body of a bearded man. I assumed he was the security company's man.

"What?" I said.

He slapped me with his empty hand and my head snapped to the left. I bit my tongue and tasted blood.

"The money. You know what I want."

"I don't . . ." Before I could finish he hit me with the gun. He let go of me and I fell back into the narrow storage unit and against the box. The box flew across the concrete floor. The gun opened a cut above my ear. I struggled against dizziness.

Contreras reached down to pick me up. I kicked at his knee and he twisted to the floor. I kicked again, at the gun, and smashed his fingers. He dropped the pistol. I dove for it but he kicked it away, then slugged me. I felt like I was about to pass out. I rolled across the floor and pulled my gun from my pants. I aimed it at him, hoping he would stop. He rushed at me. I wasn't breathing. My heart banged against my chest. The gun felt weightless in my hand.

I fired.

The gun's explosion echoed against the concrete walls. The ringing in my ears blocked out all other sound. Contreras jerked backwards from the shot. Even I could not miss at that distance. He grabbed the left side of his body under his arm, pulled his hand away and stared at his bloody fingers. He lurched towards me. I raised the gun to fire again but before I pulled the trigger, he jumped in the air and landed on me. He knocked the gun away and punched me in the ribs once, twice, three times. Pain rumbled through my chest. Blood dripped from my left ear. I couldn't think straight. One more punch would end the fight.

I'd been beaten up before, but this was the worst. My mind reeled and my body couldn't take it.

His fist stopped in mid-air. A low groan rolled from his throat. He grabbed his wound again. Blood flowed across his jacket and hand. He sat back on the floor and tried to raise his eyes to look at me.

"Where's the goddamn money?"

I struggled to regain my breath. I held up my hand to keep him at bay. He didn't move. Blood soaked his jeans and trickled on the floor. Blood from my sweater sleeve mixed with his. I picked myself up. I tossed his gun into the hallway. Sam Contreras sat on the floor, not moving. I sweated, and my breathing was ragged and rough.

"The money?" he said one last time. He slumped over and closed his eyes.

The sound of gunshots bounced down the hallway from outside the building. I wobbled from dizziness. I breathed deeply for a few seconds and regained my balance. I kicked Sam's gun further down the hallway and headed for the front door of the building.

I was almost to the door when it burst open. I raised my gun and pointed it at Gus as he rushed through the door.

"You okay?" he shouted.

I nodded. Gus saw the gun and indicated with his head that I should drop it on the littered desk. I did. Waiting outside were Jerome, Ice and Shoe. Behind them, a man in a park ranger uniform held his gun on two men I didn't recognize. I didn't see Batista.

Police and ambulance sirens wailed in the distance.

That's when I started to shake. My fingers shimmered like dry leaves in a stiff breeze. My legs trembled out of control. I got dizzy again.

I threw up on the floor of the office of Alpine Storage and Security.

33 [Gus]

well, I woke up this mornin', didn't know right from wrong

It took several days to iron out the Frisco mess. We dealt with different law enforcement agencies and the encounters were anything but friendly. In other words, standard operating procedure between me and cops.

At first, we were all arrested, including Batista as he lay in his hospital bed. He'd been shot in the side of the neck, but the wound wasn't fatal. The bullet ripped him but passed on through. The Summit County Sheriff's Office handcuffed him to the bed while the doctors worked to stop the bleeding and stitch up the hole. Luis was looked over by a doctor, then shuffled off to the local police, who interrogated him about the storage center shootout. He told the truth: he had taken advantage of the fishing trip to follow up a lead for one of his old clients, when he was ambushed and had to defend himself. Finally, the city police and county deputy sheriffs believed him. Sam Contreras also was taken to the hospital, but we never knew where they had him. Jerome, Ice, Shoe and I were thrown in the county jail.

I saw the storage unit guy, Eugene Eccles, who'd been knocked out by Contreras, wheeled into one of the ambulances, but I didn't see him at the hospital. At least, not where they had Batista.

Eventually, when he could talk, Fulgencio Batista was allowed to make a call. His superiors then contacted the Denver FBI office. A few hours more and a carload of suited agents visited the sheriff and the local police chief. Another hour and the cuffs were taken off Batista, and the rest of us were released from jail.

Two of the agents talked to us outside the jail, in the snow, in the freezing night air. We huddled together for warmth. I asked why we didn't use someone's office, but they ignored my question.

They made it clear that we were cut loose only because Batista had made a show of backing us up, which caused the Mexican attorney general to call the U.S. attorney general, and so on up and down the chain of authority between the two countries. It made sense in a geopolitical, international relations way, which I didn't understand nor did I want to. I didn't have to understand it, I simply liked it.

Batista's story was that he'd found Contreras in Denver. He waited for the man to make his move for the money that everyone knew Sam must have stashed. He made friends with our friend, Ana Domingo, and attached himself to our group because of the tenuous connection some of us had to Sam and his ex-wife. After days of watching and waiting, Batista believed that Sam was on his way to Frisco. The Mexican cop used our fishing trip as an excuse to travel to the mountain town. He told the agents that he influenced us—the Denver muchachos—to go on our fishing trip because it was "something I always wanted to do and, tú sabes, no puedo en México. Never happen in my country." The rifles we carried were simply part of the fishing, outdoor mountain adventure. He never expected the cartel men, and he was as surprised as anyone else about what went down between Luis and Sam. He said Luis wandered into Alpine Storage to warm up and look for his client's belongings while the rest of us set up for fishing.

When he was asked why Luis had his own car, Batista said the lawyer planned to leave early so he had his own ride.

I wasn't sure anyone bought his tale, but with the political pressure from D.C. and Mexico City, all in the interest of good neighbor relations, as well as a very public display of across-the-border law enforcement cooperation, it became the official version. Batista was a quick thinker.

Later I mentioned to Jerome how Batista had to have come up with the cover story while the doctors worked on his neck. "That says something about the man. But, I guess anyone who can survive cartel torture should be able to think clearly while he's bleeding and in pain and doctors are patching him up."

"Or he thought of it on the way up to Frisco," Jerome said. I asked one of the agents about Sam. "What's going to happen to Contreras?"

He looked like I had poked his eye with a sharp stick. "Who?" he said.

"Sam Contreras. The wounded man you found bleeding in the storage building."

He paused. "The man shot by your lawyer, Móntez, right? He said his name was Toby King. Whoever he is, that man's been taken into custody by our office. That's about all you need to know."

The FBI men chained the cartel hitmen together and hauled them away. They caught Sam and two other criminals in the act of serious crimes on U.S. soil. They had to be happy about that.

The two thugs, who had given up too easily, I thought, were part of the Rojos, a gang that had messed with me in the past. I felt good about that part.

"They'll use one against the others, get all three to turn, snitch, maybe become ongoing informants," Jerome told me over stale coffee in the hospital cafeteria while we waited for Luis to be released. "It's a good day for the feds."

"And a damn lucky day for us," I said.

"Yeah, if you think Luis getting beat, us almost killed by those two babosos and then all of us arrested is your definition of lucky."

Jerome had a point.

※ ※ ※

When the dust settled, and the blood dried, we tried to return to our old lives. Easier thought about than done.

Luis and Rosa trudged through the closing of his office. He seemed to be okay—no post-traumatic stress that I could see—but I worried about the guy anyway. He'd fought for his life and had almost lost. I worried because something like that would have stayed with me.

Ana focused on her work and didn't have time for anything else. At least, that's what she told me when I called and said I'd like to try for a better ending.

Jerome, Shoe and Ice had something to crow about when they went bar-hopping.

Batista returned to Mexico, without Sam Contreras. Sam departed with the U.S. feds and we assumed he spilled his guts on his old running dogs. Fulgencio Batista became the odd man out. I can't say I was sad to see him go. He'd taken the brunt of the rough stuff and been shot. He'd most likely saved Luis' life by stopping the cartel men before they made it inside the building. But I couldn't forget his play at Ana. That's just me, I guess.

I waited, not sure for what.

A couple of weeks after the Frisco episode, my waiting ended with a surprise phone call from Ana. She said she'd changed her mind and would like to "wrap things up," as she put it, and could I come over to her place.

"Sure," I said. "Later tonight?"

"Can you come now?" The urgency in her voice was out of place.

"Give me about an hour. I'm working on something for Luis. Okay?"

"Yeah. Just hurry. I'll be here."

I could've taken her request to mean that she wanted to get back with me. The tone of her words might've meant that she regretted how it had played out between us. She could've been trying to tell me that she made a mistake.

None of that was happening.

She greeted me with a nervous smile. I walked in slowly, unsure about the situation. She had me sit down on the couch and offered a beer.

"Okay, yeah."

She went in the kitchen and quickly returned with the booze.

"So what's up?" I said. She looked good, in a nervous, uptight kind of way. Something inside me moved or fluttered—whatever it was, it brought up a feeling I thought I'd buried deep.

"I'm sorry to drag you into this, but Fulgencio contacted me. He's back in the States. He lost his job. It got weird for him. The higher-ups didn't like that he came here on his own without official backing. He said they called him rogue, and what finished it for him was that he didn't have anything to show for his efforts. He didn't get his man. He thinks the cartel pulled some favors and he was kicked out. It's dangerous for him in Mexico. You can imagine. So now he expects me to help him get back on his feet."

"Yeah, that's strange." I sipped the beer. "Uh, but what can I do about it?" She hadn't eased my anxiety.

"I was hoping that you could talk to him."

"Why me?"

"He respects you, Gus. You may not believe that, after the way we treated you."

"You think?"

"But, he talked about how well you handled yourself. How you could be trusted. And how you reacted up in Frisco. He said you rescued him. He admires you. I just think you and he can talk about what's happening and maybe you can come up with something."

I gave her a fake laugh. She frowned and sputtered cuss words before she caught herself and stopped.

"Hell, I don't know," she said. "I can't deal with him. Actually, I don't want anything to do with him. We didn't part on good terms. He wanted me to go with him to Mexico. Can you believe that? Go to Mexico and do what? Anyway, I'm hoping if he talks to you he'll come to his senses and get on with his life."

"You got it all figured out, eh?"

"Obviously, I don't. I need your help. I'm asking for your help. You don't have to do it, and I couldn't blame you if you walk out now. But I had to ask, Gus."

I sat in her comfortable apartment with the photographs of her brothers and the matching furniture and drapes and a few books precisely placed on eye-level shelves. She'd wasted my time and now she wanted my help. I finished my beer.

"I have to go. I don't think there's anything I can do for you."

Her shoulders slumped and she sat on one of her expensive chairs.

Someone knocked on the front door.

"You expecting somebody?" I asked. She shook her head. "I'll get it," I said.

Batista stood in the hallway. He was in bad shape. There was little left of the imposing in-control legend who'd chased Sam Contreras from Mexico to Colorado. His hair was messed up, his eyes bloodshot and older. The scar on his cheek had dulled into a gray stain.

He wore a thin black nylon jacket that was spotted with dirt. His hands were stuck in the jacket pockets. He looked like he'd slept in his clothes. A dirty bandage wiggled on the side of his neck.

"Hola, Gus." His words sounded hollow. A crooked smile crossed his face. "I see she got you here. Bueno." He walked in. More correctly, he hurried into the room like a wounded animal.

"You okay? You don't look well."

"Sí, I am good. ¿Por qué no, eh?"

He stumbled to a chair. "It's good to see you, Gus. I never got the chance to really thank you for what you did at the lake. Mil gracias, señor." He extended his hand. His fingers shook.

His sweaty palm gripped mine only for an instant. I turned to find a place on the couch when I heard the rustle of his jacket. Then I felt his gun jam up against my spine.

"I don't want to hurt anyone. Just listen to me, and everything will be okay."

He stood up and kept the gun aimed at me. He was shaky. He walked in front of me. "Sit down, por favor. Next to Ana."

I did as he ordered. "What's this about?" I said. "What're you trying to do?"

"I have nothing left. They took away my work. Disgraced me in my country. Me, the only honest cop in Mexico." He laughed at his words. The laughter was out of place, wild.

"Maybe there's something in this country," I said. Ana glanced at me.

"Yes, that's possible," she said. "I told you that. Give me a chance to talk to some people."

He shook his head. "No. That won't ever happen. We all know that. Es de mierda."

"Then what do you want?" I asked.

"The money, Gus. What else? It wasn't in the mountains. There's nothing in your lawyer's office." Another piece of the puzzle fell in place.

"You're the one who trashed Luis' office. You knocked out Rosa?"

"I'm very sorry about that. I didn't want to do it. But, after Ana didn't get the files for me to look over, I had to do more. You left me no choice. I needed to find something that would lead me to Contreras and I knew that if I found the money, I would find Contreras. Rosa surprised me. I didn't want to hurt her, you have to believe me. But I couldn't risk being discovered."

"You were after the money all this time?" Ana asked. She squirmed on the couch like something crawled across her skin.

He shifted the weight on his legs. "No, no. It wasn't the money. I was trying to find Contreras. I had to do extreme things because we were too slow. I thought he would find his money and run, and I would miss him again. It wasn't the money."

"But now it is?" I said.

He slowly nodded. "I have no choice. The money is here, in this state, this city. You have it Gus. Somehow, you and Luis Móntez found it. That's the only explanation that makes sense about the empty storage room. You have it, and now I want it."

The man had lost it. He slurred nonsense. He looked out-of-place, undone.

"We don't have anything," I said. "You had the chance to interview Contreras before the FBI took him. If he didn't tell you anything about the money, you can bet he's talking now. The money's gone, Batista. The money's gone and you have to snap back. Remember who you were. What you did. The money isn't worth all this, isn't worth you ruining your life."

"My life is already ruined!" he shouted. His eyes opened wide.

"You can't do this," Ana shouted. Batista jerked at the screech of her voice. He pointed the gun at her. He gripped the weapon with both hands but the shaking continued. Ana hollered again. "Fulgencio!" She stood next to him, about six inches shorter. She looked up directly in his eyes. He slumped backwards, away from her.

He stared at the gun in his hand like it was the first time he'd seen it. Disgust swept over him. He threw the gun on the couch.

Ana grabbed the gun and held it on him.

"Ana, put that down," I said. "He's not going to hurt us. He's done." She took the gun to her bookshelves and set it down. Batista sat back in the chair.

"Please, por favor. I don't . . . I can't . . . "

"You want a beer?" I said. It was all I could think of to say.

He nodded.

Ana retrieved the beer from her kitchen. For several minutes we sat in silence as we finished our drinks.

He breathed deeply and occasionally a low groan escaped his wounded throat. His eyes never stopped moving. Ana and I kept our silence. A few more minutes passed. Ana fidgeted.

"I can help," she said. "I want to help."

He looked at her without any emotion on his face. "I don't believe you." He looked around the apartment. His eyes stopped when he saw me, then moved to Ana, where they stopped again.

"I'm leaving now," he finally said.

He walked out the apartment without looking back at either of us.

"You think he'll be alright?" Ana said.

"Maybe, maybe not. I think he's going home, though. That's got to be a good thing. And you offering to help him. That something. That counts."

"I hope I never see him again," she said. "After what he did to Rosa? He deserves all that's happened to him, and more."

She walked to her bookshelves and picked up Batista's gun. It was a big gun with a wood-grain grip. She held it tightly. For a second I expected her to aim it at me.

"You want this?" she said.

"Uh, no. I don't like guns."

She put it back on the shelf.

"Look, Gus. About everything . . . "

"Yeah, everything. Let's just leave it alone, okay? You gotta agree that we need a break. From everything. Right? Let's call it a night. I think that's the best we can do."

She licked her lips. "Yeah. Guess so."

I left Ana Domingo in her clean, efficient and expensive apartment with photographs of her brothers on the walls and a gun on her bookshelf. I never saw the inside of that apartment again.

It was almost time to level with Luis. Almost. Patience, Gus. Patience.

34 [Luis]

y volver, volver, volver a tus brazos otra vez

Maxine Corral's wedding happened on the hottest day in July, which made it the hottest day of that summer. Sweat trickled down my back. The collar of my blue, purple, red and green shirt was soaked. Max had decreed that all guests had to wear Hawaiian Aloha shirts (or no cake!) to the celebration. I splurged on a one hundred percent cotton genuine vintage camisa that set me back a hundred bucks. That kind of extravagance was unusual for me now that I was on a rigidly fixed income. ¡Órale! How often does someone get married for the first time?

The parrots, ferns and palm trees imbedded on my shirt felt right at home in Corrine Corral's back yard. The grass hadn't burned yet, despite watering restrictions, the last of the summer flowers were still in bloom and the deep ocean blue sky almost gave me a headache, it was so bright. I'd drunk more than a few of Corrine's homemade concoction that went by the name of Jungle Juice or Purple Passion, depending on who was talking, and so I felt at home myself, sweat or no sweat.

I sat in the middle of the party, using my Panama straw for shade. Around me, assorted people, all much younger than I, talked, danced, drank and ate. Dogs and kids ran in circles and occasionally one or the other bumped into my lawn chair. The four-piece band blasted from the far corner of the yard, under a white tent. The musicians wore their own Hawaiian shirts and cowboy hats, as well as huge smiles. Each had a beer bottle close by. They played a ranchera, then an oldies rock tune, then a country swing. I knew the words to most of the songs. The semi-sweet smell of legal marijuana, illegally smoked outside, drifted and mixed with the other smells of the reception: barbecue ribs, hamburgers, green chile, sweaty people. Corrine stood by the silver tub where she doled out glasses of her dangerous mix.

That morning I'd told her that I could kiss her for bringing Gus into my world. She kissed me on the cheek and said, "Te dije."

I looked retired, I felt retired. I also felt hot but the alcohol content of Corrine's magic mixture made the temperature irrelevant to my overall mood. I was on inactive attorney status with the state supreme court. Clients no longer called to ask "a quick question or two." My old office had been taken over by a pair of look-alike millennials who developed phone apps and had already made more money in a few months of business than I'd made my entire career as a lawyer. Rosa and I shared dinner several nights a week, as well as a few other things.

Life was good.

Jackie O walked over in an orange and teal sarong. Apparently she didn't have to wear an aloha shirt since she was the official person who performed the wedding ceremony. She did wear a huge lilac-colored hat that covered her face and hung down her back. A white gardenia peeked out from under the brim just above her left ear.

"Luis Móntez!" she squealed. "It's been ages." I smiled up at her. Marijuana smoke clung to her like the spider webs building up on the filing cabinets in my garage. "Where's that no-good partner of yours, Gus?" I pointed in the direction of the mountains. Gus was somewhere in the party.

Jackie sat down on top of a cooler. She waved her hand in front of her face. "Damn, it is hot today, no?"

"Oh yeah. What you gonna do, eh?"

For some reason that made her laugh. I chalked it up to the grass in her system. I thought for a second. "You doing okay these days? You working?"

She laughed again. Yeah, it was the grass. "Funny you should ask. I just stumbled into something new. The Safe and Healthy Initiative for Kids. SHIK. Helping kids is so chic, you get it?"

I smiled but I didn't get it. My brain wasn't working very hard.

"It's a shelter, resource center for children of addicts, abused kids, sick kids. We provide support, health care, community education. I do everything from answering phones at the main office to a lot of the bookkeeping. I track donations and do some fundraising. I'm going to organize a costume ball to help launch the project in style. It's right up my alley. I finally feel right about a job. It's all good." She paused. "Yeah, all good."

"I hope this works out for you."

"Thanks. We have a long ways to go. It's all about money, right? We don't have any, but we're working hard. We'll get there, somehow."

"You're not bartending anymore, then?"

"Not if I can help it. I hate drunks, know what I mean?"

I nodded, but since I was drunk I didn't think I should actually agree.

"Did I ever thank you for that Dynamic-Tec thing?"

"Yes, you did. Worked out okay?"

"I got a letter the other day from the district attorney. That guy, Younger? The one we met with? He said Cristelli's closed down. Facing about a dozen charges for his theft of private information, bribery, fraud, that kind of stuff. I'll have to testify. Looking forward to that. I'll stare that jerk right in the face and let him have it."

"Sounds good, Jackie. Sounds real good."

Jackie floated away, humming to herself. I had an overwhelming desire for some of Corrine's ribs smothered with her green chile. Before I could make my move to the food table, Gus sat down where Jackie had been.

"I need to talk with you," he said. He looked agitated—not the emotion I expected from the bride's brother.

"Sure. But if it's work, save it. I think I had one too many glasses of whatever it is that Corrine puts in that tub."

"It's not exactly work. But it is important. Can you focus?"

He looked around the yard, pulled his chair closer to mine.

"Yeah, sure. I'm all yours for the next five minutes." Gus wanted to be heard by only me. With the band playing full tilt and the boisterous crowd reaching the peak of its partying mood, I doubted anyone could hear what we said to each other. Corrine told me during the ceremony that Gus was moving out. He'd saved enough money for a security deposit on an apartment in the Edgewater area, west of Sloan's Lake. And he'd bought a car. Coupled with his new business, Gus Corral looked and acted like a reborn man.

"Congrats on everything, by the way. Corrine told me about your new ride and your move. Glad that you saved your money. Leaving the Northside?"

"There is no more Northside."

"Not like it was, for sure. Change happens. At least you can afford to move now."

"About that. You need to know something. I should have told you a while back, but I wanted to wait, to make sure."

"Make sure about what?"

"That the whole thing with Contreras and the money is really over."

"Yeah, it's over. Been over for a few months. Contreras is gone, and with him, all the bullshit he brought. The money was never found. That's all done, Gus. What is it that's bothering you? What should you have told me?"

He squirmed in the lawn chair and pulled it even closer to me. "Uh. It's like this. Uh, the money, it was in the, uh, storage unit."

"What are you talking about? You and I made that up, to trick Contreras. We wanted to flush him out of hiding and acting like we were going after his money was the best way to do that. That was your idea. It was a good one." It might have been the booze, or my lightheadedness from too much sun, but Gus' words didn't make sense. I couldn't understand why he said what he said.

"Yeah, that was our plan. But it was based on a reality. You remember that I visited the storage unit early on? Right after María went missing? I searched her house and found the key, along with some other papers?"

"Yeah?"

"Yeah. I followed up. Put two and two together to get to Alpine Security, like we told the others that we'd done. Only, it was just me back then."

"You did this without letting me in on it?"

"I didn't know what was going on. I didn't want to cause any trouble for you. So I checked it out myself. One weekend I drove up to Frisco, opened the box and found the money."

"You found the money in the security unit? It really was there?"

"Yes. I didn't want to leave it there for Contreras to find. So, I threw the money into two big trash bags and loaded them in the car. The money's been in Corrine's basement ever since."

"Jesus!" I almost fell off the lawn chair. "How could you do that, Gus? What's wrong with you?"

He waved his hands to get me to tone down the volume. "Easy, Luis. It's not as bad as you think."

"Screw you." I stood up. "I think that's it for us, Gus. I can't trust you."

"You firing me?" That was the second time he'd asked that question. I hoped it was the last.

"You don't work for me anymore or I would."

From over Gus' shoulders I saw Corrine looking at us. The look on her face couldn't have been as worried as mine.

Gus stood up and grabbed my shoulders. I tried to jerk away but he had me in his grip. Words rushed out of his mouth. "Luis. Listen. I didn't do anything with the money. I've been waiting. I think I've waited long enough. The money's yours. You figure out what happens to it. I don't care. I just know I don't want it. That's why I'm telling you this."

I sat back down. He stood over me.

"You want to give . . . " I mumbled. "How much was in the unit?"

Now he sat down. Corrine went back to serving drinks. "Not all of it, of course. At least, not as much as Batista said there should be. Nine hundred thousand, give or take. That's why I could carry it out in two plastic bags. Wherever María hid the rest, we'll never know. It's all yours. You can give it to the feds or Batista, or Rosa for that matter. I just know I don't want it." He stood up again. "One thing. Full disclosure. I used a thousand dollars for a security deposit on my new place. I'll pay you back, a payment every month." I had a hard time coming up with the right words to respond. "Whenever you want it," he said, "let me know. We'll figure out how to move it. It'll be here until then." He waited for a response. I managed a weak nod of my head. Gus slowly walked to Corrine, where he helped himself to a glass of the purple drink.

It took a few minutes to get my bearings. Jackie O danced near the band with a young man whose face was flushed from trying to match Jackie step for step.

I strolled to the tub where Corrine and Gus talked.

I leaned in close to Gus. "Jackie. Her charity."

"Okay," he said. I returned to my seat in the summer glare.

I stared into the sun. The music at my back vibrated my chair. The newlyweds Maxine and Sandra sang at the top of their lungs— "Y volver, volver, volver a tus brazos otra vez . . . " I heard children laughing and dogs barking and my heart pounding.

I looked over the crowd until I saw Rosa standing near the singing sweethearts. I wobbled to her side and grabbed her hand. She clung to me like frosting on a wedding cake.

"I saw you with Gus," she said. "What was that about?"

"María Contreras, if you can believe that. Some final details. But it's all over now."

"I guess I was wrong. He worked out, didn't he?"

"I don't want to talk about Gus Corral."

She kissed me and I kissed back. All around us I imagined kissing couples and I didn't feel like an idiot.

"You know what," I said when we came up for air. "Now's a good time for a vacation."

"I'm for that," she shouted. "Where we going?"

"How about La Paz, Mexico? I hear the fishing is great."

35 [Gus]

quiero que sepas, que yo reconozco, que tuve la culpa

Corrine's mad mix of alcohol hit me as soon as I swallowed it. My system wasn't used to it. I stood immobile as I listened to the music and thought over my conversation with Luis.

The guy treated me like a brother. A troublemaker brother, maybe, but still family. When he finally shut the door on his business, he helped me start up my own. He did the paperwork I needed for Gus Corral, Law Office Support, LLC. He spread the word to the Hispanic and Denver Bar Associations that I was a reliable and effective investigator, process server, witness interrogator and whatever, at rates even the solitary lawyer on his or her own could afford. I had to take out a loan, with Luis as co-signer, but the first few months of my business were good and I was already ahead on my bank payments.

I borrowed some of the Contreras money for the new apartment. I told Luis about that. I also spent some of it for the down payment on the used Suburban I needed for business, camping out, fishing trips and maybe even a hunting trip or two. I didn't tell Luis about the money for the van. What he did know almost gave him a heart attack. I didn't want to pile it on. I promised to pay him back and I would keep my promise.

When I told Corrine I was moving out, she immediately thought the worst. She had too much of the street left in her not to figure out that something was going on with her brother. She grilled me, in her own way, about how I managed to save enough money for the apartment and the car. I told her I gave up beer and I put away most of my check from Luis every week, and then my own business had opened with a bang. She said, "That's not like you, Gus Corral." I agreed, of course, but only to myself.

Finding the money and then not revealing it to anyone, including Luis and Corrine—my bad. The ideas that went through my head tripped me out for a long time. That money tempted this Chicano homeboy like nothing else ever did. The thing that kept my head on straight was when I remembered where the money came from—the pain and grief it caused, the wasted lives it represented. I waited, watched. At the end, it all worked out. I finally accepted that the money wasn't for me, but it wasn't going back to the hoodlums. That I knew for sure. And the feds? What would they do with it? Nothing that really mattered, nothing that could help balance the karma of how it was collected in the first place.

I guess I could've played it a little more straight with Corrine, at least. Like I said—my bad.

That María Contreras—she was smart. Too smart for her own good. But I thought I had her figured out.

Corrine jabbed me in the ribs with her elbow. She wanted to dance. The band jumped into an old favorite.

Rick Garcia's perfect voice blasted over Corrine's sunny back yard and streamed through the neighborhood.

"Quiero que sepas, que yo reconozco, que tuve la culpa en perder tus amores."

The song about accepting blame, about responsibility, stirred the wedding guests. We joined hands and formed a circle on the lawn. We weaved in and out, around and around. Couples took turns showing off their best dance moves in the middle of the undulating mass. Maxine and Sandra hugged and kissed while they danced, but the music was too fast for slow romance. Luis and Rosa stood in the shade, clapping their hands to urge on the dancers. Corrine twirled me into the middle of the circle and we shook, dipped and twisted like teenagers. Sweat oiled Corrine's face. The band played louder. The sun melted all of us into a ball of laughing, happy people.

Luis had the right idea. Hand over the money to SHIK. That was the promise I made to myself while Max and Sandra celebrated their love in the bright hot sunshine, while Luis and Rosa began something new and while Corrine and I danced away the afternoon, the past and the rest of our lives.

I finally believed I was free.

Soundtrack

1. "Stone Free," Jimi Hendrix
2. "Can't Be Satisfied," Muddy Waters
3. "It Hurts Me Too," Elmore James
4. "You Can't Lose What You Ain't Never Had," Muddy Waters
5. "Get Out of Denver," Bob Seger
6. "One Time, One Night," Los Lobos
7. "Play With Fire," Rolling Stones
8. "El Tiempo Pasa," Antonio Aguilar
9. "Running on Empty," Jackson Browne
10. "Born under a Bad Sign," Albert King
11. "The Same Thing," Willie Dixon
12. "My Time Ain't Long," Canned Heat
13. "Jesus Make Up My Dying Bed," Blind Willie Johnson
14. "Don't Start Me Talking," Sonny Boy Williamson
15. "Thin Line Between Love and Hate," The Pretenders
16. "Hoodoo Man Blues," Junior Wells' Chicago Blues Band
17. "Nine Below Zero," Muddy Waters
18. "Nowhere Man," The Beatles
19. "Mercy Mercy Me (The Ecology)," Marvin Gaye
20. "People Get Ready," Curtis Mayfield and The Impressions
21. "El Tejano Enamorado," Ramón Ayala y Sus Bravos del Norte
22. "Bad to the Bone," George Thorogood and the Destroyers
23. "Get Along Little Doggies," Chris LeDoux
24. "La Vecina Me Puso El Dedo," Ramón Ayala y Sus Bravos del Norte
25. "Anselma," Los Lobos

26. "Nobody Loves Me But My Mother," B. B. King
27. "If Trouble Was Money," Albert Collins
28. "Smoking Gun," Robert Cray
29. "My Back Pages," Bob Dylan
30. "Why I Sing The Blues," B.B. King
31. "Fishin' Blues," Taj Mahal
32. "Lawyers, Guns and Money," Warren Zevon
33. "Rollin' and Tumblin,'" Muddy Waters
34. "Volver, Volver," Vicente Fernández
35. "Quiero Que Sepas," The Rick Garcia Band